QUROAK
THE JOURNEY HOME

JOHN CULBERSON

iUniverse, Inc.
New York   Bloomington

Quroak
The Journey Home

iUniverse books may be ordered through booksellers or by contacting:

iUniverse
1663 Liberty Drive
Bloomington, IN 47403
www.iuniverse.com
1-800-Authors (1-800-288-4677)

Because of the dynamic nature of the Internet, any Web addresses or links contained in this book may have changed since publication and may no longer be valid. The views expressed in this work are solely those of the author and do not necessarily reflect the views of the publisher, and the publisher hereby disclaims any responsibility for them.

ISBN: 978-1-4502-1461-2 (sc)
ISBN: 978-1-4502-1462-9 (ebk)

Printed in the United States of America

iUniverse rev. date: 03/10/2010

To Irina, for shining your lovely light
into my night.

CHAPTER 1

"I'm coming!" Quroak thought-yelled to his friend and he made himself fall downward through the green sky-tunnel as fast as possible. He didn't know if his friend was conscious or not so he telepathically shouted again, "I'm coming!"

Tsin was falling totally out of control down the inside of the raging, dark green cyclone, bouncing down the almost solid wall of the upward spiraling winds of the twister and Quroak flinched at each impact, knowing his friend was being badly hurt each time. Quroak flew deeper into the relatively calm center of the cyclone where he could fall faster against less wind resistance. He needed to reach Tsin before his friend slammed into the ocean surface below, for striking the water at this speed would surely kill him.

With the strong winds whipping all around in a howling frenzy, Quroak couldn't stop replaying the

1

accident in his mind even as he desperately raced to save Tsin. The dark green twister had appeared out of nowhere in the light tea-green skies which were perpetually overcast with white and mint green clouds. Quroak and Tsin, along with most Cloudotians, loved windstorm surfing and as they were casually returning home from a day of goofing off, they decided to not let this opportunity pass them by.

So they had attacked the cyclone from the top, riding the 240 kph winds, reducing their density just enough to penetrate into the center via an inward flowing current. The goal, of course, was to slip into the eye where it is calm, change their weight to be at their heaviest and drop down through the eye as fast as possible while skimming the inside wall, in a controlled fashion, and then just before hitting the ocean surface, dive back into the winds while lightening themselves to surf *up* the spinning cyclone on the outside.

Quroak remembered thought-shouting to his friend, "Look, there's the current we want!"

Tsin had locked two of his arms together in acknowledgment, thought-yelled "Follow me!" and dove into the quick moving current.

With the lamenting wind so loud Quroak could barely hear his own thoughts, he had followed Tsin into the inward current with his skin turning turquoise from his excitement with the torrents buffeting him about like a piece of seaweed upon a stormy sea.

Then suddenly, Tsin's joyful thought-shout "Great Clouds!" had echoed through his mind as they both entered the calm of the storm's eye where without hesitation, Tsin had dived down the inside whirling wall of the cyclone, maximizing his weight in order to free-fall as fast as possible while surfing down against the upward spiraling inner winds of the twister's wall.

Quroak had hesitated a moment, then followed his friend with his skin flushed a dark turquoise for he had always loved cyclone surfing because it made him feel alive inside, as if the whirlwind's energy was somehow absorbed into his soul.

But that joy had quickly changed to horror, coloring Quroak a light blue, when a storm-rider had suddenly appeared from within the cyclone wall colliding with Tsin at full speed, if not knocking him unconscious, then at least stunning him for he became limp and fell out of control. Even as his three hearts froze, gripped with fear, Quroak instantly dove for his friend.

Quroak knew storm-riders were not dangerous animals. In fact, they were quite rare and usually steered clear of people. However, they were twice as massive as the average Cloudotian and being hit by one was almost as bad as slamming into the ocean at 100 kph while at full density. Also, storm-riders were not known for their intelligence as they always acted out of pure instinct.

After the storm-rider slammed into Tsin, being unharmed, it immediately flew back into the cyclone wall, leaving Tsin tumbling helplessly towards the stormy sea below with Quroak desperately trying to reach him before it was too late.

Quroak tried to shape his body as aerodynamically as possible while increasing his mass to the maximum, wishing his body could be as heavy as his central heart felt right now. It seemed like it was taking an awfully long time for him to catch up to Tsin but it was probably the fear thundering through his veins that stretched his perception of time into eternity.

Quroak mentally sighed with relief as he caught up to his friend about two kilometers above the ocean surface. He quickly grabbed four of his friend's arms and then Quroak lessened his mass in most of his body except for his own arms, four of which he used to hold onto Tsin and the other four to claw at the cyclone's inner wind-wall trying to slow their descent. He kept mind-shouting to his friend but so far there was no response at all and despairing thoughts darkened his hopes once more.

While their rapid descent decreased somewhat, Quroak knew it still wasn't enough for though he now weighed a fourth of normal, Tsin was still at his maximum mass and he couldn't do anything about it. By the time they were only one kilometer above the waiting waters (an image of the sea as a hungry monster opening its maw wide to receive its dinner flashed through his mind), Quroak was filled with desperation and his mind howled in frustration, making the roaring wind seem as silent as a soft breeze in comparison.

That mind-howl was his salvation for it scared the storm-rider out of the storm's wall where it had been hiding and flew right below Quroak & Tsin. As they were dropping past the fleeing animal, Quroak grabbed one of its clawed feet with all of his strength. As his direction suddenly went from downwards to sideways, Quroak thought-screamed in agony as his arm was almost wrenched from his body. Later, Quroak was both amazed and proud that he hadn't let go of the storm-rider at that moment. He quickly grabbed the creature's other three taloned feet with his other three arms that were no longer clawing at the twister's walls.

With all eight arms protesting in agony and strained to their utmost, Quroak closed his mind to the pain and willed his body to hang on, to both the frightened animal and to his friend, while caressing and poking at Tsin's mind with his thoughts, trying to get Tsin mentally alert.

Finally, when Quroak didn't think he could hold on any longer, Tsin responded groggily enough to reduce his mass to ease Quroak's numb muscles. The sudden relief that swept through Quroak's body was so unexpectedly strong that he lost his grip on the storm-rider and they started to fall. However, Tsin had made himself weigh next to nothing, so Quroak quickly gained control and flew them both out of the frenzied cyclone.

Quroak started to fly homeward while calling out for help with his mind. He wished he had called out earlier but events had been too fast and violent for him to think of it before. He continuously tried communicating with Tsin, but his friend's mind was disturbingly quiet. Fortunately, he didn't have to go far before he was met by a medical team sent by the hospital. After probing Tsin's mind, much deeper than Quroak was capable of, to gauge his physical and mental condition and reviewing the chain of events burned in his short-term memory, the medical team flew off with Tsin towards the hospital while tending to his injuries, leaving Quroak alone with a single medic.

Since it was unethical to probe another's mind except in an emergency when the person could not respond voluntarily, the medic thought-whispered to Quroak, "How do you feel?"

Quroak was shaking from the weakness of his strained muscles. Plus his body was now crashing after the adrenaline rush that had provided him with the strength to rescue his friend from almost certain death. He weakly answered, "I'm alright, just tired. Is he going to be okay?"

The medic said gently, "He is in a very bad way. But yes, with time he will make a full recovery."

At this confident announcement, Quroak felt the ice of fear constricting his heart slowly melt away, leaving him emotionally drained as well as physically and mentally exhausted. Tsin was Quroak's best friend. They had been friends for most of their lives ever since meeting in a wave-hopping competition where Quroak had narrowly beaten Tsin in the final challenge. They had admired each other's technique and soon became inseparable, going through schools and the trials of adolescence together, always being there for each other.

Yet for all of that, Quroak still felt an intense loneliness for he could only get so close to Tsin, or anyone else he had ever known. He felt he was like an iceberg where he could let others know the surface of him, yet the majority of himself, his true self, was hidden below, unknown. He dreamed of finding someone he could truly be emotionally intimate with, be open with and share himself and life with. This loneliness haunted his heart mercilessly, like the dark grayish green clouds that blocked all sunlight over the South Pole, keeping the ocean there completely frozen.

Quroak was able to keep the cold darkness at bay most of the time by staying busy, keeping himself distracted, yet it always returned whenever he mentally relaxed or was exhausted. His mind created a force field protecting himself from this loneliness, but when he was too tired to maintain the mental energy required, or he allowed himself to fully relax, it always attacked with the hunger of a winter wind draining body heat.

He didn't understand why, but this depression usually managed to slip through his defenses after he helped someone or simply did a good deed. He just didn't get as much satisfaction as one would expect from doing good towards others. Quroak figured it was because he didn't have someone to share the experience with. Or maybe it was because he thought helping others would form a connection to alleviate his loneliness, but the connection was always fleeting, leaving him disappointed.

So now that he knew Tsin was going to be okay, plus being totally exhausted in every way, the cold loneliness swept through his heart like a ghost reclaiming its deserted home, having chased away livelier occupants. His mind went numb as his thoughts froze, and then shattered into useless shards leaving him without the ability to reply to the medic, so he silently flew towards the hospital with the medic hovering over him with concern.

Then slowly penetrating the numbing haze of his mind, he felt a sweetness gently caress his mind. It was a kind of touch he had never felt before and he found his mind responding instantly to the caress, welcoming it in deeper. It was like a warm light was slowly and tenderly sweeping the darkness out of his mind and a calmness he had never felt before started to settle in his soul. Not only did his mind welcome the warm light, but he was hungry for it, absorbing all of it with desperation, as if his subconscious knew this was what he had been searching for all along. Quroak was so entranced by these new sensations, it took him a while to realize that it was the medic flying by his side that was caressing his mind. He turned to her in wonder.

When she noticed she had his attention, the medic thought-whispered to him, "That was a very brave thing you did for your friend."

Quroak found himself speechless, feeling a little dazed from really seeing her for the first time, thinking he must be more exhausted and traumatized than he realized for there was something special about her that under any other circumstances he would have noticed right away.

She was very pretty but her beauty seemed to shine from within her heart, no, from her soul, he decided. He had never believed that old saying that a person's soul was reflected in the eyes, but she made him an instant believer. Her large bronze eyes were extraordinarily expressive and shone with an inner light that somehow promised mysteries and wondrous beauty if you cared to look deep enough. And as he looked deeper into that wonderful light, his heart leaped for the stars above in joyous wonder and his mind froze again, not from exhaustion this time, but from being stunned by her soul's beauty. He felt like he had lived his whole life in darkness, never having known light and all of a sudden the sun appeared out of nowhere, blazing at full strength only an arm's length away! He couldn't help but dive deeper and deeper into the wonderful light of her eyes, wanting, no, *needing* to drown in her beauty, instinctively knowing he would only truly feel alive inside with her light filling his heart.

All of this hit him in a flash like a bolt of lightning. He slowly realized he was just staring at her in a daze as she gazed at him with a questioning look. He felt himself flush a dark blue from embarrassment as he reluctantly swam up from the wondrous depths of her light-filled eyes. He hastily gathered his scattered mind, hoping she wasn't doubting his sanity as he struggled to remember her statement before he managed to thought-reply, "No, I didn't have time to be brave: only to react."

"What would you have done if you had time to think before taking action?" she inquired with quiet amusement.

"I would have done just as I did", Quroak admitted, avoiding her tempting eyes.

"So there you are then: brave".

"No, you're wrong. I just did what had to be done, no more", he insisted weakly, still trying to recover from her sun-blossoming light.

"But not everyone would have risked their life so quickly" the medic insisted. "Not in this day and age. Oh, everyone is polite and helpful to each other, but only up to a certain point. Ever since the Mind Invasion Wars sixty orbits ago, everyone is very cautious and closed, even to supposedly close friends. No one opens themselves, makes self sacrifices or even help others beyond the etiquette for good manners."

Quroak sighed and asked tiredly, "What is your name?"

"Xelrine".

"Well Xelrine, if you don't mind, I'm much too exhausted to think straight, much less have a deep, meaningful conversation about our society. Can we continue this tomorrow, say, over dinner?"

Xelrine replied, "I would enjoy that" with kind amusement lighting up her eyes, recognizing he was really asking her out.

Quroak took a chance and glanced at her eyes, and the next moment found himself using all of his remaining willpower to extract himself from the depths of her eyes where he felt like he was drowning, though happily. His heart leapt at her easy acceptance. He realized he must really be dazed and exhausted, otherwise he probably would not have found the courage to ask her out so easily.

Quroak barely had the physical strength to make it to the hospital under his own power, for though Xelrine's mind-warming caresses helped tremendously, he still felt the coldness washing through him, sapping his willpower, making him feel hollow inside, as if he were a robot without conscious thought, following some long forgotten instruction. Once there, he immediately collapsed into a waiting bed where he passed out from exhaustion.

Quroak's next awareness was of slowly swimming up from the deepest sleep he had ever experienced. It took him a while to swim up from the depths, mostly because he didn't want to leave this warm, quiet and safe place. He felt wonderfully relaxed with a sense of warm well-being throughout his mind. He felt like he was flying high and free on a nice warm, breezy day. Before greeting whatever day or night it was, he reached out with his mind to determine the condition of his friend, Tsin, and once satisfied that he was stable and in no immediate danger, Quroak took a few precious moments to think about Xelrine and his heart couldn't help but smile.

He finally opened his eyes to find himself in a hospital room (he only vaguely remembered coming to this place) with a nurse checking his vital signs. He looked around but didn't see anyone else around.

The somewhat plump male nurse noticed Quroak was awake and asked, "How do you feel, Hon?"

"I feel really good," answered Quroak wondering yet again why all nurses always addressed their patients as 'Hon'.

"Well, you should feel good. You've been sleeping for four days."

"Four days? No wonder I'm so hungry!" His stomach growled in agreement.

"Don't worry, Hon, we'll get you something to eat. For now, drink this nutrient drink", said the nurse as he passed Quroak the cup.

As Quroak drank the foul tasting concoction, he thought-asked hopefully, "Do you know a medic named Xelrine? Do you know if she is on-duty now?"

While multi-tasking with five of her arms adjusting several machines and cleaning up, the nurse replied somewhat distractedly, "Hon, there is no medic here named Xelrine. In fact, we don't have any female medics currently at this hospital."

"Oh, well, then maybe she works at another hospital in the area and just happened to have responded to my distress call."

With an amused look gleaming in his eyes, the nurse replied, "Listen, I know every medic in all the hospitals in the closest forty cloud-cities and there is no medic named Xelrine. Maybe in your exhaustive state you were fantasizing. Where do you imagine you met this Xelrine?"

"She accompanied me to the hospital!" Quroak answered, rather defensively he realized as he suddenly found himself floating a meter above the bed.

With the amusement slowly turning to concern, the nurse stopped his busy activity and turned to give Quroak his undivided attention. "Uh, I was here when you arrived and you were not accompanied by anyone. You were definitely alone."

As this news slowly filtered through his agitation, his body sank back onto the bed as his mood suddenly descended from his lofty sense of well-being. Had he dreamed his encounter with Xelrine? Softly cursing himself for being a fool, he realized what had happened, flushing a dark blue from embarrassment. He felt like curling up into a ball but pride stopped him.

All his life he had always dreamed of sharing love and life with someone. Not just *someone* but a specific someone, though he had never met her or even seen her before, at least, not outside of his dreams.

He knew exactly how he felt in these dreams, how their love had a life of its own and how life felt so wonderful and magical. He was totally free with himself with her, sharing and giving all of himself with and to her, holding nothing back because that was the way he needed to love and it was what his heart craved for. With her, he felt as alive as he imagined electricity felt.

He dreamed of all kinds of life situations they shared, from the mundane of routine life to holidays and unexpected surprises where it all felt 'right' and good as long as they experienced everything together. They enjoyed each other so much and knew each other so intimately that they knew what the other was thinking with just a look without the need for telepathic communication.

And these dreams always felt so real to his heart, as if he were actually remembering a cherished memory. In these nocturnal visitations, he sensed what she looked like: her flowing graceful arms, her round face, her smiling bronze eyes and especially the look in her eyes when she laughed or looked at him tenderly. He knew the flowery scent of her skin and could taste the sweetness of her thoughts caressing his mind. But most of all, he knew the beauty of her heart and the glowing light of her soul. He also knew in his heart that they were soul mates.

But his dreams had never provided him with a name before. He must have dove deeply into his dreams of her to escape the trauma of what he had gone through rescuing Tsin and from his overwhelming exhaustion. He must have really needed to share his experience with someone and the only one he felt safe with was her; the girl of his dreams which, as far as he knew, didn't even exist.

Since he had never hallucinated before, he realized he must have pretty much passed out from exhaustion and had sleepflew to the hospital, dreaming of her escorting him safely there since he always felt safe and a calm peacefulness when around her. Well, in his dreams anyway.

He wondered where the name Xelrine came from and if he was starting to go a little crazy. What he really hoped was that somehow, somewhere, at some time in his life, his mind had felt her presence, like while they were in the same crowd like at a concert or sporting event. Or that they had been at the same place at some time without ever meeting. That their minds had touched on a subconscious level, with his heart captured by the flavor of her essence and that his heart's awakening from her ethereal touch was manifesting itself in his dreams. Basically, he was just hoping she was real and not just a hopeless desire never to be fulfilled.

With his previous flight of high-spirits now grounded by the weight of disappointment kindly dished out by that unavoidable laughing mistress called Reality, Quroak wearily closed his eyes and tried to dull the sharpness that was slicing through his heart.

"ME!" I said firmly. Then I exited the small privacy kiosk and withdrew from the quiet memory library.

CHAPTER 2

My name is not important. What I am is not important. I could be the wind on Jupiter, an Earth coyote, a blue-winged sunsurfer from Saturn, a moon cat from Epsilon IV or like you, an Earth human. Since this manuscript has recently been published only on Earth, for now I'll assume that any reader is human. Though if you ever left your spy camera on at home, you might he surprised at what your cat is doing during your absence, though they are usually much too clever to be caught by such low-tech toys. But if you are a feline, then I apologize for my assumption; however, you should have received this via the usual secret communication channels and therefore have no need to read this account in such a primitive fashion.

What I *feel* is important. I am a creature of emotion. Emotions carved out the path upon which I have traveled throughout my life thus far. Emotions are the spice of existence, giving life flavor. It is through emotions that life is fully experienced and savored. Can you imagine experiencing the beauty of the Orion Nebula up close, the haunting music of Saturn's rings or the blazing wonder of a fiery sunset in the purpling sky while peacefully lying on the beach without emotions? The experience would be interesting but hollow, flat, without substance. It would be like seeing a rainbow in gray or only hearing C sharp in a symphony. How can life be exciting without passion, whether its passion for an interest or for a beautiful woman? How can life be fulfilling without joy? Or love?

Emotions are the driving force that compels me onward, and my compass seems to be an insatiable need to "connect". However, steering my course is a bizarre map consisting of detours where I abandon myself, trying to help others with their path. Either abandoning myself to help others is an avoidance technique on my part, or I feel that helping others is my path to that "connection" I seek. I haven't figured that out yet.

In any event, my emotions are ocean deep, and like the tides to the moon, my heart follows that elusive dream for intimate connection and real love. Every living creature wants to be loved, though their definition of love may differ from yours, like your black widow spider where the female makes a meal of the male. Talk about giving your all!! But I will go to extraordinary lengths for the mere chance of love. I have kept my heart completely open while enduring constant spears of disappointment and indifference slicing through my heart just on the slim hope my steady persistence would finally forge that intimacy so craved for by my soul. If you have ever floated naked in the middle of a Neptunian storm with the winds racing at 900 kph, whipping diamond raindrops through your body while you kept your arms wide open and a smile on your face (though sometimes with gritted teeth) then you know what I speak of. My heart chases this dream as if my life depended upon it, which in a way, it does. By the way, I do not recommend the Neptunian diamond bath.

Though I search for this connection and form temporary bonds, my heart is open yet protected and therefore I remain a mystery, an enigma. My heart is fragile yet resilient and strong. Fragile because I care too easily and too much and therefore easily taken advantage of by vampiric or selfish souls. My heart bleeds kindness like blood into the ocean drawing sharks to circle, hoping for the chance to appease an insatiable hunger. Therefore my true heart is hidden under a layer of control, albeit, a thin layer, so that most won't discover who I really am. My inner nature is too alien for most to comprehend, for you live in a world of questioning mistrust due to ubiquitous selfish motivations that surround you every day trying to beat you down. My heart is too honest for most to comprehend. My intentions are always as stated with no hidden agenda; no secret desires to build myself up by tearing another down. My heart is open for any to see but unbelieved by all who are unaccustomed to such honesty, especially within themselves.

Where do I hope my path will lead me? The answer is deceptively simple: my home. A home I have never even seen before. A home I have only felt in my heart as a longed for place. It's really only a sensation of what my home should be like. This sensation, this hope, has been a ghost of a dream that visits me deep in the lonely night. The place in the dream is not clearly seen but leaves a *feeling* that haunts my heart and soul. This homey *feeling* also caresses my wanting heart via the soft melodies of certain songs. It's like these magical songs don't bring back memories from the past, but are showing me memories yet to be forged in the future. I know this is where I belong, and not where I've been. In case you have not figured it out yet, my home is the warm intimacy of real love that my heart yearns for. I did warn you that the answer was deceptively simple, for how can this be?

Until recently, I had not even found the right world upon which my home resides. Let me tell you, the universe is a mighty big place in which to be lost. I mean, if you take a left at the Orion Nebula when you should have gone down, you end up in the center of the Virgo Galaxy when you wanted the Milky Way. Then you're trapped because that place is being swallowed up by a monstrous black hole as big as the solar system around Sol. Then your whole day is ruined!!

Fortunately for me, I've never been beyond Sol's Solar

System so I've never made that particular mistake, but I probably would have. No, I have slowly circled Sol searching for my home, sensing it was here somewhere. And though minuscule by universal standards, it's still a big place for one lonely traveler to search. It's taken your Voyager 1 probe, currently rushing along at 61,000 kph, 30 years to reach the outer limits of Sol's spatial influence where it will soon dip its metallic toes into the cold vast interstellar ocean. So I think you can understand why it's taking me a long time to find my home in Sol's immense sea.

So, I'm a creature of oceanic emotions with a thinly veiled, sensitive alien heart searching the local cosmos for my hitherto unknown home built from a foundation of intimacy and warmed by the light of love that I've only sensed in a dream that haunts my soul like a ghost lost in a deserted mansion. But unlike that ghost lamenting over what was, my heart weeps over what is not and yearns for and is driven toward what could be. How messed up is that?

Not only are my emotions the lightning bolts cutting my path through the mysterious clouds of life with thunder rolling through the heavens searching for my home like some kind of sonar, but their unusual intensity and depth drove me to choose my profession: emocology.

I study emotions. I have always been fascinated in understanding the underlying emotions behind a person's character and actions. What emotions drive a person to do what they do? That is always the first question that comes to my mind when I meet or observe someone.

I'm what you humans would call a 'people watcher'. Most everything a person does is driven by some kind of emotion, whether they are aware of the emotion or not. Even when a person claims they feel nothing, it just means they do not know how they feel. And, of course, the act of suppressing an emotion is done out of fear of feeling the pain associated with the emotion. Emotions can be subtle like a barely heard whisper or they can be overwhelming like a tornado rampaging through the heart and soul.

Though other emocologists tend to study the more glamorous aspects of our field, like what emotional sickness causes a person to such uncontrollable hate that mass murder becomes the only answer for that individual, I tend to study individuals that are good-hearted but for some reason deal with a disproportionate amount of emotional pain. I also drift towards those that feel emotions as intensely as I, in the hope of better understanding myself. After all, I believe we are not really alive to discover the secrets of the physical universe, since I believe our thoughts create everything we see, hear, smell and touch, but that we are here to uncover the secrets of ourselves. And Quroak falls into both categories of what I choose to study.

The name Quroak is well known throughout Cloudotian society, at least in a legendary sense. Though he is still young, Quroak's adventures are envied by older generations and his positive attributes, such as emotional strength, sensitivity, bravery, courage are held as standards to which the young should aspire.

I first heard about Quroak while visiting the Jovian moon Europa where an ocean miner relayed to me the story of Quroak's rescue of Tsin. Anyone mining Europa's ocean deals with danger on a continuous basis and so the awe in the miner's voice impressed me and inspired me to seek out Quroak for an interview.

I probably would have tried to meet Quroak simply out of curiosity after hearing this adventure but the truth is I sensed something deeper here. The story I just related to you was directly from his memories which I obtained after meeting him. Though the minor's version did not have Quroak's point of view or his emotional flavoring, I felt that there was more to Quroak than simply someone saving his friend during a crisis. It was just a hunch but it drove me to seek out Quroak.

Before I met with him, I sought out some Cloudotian friends of mine to learn more about Quroak. That's when I heard the adventure which made Quroak legendary among his people. This adventure, which I will share soon, validated my hunch that there might be some deep emotions roiling within the young Cloudotian.

When I actually met Quroak, I was initially surprised to find a normal, young Cloudotian male with no really outstanding physical qualities. But when he starting telling me the story of how he dreamed of Xelrine, his clear, polished copper eyes were like vault doors that rolled open to reveal the rich, shining emotions of his heart. The intensity was such that I felt I'd been blasted by a solar flare.

It was quite obvious that the event that had the most emotional impact on Quroak that day was receiving the name Xelrine to associate with his heart's dream and that his incredible rescue of Tsin was almost incidental. I now knew that Quroak and I were similar, at least emotionally, and I couldn't wait to dive into his emotional ocean to hopefully discover new currents that would help me to understand or deal with my own stormy seas.

Unfortunately, Quroak didn't have much time to spend with me but I did convince him to upload his memories into what you can call a memory database. Now, most memory libraries are rather rudimentary where they can only contain one dimensional memories where only the events are recorded without any of what I call *flavoring*. By *flavoring*, I mean there's no emotional coloring, no olfactory or tactile sensations to the events. It's akin to humans watching their television programs.

However, I have created an uploading process and storage method where all dimensions of the memory are captured perfectly intact. And when I connect into the library, I'm not just watching the memories; I'm actually experiencing them as if I'm living them. Everything the original owner felt emotionally and physically, I feel. Everything he smelt, heard, tasted and saw, I smell, hear, taste and see.

At first, it's pretty weird living someone else's memories in your mind. It's especially weird when you're not even the same species and are totally different anatomically. For example, Cloudotians have eight arms. I don't. So when Quroak uses those arms, it feels like I have eight arms and believe me, it takes some getting used to!

Though it may sound like fun experiencing another's memories, it is also very dangerous. As I said, you are literally living that person's experiences, feeling everything they did, especially their emotions. If that person felt love for another, then you will feel love for that person as well. This is usually okay because once you disconnect from the memory library, those emotions fade and you are able to separate the memories you just experienced from your own memories. However, during the experience, you must have a strong sense of self or you may lose yourself, your identity, while immersed in another's memories.

Now, part of the thrill of living someone else's memories *is* to lose yourself into their life. However, you must have a strong anchor firmly embedded in the bedrock of your identity with an unbreakable chain leading you back to your true self when necessary.

If you have ever gone through intense emotional pain, then you will have experienced that feeling where a part of yourself becomes *detached* and seemingly hovers over you, watching the rest of yourself crying in agony. You actually feel like you are in two places at once, where one is watching the other. It is the same concept in memory immersion where you lose yourself in the memories but a part of yourself, the deepest part of your ego, is detached, watching, and ready to reel you back in when you're in danger of losing yourself altogether. To re-establish your identity completely and resurface from the memory immersion, you simply have to create a firm thought of *me*.

If you have a strong personality, a firm sense of self, then you really are not in any danger. Individuals not as strong will have a much harder time withdrawing back into their own personality. However, it is dangerous for *anyone* if the originator of the memories was deeply and intensely emotional where Mars-sized dust storms howled through their soul or Jupiter-sized oceans flooded their heart. In this case, no one is absolutely safe.

I remember it took an Earth year for one poor soul to really recover his identity after a particularly intense emotional memory journey. In fact, the affects of the memory immersion still haven't completely worn off for he still has uncontrollable cravings for rainbow mint pie which doesn't even exist within the Solar System and it's quickly driving him insane because his body is going through withdrawal symptoms. His body shakes so uncontrollably he can't hold anything or even walk. He is fatigued all the time and his brain has been affected so that everything he says comes out backwards; his words and sentences. So he's struggling with severe addiction withdrawal from something he has never actually even seen, much less ingested! That should tell you how *real* memory immersion feels.

Being intensely and deeply emotional myself, even though I give myself up completely to memory journeys,

I have never been in any real danger of having my identity swept away or drowned in another's emotions. However, my emotions have allowed me to be more empathic than most emocologists. I am able to pick up and decipher the underlying emotions driving the person's actions, even when the memory originator wasn't aware of the feelings hiding from their consciousness.

Now, you may think that emocologists deal with memories from the deceased; individuals long gone. While it may be true for some, I almost always deal with memory journeys from those that are still living. Sometimes I get interested in a historical figure and will do a journey just to better understand their motivations.

However, emocology is not my career only because emotions fascinate me or because it helps me to better understand myself. No, I also do it for a third reason, which may even be the most important to me: to help others better understand themselves. Since it's hard to help someone who has already slipped away from this plane of existence, I study emotions of the still living. After journeying into whatever part of their life they chose, I provide insight into their hidden motivations so that they can change or correct their path, if they so desire, in order to find what they are truly looking for in life. Or I point out what is blocking them emotionally from achieving their desires. What people are usually looking for is fulfillment of some kind, whether in a career, love or simply finding peace with themselves.

Not everyone needs help with their path to fulfillment. In fact, many people find their own way, some easily and some with much difficultly. And, of course, some just don't care or aren't motivated enough to do anything about it. And not everyone is comfortable having someone else re-live their memories. I can't imagine anything that's more intimate than someone living a part of your life, having your thoughts, experiencing your emotional urges and physical desires and, of course, feeling your emotions.

Plus, as my process captures the full spectrum of memories, I also see the negative thoughts that everyone has but usually don't act upon because it goes against their true nature. Still, people are embarrassed for having these thoughts which I call 'thru-way' thoughts. These thoughts are usually fleeting, zipping through the mind like passing cars on the highway where they appear and disappear without stopping for there is no substance to them. These thoughts are pure garbage and can't be taken seriously given a person's true character and so I never embarrass any client by mentioning them. No one has really determined where these random thoughts originate from, but it's currently believed it may be from a species' group consciousness that's buried in every individual's subconscious mind going back many generations. This is probably why it takes a long time for a society to accept new social ideas or to drop prejudices.

However, other people like to share their experiences for a variety of reasons. You will always find self-important individuals in any given group of sentient beings who believe the universe revolves around them. I tend to steer very clear of these people for their experiences tend to be the most mundane, not the world-shattering catastrophes or epiphanies they believe.

Some do it just so that they know they are truly understood by at least anyone who lived their memories. It makes them feel less alone, which I can empathize with. I think most people feel alone in some way and to a certain degree.

And then some people download their memories just in the hope their experiences can help others with their lives. Quroak is one of these individuals that like to help others and so he not only gave me his memories but also gave me permission to publish them in order to reach as many people as possible in order to encourage them to strive for their dreams and to give hope in achieving them.

Before I dive into the adventure I wish to relate to you, I'll just let you know what happened after Quroak's memory we just shared. His friend, Tsin, fully recovered from his injuries and though he and Quroak remained good friends they eventually drifted apart as Tsin pursued a career in oceanography and spent most of his time undersea.

After leaving the hospital, Quroak did search for Xelrine, hoping the nurse had been wrong, but it was in vain for he didn't find anyone who had known a medic by that name. For months, he drove himself crazy thinking every woman he saw might be the unique soul his heart believed existed for him to meet. But as time went by, he eventually calmed down to the point where he practically lost all hope of finding her.

Four years later, after being in a couple of unsatisfying relationships where he just felt more alone than ever, he was quietly admitting to himself that he would probably always be alone, at least emotionally, if not physically. Then events transpired causing the experience we are about to share which both confirmed and changed his assessment in this regard. Instead of going into more details, we will learn more by immersing into his memories.

However, before we do, I think I have to clarify your current understanding regarding your own Solar System. I do not mean to shock you, but I think it will be helpful for you to understand what's happening in your own cosmic neighborhood, and even right under your own nose, if I understand that idiom correctly.

CHAPTER 3

The whole Solar System is very much aware of you humans and the events occurring on your blue and white ocean world. However, it seems you are not really aware of the rest of the Solar System.

I don't like to judge people and I never characterize a civilization as a whole, however, you do make it tough not to pass judgment with all the *noise* you send out into the cosmos. And by *noise*, I mean your electromagnetic radiation pouring out into space, i.e., your radio and television transmissions. Based on these transmissions, especially from your media, one would think that you are obsessed with blond women, like what Britney Spears wears (or doesn't wear), what Paris Hilton is doing (she is kind enough to show you on the Web), who's the father of . . . and so on. Or fighting over such nonsense as to whether or not Pluto is a planet.

Well, for your first surprise, I have to tell you that

there are ten planets in the Solar System, if you include Pluto. Whether or not you count Pluto, you are still off by one. The missing planet orbits between Mars and Jupiter where you see the Asteroid Belt, which I hope proves to you that you can't always believe what you see. I mean, look at your feline friends.

What you perceive as thousands of little asteroids chaotically tumbling through space between Mars and Jupiter is really a full-size, intact planet called €ꝏ⊖ꜱꝋ ꝋ ⅄ꝋ☺ꝍ ⁄ which translates to Sea of Clouds. The ꝍ ⅄ꝋꝍꝏ, (Cloudotians) have the ability to shroud their planet within an illusion. No asteroids, just one planet about the size of Mars. It is a beautiful planet completely covered by an emerald green ocean shrouded by swirling white and mint green clouds.

The asteroids you call Ceres, Eros, Vesta, and all the others are really just pieces of their world projected as separate uninteresting space rocks so that Earthlings will ignore them. Your scientists believe the "asteroid belt" is either a planet destroyed in the past or a planet that couldn't form due to Jupiter's gravitational hunger. The Cloudotians believe that if this area looks like a destroyed planet, you will leave it alone.

Why do the Cloudotians want their world left alone? Everyone can hear Earth crying out in pain from your treatment of her, except humans. It is gratifying that you are starting to listen to her, albeit slowly. As one of the last civilizations to join the Solar community, you have been watched for centuries and your violent and neglectful nature has been duly noted so the rest of us have preferred to remain unknown to you until it is felt you are mature enough to join us.

In fact, I'm breaking rules and protocol by sending you this manuscript and since I don't want to be tracked down by the Solar Enforcers, that's why I can't tell you who I am. However, though I don't believe you are ready to join the community, I do think that knowing you are not alone in the cosmos (far from it) you may decide to become less arrogant and more responsible not only to each other, but also to Earth and to your future generations. Basically, I have hope for you which is not widely shared.

Plus on a more personal level, I believe this manuscript may be helpful to some of you as individuals on your life's journey.

However, the main reason why the Cloudotians shroud their planet in space rocks and dust is because some of your probes to other planets have not been as bacteria free as you believe and they wish to leave their pristine ocean world left untouched.

Also, the Cloudotians are highly advanced culturally and aren't really sure if they want anything to do with a species that spends hard-earned money and precious time looking at pieces of junk haphazardly thrown together or randomly splashed canvases all labeled as 'art' to represent the human condition. If that's the state of the human condition, Mr. Jasper Jones, then it will be a lonely condition as far as the Cloudotians are concerned. They're not snobs, but they have to draw the line somewhere. Actually, come Cloudotians are very snobbish.

The Cloudotians are a very interesting people. They originated in the sea but around 144,000 years ago left the ocean currents for the safer air currents to escape the ferocious marine predators. Gravity on €ᎭƆ⊖ᏚᏅ◇ᏔᏺᏕᏅ𝒩 is only about a quarter of Earth's and the winds always blow at a steady 70 – 100 kilometers per hour with occasional cyclones up to 240 kph. Given the strong winds and the weak gravity, it wasn't hard to evolve from ocean to clouds.

They live in small transparent cities that float within the clouds. The cities themselves are alive, as they are just carefully shaped sea plants. The Cloudotians do much traveling between these cities. Since each city is on its own cloud and the clouds travel at different speeds around the planet, two cities that are four kilometers apart one day may be forty kilometers apart the next day. But somehow the Cloudotians can instinctively find their way around with no problem. And here I am getting lost in a simple detour around my own neighborhood where the blocks stay in the same place! And I'm using a GPS unit!

The Cloudotians have the amazing ability to change their density to make themselves lighter or heavier at will by transferring their mass between this dimension and another. When they want to be lighter and nebulous they transfer their mass to the other dimension. Don't you wish you could lose weight that way?

As you learned through Quroak's memories from the day he saved Tsin, the Cloudotians use this ability to practice their favorite pastime, windstorm surfing. They especially love surfing cyclones. The more adventuresome travel to Jupiter to surf the biggest storm in the solar system: the Great Red Spot. The winds of the Great Red Spot, which is big enough to hold three Earths, whip around at 430 kph and takes days to surf properly to get the most intense surfing experience. For some strange reason, the Cloudotians like to claim they created the Great Red Spot for their surfing pleasure but the truth is the Jovians created this swirling red storm as part of their planetary artwork and they just tolerate their visiting neighbors' wild antics.

How are you doing so far? In the past few minutes I've informed you of a planet you didn't know existed in your own backyard, of the denizens of that mysterious planet, the Cloudotians, and that there are intelligent creatures on Jupiter that create world-size artworks. Though I've unbalanced your egocentric fantasy regarding your place in the universe, I don't think I'll clarify your misconceptions about the creatures you think you have as pets that you call *cats*. Though you may want to rethink your position on why felines act like they are superior to you.

So yes, Cloudotians travel to Jupiter. They have the ability to travel in sea, air, and space without need of submarines, planes or spacecraft. You are probably wondering right about now why they haven't come to Earth to visit humans. Right? The truth is some Cloudotians are living on Earth right now and have been for about four thousand years.

Now you are probably pondering about the strange habits of your spouse that seem more animalistic than your cat's behavior. Or about that co-worker with the social skills of a Cro-Magnon. Or the one who seems to see reality in a totally different dimension because it doesn't match your reality in any way, shape or form.

Well, before you convince yourself you can easily spot the aliens among you, you should know that the Cloudotians aren't even humanoid. You know those superior acting furry felines? Just kidding, they're not Cloudotians infiltrating your house to control you in ways you can't imagine. No, those aloof fur balls are something else altogether which I don't have time (or authority) to tell you.

Anyway, the Cloudotians are really the creatures you call octopuses. Well, kind of. You're really not going to like hearing this. You see, well, how do I put it? Earth is being used as, well, kind of being used as a penal colony. Now, before you get all indignant, just remember your British used the colony of Georgia (yes, what is now part of the U.S.A) and Australia for the same purpose: a place to deport prisoners. Actually, penal colony is not quite the proper term in the Cloudotians' case for these prisoners are not forced to work unpaid till their deaths like your penal colonies.

It's more accurate to say that the Cloudotian criminals are *exiled* to Earth. No, they are not dangerous to you. Before exile, the prisoners are de-evolved in a few ways: 1) their ability to change density is removed; 2) they must remain in an oceanic environment where they can only survive outside the water for a short while; 3) their intelligence and mental abilities are restricted and; 4) their life spans are reduced to just a few years.

So with all these changes, these once extremely dangerous criminals on Sea of Clouds are no threat at all to you by the time they are exiled to your oceans. They still maintain enough intelligence to amaze your scientists and to survive in Earth's predatory oceans. They also retain the ability to communicate with each other via color changes of their skin. Eons ago, the only way Cloudotians could communicate was by flashing color patterns upon their skin. Now the Cloudotians only communicate this way during intense emotional moments. They are a very emotional and passionate people and watching their bodies ripple with flashing colors when they are excited is like watching rainbows belly dance! However, the Cloudotians have evolved into telepathic beings and now primarily communicate in this convenient manner. This telepathic ability is also stripped away from the exiled individuals during the de-evolution process.

Once you've had time to absorb all of this, you might

realize that I've put you on the path to solving one of your unsolved mysteries: UFOs (Unidentified Flying Objects). Since these prisoners are de-evolved, they can't survive in the cold vacuum of space anymore so they must be transported to Earth somehow. Which brings me to the fact that there is not just one species on your planet that actually evolved on Sea of Clouds, but two!

The Cloudotians create their spacecraft from living creatures, not metal. There is a creature on Sea of Clouds that is actually composed of hundreds of smaller versions of itself. This creature, called ഔℋ♌ᚷ᳚ (the giant small-one), are hundreds of individuals connected together to great one giant creature containing one hive mind that controls the whole. It is not intelligent, this occurs instinctively as a survival method.

The Cloudotians use the ഔℋ♌ᚷ᳚ to transport the banished prisoners to Earth. This becomes strictly a one-way trip for both the prisoners and the 'ship' in which they ride. The salt in your oceans prevents the ഔℋ♌ᚷ᳚ from staying connected together. So once the 'ship' plunges into the ocean, it dissolves into its hundreds of individuals who then live out their lives as single small creatures. So what you call UFOs are really ഔℋ♌ᚷ᳚ transporting prisoners to your oceans. Most of your UFOs are described as being round and saucer-like which is the shape of the ഔℋ♌ᚷ᳚. And you never find evidence because the 'UFO' dissolves into small creatures that you call jellyfish. Yes, jellyfish. Okay, okay, I agree you can be upset for the Cloudotians every time you get stung at the beach!! Other than that, they are pretty harmless.

The Cloudotians only use the ♏︎♓︎♌︎♈︎ॐ to transport exiles to Earth. They don't actually do too much space travel, and when they do, they stay in the general neighborhood of their own planet with only trips to nearby Mars and Jupiter. For these adventures they don't need the ♏︎♓︎♌︎♈︎ॐ as they are perfectly comfortable in space au natural for these relatively short journeys. However, they can't travel much beyond Jupiter without serious danger to themselves where death becomes their destination.

Okay, I think that's enough background for now so let's immerse ourselves into Quroak's memories again. Though I will immerse myself thoroughly into his actions, emotions, and life, during the journey it is always safest to not use the first person but the third person. Otherwise, the chance of losing your identity is much greater. Besides, it would be confusing to you, the reader, if I were to use the first person to refer to both myself and to Quroak.

CHAPTER 4

"Don't worry Xelrine, I know they will accept you," Quroak reassured her for what seemed like the eighth time. "They are very perceptive. They will see what I see in you and love you."

"But you said they aren't comfortable around most people," she worried.

"That's true, however, I'm positive that you have nothing to worry about," he replied tenderly but with a barely concealed exasperated sigh. He sent her warm and loving thoughts to try to reassure her.

"Well, you are a little biased," Xelrine thought-said happily.

Quroak's answer was to entwine their fourth and sixth arms in the Cloudotian equivalent of a human hug with devoted love shining in his eyes and his skin flushed a warm turquoise.

They had just left Sea Of Clouds' atmosphere on their

way to ♌ ♈ ♉ ♋ ♌ (Curon) which is the largest and closest of the three small moons that circle their homeworld. Curon means 'Blue Guardian' because it shines like a bright royal blue orb during the dark night looking like God's eye watching over the Cloudotians. Quroak could see why the superstitious ancient Cloudotians believed this. Especially since every night, a bright golden circular light traveled across the face of Curon, making it look like the eye was gazing down from the heavens upon their world searching from one end of the sky all the way to the other, making them feel watched over during the long cold night. Of course, it was discovered centuries later that the golden 'pupil' was really millions of glow-bats that migrate around the moon every night.

It was to visit the enchanted glow-bats that enticed him to fly to Curon as often as possible. He loved to fly with the glow-bats during their long nocturnal flights. The golden glow-bats are as intelligent as Earth's dolphins and are very sensitive to other's emotional state. He felt a connection with these lovely creatures for he felt they understood and accepted his deep emotions.

The glow-bats do not like intruders but accepted him as one of them. Throughout his life, he would find he was often the exception to the rule for a lot of people who would treat him differently, much to his confusion for he didn't feel he was special in any way. Anyway, when gliding with the glow-bats he felt at peace with the world.

And now, he wanted to share this experience with Xelrine. He had never shared this part of himself before and he was excited to be able to experience this with her. He knew she would be moved by a flight with the glow-bats, be totally absorbed in the mood-shifting experience and truly *get* it, why he loved doing this. This thought made him flush turquoise again with a wave of love for her gently washing through his heart.

Still holding her, he asked gently, "Are you okay?"

She turned her gaze towards him and with warmth in her eyes, "Sure, I'm okay."

As her skin was flushed a light yellow, he knew she was nervous as this was her very first time leaving Sea of Clouds' atmosphere. "You are doing great, Xelrine."

Laughing softly, she replied "Why thank you, kind sir. I feel safe with you."

Feeling happy, he declared in a solemn-flavored thoughtwave, "My lady, I will never let harm come to you nor let darkness shadow your soul's light."

"My hero!" she exclaimed. Then turning more serious, "It's just that after that time I was lightsick, I've just been afraid to go into space."

"I don't know too much about that disease. I just know that it's rare and it has something to do with your body shutting down because of too much or too little air. What was it like?"

"No, no, no. You know how our bodies immediately adapt to whatever environment we put ourselves into? If we are in ocean then our bodies extract nutrients from the water. When we're in the sky, as most of the time we are, the atmosphere is our main source of certain vitamins and energy. But when we go high up in the atmosphere where the air is very thin or when we go into space where there's no air, our bodies then gets what it needs from sunlight."

"Yes, I kind of knew this. Where does lightsickness come in?"

"When I was a child, I got the light-inhibitor disease where my body could not extract nutrients from light. I knew I was sick but I didn't know from what and I went with my parents up to the cloudtops to watch a comet. Well, I immediately felt weak, my whole body was convulsing while my head felt like it was going to explode and then I lost consciousness. My parents told me later that my skin turned a deathly pale blue as they rushed me down below and then to a hospital. The doctors said if I had been in the thin atmosphere for a minute more, I would have died."

"Oh, sunghost! That was horrible. No wonder you weren't in a hurry to try to go up again."

"Oh, they did cure me but after that experience I was just too scared to try again." Then she looked directly into Quroak's eyes saying quietly, "Until now."

He turned a dark blue with embarrassment, tinged with sea green to show his happiness. He had to remind himself to look away after a few moments. He was always finding himself lost in her in some way: her smiling eyes, her beauty, her mind's voice, her scent. Forcing himself back to a state where he could function was always a concentrated effort.

He couldn't believe these past couple months where he had been incredibly happy for the first time in his life. He was pretty introspective and thus knew himself pretty well. He knew his emotions ran deeper and stronger than most people's. His emotions were an ocean that overwhelmed him where whirlpools of depression would pull him to the deepest depths or storms of loneliness would batter his heart with waves of tortured agony. Yet at times, the ocean was so calm that it was a smooth mirror reflecting the warm, clear, green sky above where he felt so at peace, so at *one* with the world.

However, he had discovered something new about himself and it had surprised him. He always knew he was capable of love but never realized that it would be one of his strongest and deepest of emotions. His love for Xelrine was a physical force and he knew it would drive him to any lengths to fulfill that love where she was the center of his universe and he would do anything to protect and cherish her.

And the time spent with her always flew by so quickly, as if someone was playing around with the laws of physics. Everything with her just seemed to be so . . . the only word he could think of was *right*. It was like he finally found a piece of himself with her that had always been missing before.

Oh, sunghost!

Quroak gave a heavy sigh, subconsciously flattening his arms' suction cups reflecting sadness and tried to refocus his mind away from his daydreaming heart. A while ago, he had gotten into the habit of imagining Xelrine being with him, sharing experiences with him. He knew he did it purely out of loneliness and sometimes wondered if it was healthy or if he was slowly going crazy. He usually tried to stop doing it as soon as he realized he was having conversations with an imaginary partner, but sometimes he just couldn't help it. Sometimes it helped alleviate his pain of loneliness, other times it sharpened it.

But the love he felt *was* real, which confused him to no end. If she was imaginary, how could he be in love? Was she real and communicating with him from afar? He was going crazy trying to figure out was going on. He even wondered, well, really more of a passing thought, that maybe she was someone who had died and her spirit was trapped in this plane of existence somehow and her energy was attracted to his brainwave frequency, not only giving him her thoughts but also images of her now gone body.

All he knew was that he was talking with someone, whether real or imaginary, and that he was in love, real not imaginary. He figured this made his happiness an illusion, but when he was immersed in sharing with Xelrine, it just felt so great that he couldn't resist. *I'm really in trouble.*

As he was leaving the light green atmosphere embracing Sea Of Clouds, the stars slowly appeared as differently colored, cold points of light punching holes in the absolute blackness of space. The wonderfully multi-hued, banded Jupiter shined majestically in the distance with its slender rings glittering like a belt of diamonds encircling its center.

As he slipped from the atmosphere's glow, he transferred a portion of his mass into the other dimension until he felt comfortable in the vacuum of space. He paused for a few moments to float in quiet awe above his world, watching with wonder the clouds of light green and white lazily swirl. Occasionally, the clouds would part briefly to show a portion of a floating city before shrouding it again in ghostly mystery.

In the far west he could see a huge cyclone silently rage, pulling clouds into its funnel like a giant whirlpool. It was eerie watching such a storm in complete silence, especially since Quroak's body-memory could almost feel the crushing wind pulling him inward.

Quroak imagined Xelrine was with him and that he turned to look at Xelrine and his heart suddenly melted into a warm pool of love as he saw the world reflected brightly in her wonderfully bronze eyes with the pale green light of the planet shining upon her skin. But it was the smile in her eyes and the look of reverence on her face that made his central heart do things it wasn't accustomed to doing. At the touch of his tender warm thoughts, she turned to him, gracing him with the full light of her soul beaming from within, numbing him with pure emotion.

After a few moments, he thought-whispered, "You have to stop doing that to me".

"Doing what?" she innocently asked while he used all of this willpower to pull himself from the depths of her alluring eyes that promised magic and wonderful mysteries.

He swept her up in his arms and they danced to the humming of his heart with the planet's glow their dance floor, the stars the mood lighting and Curon their approving chaperon. He loved holding her in his arms for so many reasons but mostly because it was where he felt he belonged in the entire universe.

Reluctantly he let her go so they could continue to Curon. As they traveled, Xelrine was telling him about something that happened yesterday but he was barely aware of what she was saying because he was caught up in the way her thoughts softly caressed his mind with a warm sweetness, like a spring breeze blowing over the mint-apple cloudbeds of the North.

With a sigh he quietly chastised himself; *I have to stop doing this.* These imaginary scenes were occurring more and more often and each one always felt more real than the last. He couldn't really explain why. He tried not to think about her but she came to his mind unbidden quite frequently now. Somehow, something had changed four years ago during the cyclone accident with Tsin. How could he be in love, especially so deeply in love, with someone he never even met, with someone he didn't even know really existed? It was driving him crazy and at times he wished he could cut his own heart out so he could be at peace. He had done research into psychological cases and theory but hadn't been able to find any examples where this had happened before. Maybe he had a new type of insanity!

He forced himself to concentrate on the here and now and focused on what the current local conditions were, which he had checked this morning. His father had always stressed the importance of knowing what was happening in the solar neighborhood before venturing beyond Sea of Cloud's atmosphere and that was one lesson Quroak took to heart. His grandfather had died because he had not known Sea of Clouds was passing through a comet's path, wasn't paying attention and was skewered by a rain of ice particles, killing him instantly.

So Quroak knew Sol was acting up with massive solar flares throwing out an intense dose of high-energy particles. This proton storm was traveling at about one-third light speed but he was sure he could ride it out with no problems.

He also knew Jupiter was at its closest point with his world which many believed was the cause of the severe storms currently bedeviling his people. Scientists always said this was mere coincidence but since the cyclones always occurred more often with greater intensity when the king of planets grew to its biggest in their sky, he knew there had to be some connection that just wasn't found yet. The ancients had believed that at such times the banded giant was displeased with their civilization and was punishing them.

The cosmic report had also stated that fiery Io (moon of Jupiter) was right in between its master and Sea of Clouds and indeed he could see that yellow and orange mottled moon floating before the lighter oranges and browns of its giant parent. However, he could not see Prometheus, one of Io's largest volcanoes, erupting frozen sulfur dioxide snow 500 kilometers above its surface which was also mentioned in the report.

However, he couldn't see how any of these events could impact his short journey to Curon so he dismissed these facts as interesting but irrelevant.

He was flying through the quiet darkness with his mind drifting when he suddenly felt something odd. It felt like he was near a giant mass where there should have been empty space. He swirled around trying to locate the mysterious object when suddenly he saw a swirling current in the blackness of space where no current had any right to be. In fact, he realized with detached interest, the blackness of space was not so black anymore for the unexpected whirlpool shined a definite yellow.

Before he was able to rationalize what he was seeing, he was sucked into this yellow maelstrom. But even as he struggled for control, the phrase *black hole* popped into his whirling mind. Black hole! He knew giant black holes had been discovered at the center of most galaxies but no one had ever found one outside of a galactic center and certainly not within the solar system. And while galactic black holes were immense, at least in terms of mass, this one was extremely small; a rogue micro black hole! All of this flashed through his mind in an instant, barely noticed by his consciousness for Xelrine's image appeared quite clearly in his mind urging him to not panic as he was sucked deeper into its hungry grip.

"Xelrine?" he thought-whispered confused, as he tried to regained control of himself by decreasing his density to almost nothing. However, though his mass was now a tenth of normal, he still felt the hungry grip of the insatiable spatial drain spiraling him around its center.

He frantically looked around for Xelrine, but he couldn't see her anywhere! Had she already been swallowed by this cosmic monster! No, that can't be his heart screamed! Then a small part of his mind, a very detached and small part, told him that she couldn't be trapped in the black hole, otherwise she would be within the event horizon and appear to be frozen in space and time, at least to him. Then where was she?

His thoughts were like a cascading waterfall crashing upon rocks far below, throwing up a mist of confusion with the thundering roar deafening out his reasoning capabilities. He desperately tried to collect his thoughts into a cohesive flowing river again.

Fortunately, he was still at the top of the intense gravity well and lucky that the black hole was so tiny; otherwise he would never have been able to escape. Though, being an adventurous young lad, a part of him did want to surf the black hole. After all, he thought, how many people can say they have surfed a black hole!

Also, he was still above the event horizon, otherwise he'd have to deal with that whole crazy time dilation mess which he really didn't understand very well. Actually, he didn't comprehend it at all, though he seemed to be getting a lesson now since his growing fear for Xelrine was making his perception of time slow down to a crawl.

Then he remembered that he was alone, Xelrine wasn't with him. But her image had been so clear, much clearer than ever before and he could actually *feel* her presence. What in the name of *Guiding Star*'s moons was going on here? However, he soon became more worried about the event horizon as his confidence of escaping quickly evaporated like raindrops on the sun. He wasn't moving away from the center at all but was just traveling around and around in ever smaller circles with the stars in the background whirling by.

He frantically tried to fight the pulling force of the spatial whirlpool with all three of his hearts racing out of control and his arms flailing all around him. With his flesh shaded a light blue from fear, he tried to get his tumbling thoughts and body under control.

He had just barely regained control when he saw without comprehension the yellow whirlpool collapse upon itself in a flash, pulling him in and then the universe seemed to explode in eerie silence with the shockwave hitting him before he could even register the explosion itself, knocking him senseless and sending his limp body hurtling through space like seaweed before a tsunami.

CHAPTER 5

"Your honor, I intend to prove to this court that by definition Pluto is a planet," Quroak thought-said in a serious baritone voice to the judge who suspiciously looked like Xelrine dressed in a black gown sitting behind a wooden desk.

"Well, be quick about it. I have a full case load this morning and I don't want to miss Judge Judy", commanded the judge, waving her gavel carelessly about.

"Uh, yes, your honor. Gentle beings of the jury, the latest definition of a planet is, quote, a celestial body that 1) is in orbit around the Sun; 2) has sufficient mass so that it assumes a hydrostatic equilibrium (nearly round) shape and; 3) has 'cleared the neighborhood' around its orbit, unquote."

"I object!" shouted the prosecutor who jumped out of his chair as if it was on fire.

After a few moments of silence, the judge growled, "Well, what's your objection?"

"Oh! I just thought I was supposed to object. Well, never mind," as the prosecutor, who sounded a lot like Tsin, sat down.

"The jury will please erase the non-objection objection from their memories", instructed the judge wearily.

Quroak floated over to the jury box and began with sarcasm dripping from each word, "Well, the last time I was *there*, Pluto both orbits the Sun and is round!"

Laughter from the jury and audience echoed throughout the immense courtroom, which actually seemed to have no dimensions since the walls, floor and ceiling were hidden in a strange fog. The incensed judge pounded her gavel upon the desk screaming, "Order! There will be order in my court!"

"You will watch your tone while in my presence and conduct yourself in a manner showing respect and the seriousness of this case. Do I make myself clear, Mister Quack?" stressed the judge after quiet once again reigned in her minor kingdom.

"Uh, it's Quroak, your honor. Yes I understand."

"Whatever. You may continue."

In a more subdued tone, Quroak continued. "Anyway, that takes care of two out of the three conditions for a planet; orbiting the sun and being spherical. So that brings us to the question of the neighborhood being cleared. Well then, let's look at Earth. Earth is both preceded and followed by what the humans call Apollo asteroids, accompanying that planet every meter around its orbit. Should Earth be classified as a non-planet? What about Jupiter? Which is accompanied by the Trojans, should that be a non-planet? While you may argue about Earth, I dare say that no one in their right mind would contemplate saying Jupiter, the king of the planets, is not a planet!"

The jury reacted with shock at this declaration. Quroak knew full well that Jupiter was revered by all Cloudotians, if not by every sentient being in the solar system.

"So in conclusion, your honor, members of the jury, Pluto is just another planet that has company on its journey around the sun. The defense rests, your honor." With that, Quroak floated back to his chair with satisfaction and confidence that he had just won his case.

The judge turned to the jurors and instructed, "You now have to take everything you have heard in this case, evaluate and discuss it carefully and then return with your verdict."

The juror in the first row on the far right tentatively raised a hand, "Um, your honor, we have already come to a decision. We side with the prosecutor and declare that Pluto is not a planet!"

"May I ask how you reached that conclusion?"

"We found the witness from Earth to be most interesting and convincing in his story of how Pluto pals around with that Mickey character and getting into all kinds of mischief. Obviously, Pluto is a four-legged, long-eared, fun-loving carnivore and not a planet."

"Very well, then. The verdict has been given, received and entered into the books. Case closed." The judge rapped her gavel, arose and floated out of the court room, disappearing into the clouds as the jurors, prosecutor and audience just seemed to fade away.

Quroak floated at his desk, stunned with disbelief that the jury had been persuaded by a three year old human boy brought forth by the prosecutor. He held his aching head in his arms as the clouds disappeared from view and seemed to rematerialize within his mind as a hazy heaviness.

Then he dimly realized he was dreaming and strove to awaken fully, but the more he did the more his head felt like it had been slammed against a mountain; several times. Plus every muscle in his body was both stiff with agonizing pain and mushy from weakness.

As full awareness slowly returned, he kept his eyes closed while he tried to focus his mind to both think clearly and to reduce the blazing pain down to a candle flame to be compartmentalized in a deep dungeon of his mind so that he could function. He was usually pretty good at locking pain away but this time it was a long while before he was able to mentally sigh with relief and open his eyes.

He immediately wished he had kept them closed. Though he was shocked at what he saw, he put that aside for the moment because he was even more surprised at what he felt. Actually, what he felt was an absence, but he didn't understand right away what was missing. There was a huge emptiness, bigger, deeper, and darker than usual within. There was a dull quietness, a stillness that somehow seemed unnatural. But what was . . .

Then the reason boomed out of nowhere and echoed throughout the emptiness like a shout in the fabled bottomless caves of Miranda, moon of Uranus, where a whisper was amplified a hundredfold and bounced around undiminished for a whole day. XELRINE!!! She was no longer there with him in any way. He couldn't feel her presence. He couldn't feel the caress of her thoughts warming his mind, even in his imagination. In fact, she was now less than the dream harbored in his heart. She was like a faded photograph of a time long forgotten, once bright and clear but now clouded with age. There was nothing except his memory of her and the love in his heart. His heart felt like it was being ripped apart by ice-hard . . .

His heart? The *heartlink*? He had been part of a heartlink, the psychic link that forms whenever Cloudotians emotionally bond, and he hadn't even known it until now, now that the bond was broken. How was this possible? No, it couldn't be. The heartlink was a warm physical sensation where partners could always feel the other's presence in their heart when they were nearby, with the sensation weakening with distance but never dissipating altogether. And when one died, the heartlink was broken and the survivor felt a sharp coldness in the heart as if pierced by an icicle, just as he did now. But Xelrine wasn't *real*. She was just a dream, wasn't she?

Most thought it strange that the psychic link was created by the mind but was actually felt in the main heart; however, he had always found it appropriate since it was only formed from love. But he had never heard of his situation occurring before where a heartlink formed between two people that had never met.

It had always been believed that no distance was too great for the heartlink, but of course, no one had been as far from home as he was now. So either the distance was too great or Xelrine was . . .

"Sunghost!" he thought-shouted as loud as he could, hurting his mind. What is happening to me? She was never real! She was never with me! How can I feel her absence when she was never here? How could there have been a heartlink in the first place? Quickly spiraling in confused despair, he shouted and swirled his arms in rage while a deep part of his mind shivered in fear for his slipping sanity.

He slowly fell into a quiet state as he tired himself out. Actually, he fell into a state of numbness where he just didn't have the mental, physical or emotional energy anymore. He felt really, really lost right now and the nonsensical aspect of why made his mind whirl in circles. He decided he couldn't worry about this right now and needed to turn his attention to what he had seen when he had first opened his eyes, though it was so hard to think because his brain felt like it was swimming against a strong current deep in the ocean.

Floating in the vast blackness of space, he turned until he was facing the sun and he let the full implication of what he saw sink in: the sun looked *so small!* Though it was still brighter and larger than the pinprick stars awash in the sea of ebony, it no longer stood out as the center of the Solar System, afire with life-giving warmth. Instead, it was a small ball of cold light that at this distance only gave the memory of warmth and also dim hopes, but no promises, of heat if you got closer, *years* closer.

Despair sank his heart as he finally thought aloud what his subconscious had known: he was far beyond all the planets, far beyond Pluto and was near the outer edges of the Solar System! This is why he had dreamed that ridiculous Earth court scene regarding Pluto; his subconscious was trying to tell him where he was. He was stuck in the middle of the Kuiper Belt, floating lost in the hard vacuum of space without a ship! No Cloudotian had ever traveled much beyond Jupiter except within their living ships, the ♋♓♌♈ॐ. Even with the ♋♓♌♈ॐ, they had never traveled beyond Uranus, never mind Neptune and Pluto.

Unbidden, a masochistic part of his mind did the calculations just so that it would really hit home. Earth is one AU (Astronomical Unit) from the sun, which is

149,598,000 kilometers and it takes sunlight just over 8 minutes to reach Earth. He guessed he was now about 42 AUs (almost 7.5 billion kilometers) from his home where it takes sunlight 6 hours to reach! He was now 1.6 billion kilometers beyond Pluto, 4.6 billion kilometers beyond the furthest frontier explored by his people. Without a ship. And no snack food. Well, at least he still retained his sense of humor, he wryly thought.

But he found that he couldn't move a muscle as his very being just seemed to be frozen in shock. This was just too much! First losing contact with Xelrine, even though he knew it had been imaginary, and now this! He might as well have been thrown to another star system for all the chances he had in getting home in his lifetime! No, he couldn't think like this, it would just lead to the deepest depths of despair which would only beget defeat. He needed to think constructively.

But floating here in the unimaginable vastness of dull ebony, he couldn't help but feel incredibly small, so insignificant, so lost, like a grain of sand on the planet-wide dunes of Mars or a drop of water of his own ocean world. The stars stared unblinkingly at his plight, uncaring from their cold distance. He couldn't see any of the planets worshipping the faraway, incredibly shrunken sun. Ironically, he felt crushed in all of this emptiness with the loneliness squeezing his heart like a vice.

Even though he was so stunned he couldn't move, only stare at the tiny sun, his mind frantically raced, trying to piece together what happened. His mind jumped around in a near panic, barely putting together any coherent thoughts. He slowly forced his thoughts to construct a picture of the cosmic neighborhood at the time of the black hole explosion. Actually, more like a movie that a part of his mind cobbled together with both a shaky panic and a strange detachment.

He could see himself about three-fourths of the way to Curon with Sea of Clouds behind him and the brilliant (and much bigger) sun to his left with the proton storm racing towards the outer Solar System, towards him. Millions of kilometers beyond Curon was Io, seemingly floating high in Jupiter's ochre clouds, with the erupting Prometheus facing Curon.

Then he saw the rogue micro black hole appear halfway between his homeworld and Curon and it pulled the erupting sulfuric snow from above Io towards itself creating the yellow whirlpool draining into the back hole. He saw himself sucked into the whirling current and then his ineffective struggle to escape. Frustration made him silently scream in his mind and every muscle in his body tighten into balls of anger because it seemed that the black hole had appeared out of nowhere which was not possible.

But then the proton storm hit the whirlpool! In an instant the black hole collapsed upon itself and then exploded outward, creating a shockwave traveling at what must have been two-thirds the speed of light, almost

200,000 kilometers per second! He saw his limp body carried by the shockwave until he was thrown into the Kuiper Belt where he suddenly stopped.

He knew the shockwave would not have dissipated so quickly so he assumed his subconscious must have regained control to reduce his mass to next to nothing to escape the shockwave's grip. But even at two-thirds light speed, it would have taken something like ten to twelve hours to reach where he was now. So it took that long for his mind to regain control during which his body had been at the mercy of the solar storm and though the shockwave front would have knocked away space dust and rocks thus protecting him while being propelled outward, he still felt like he had been beaten to a pulp.

Though he was not a physicist, he was pretty sure black holes don't usually explode. They either grow more massive by sucking in more and more matter or they evaporate slowly into extinction. He thought that maybe the combination of the proton storm and the sulfur dioxide somehow created the impossible: an exploding black hole. But it just didn't sound right. There must be another explanation but he wasn't scientist enough to figure it out.

He knew this had never happened before in the history of his people. No one knew that a black hole could explode. In fact, no one had ever been close to a black hole before. So, on the one hand he felt proud for being the first to surf a black hole! On the other hand, he wished he had listened to that small voice in his head telling him to sleep in that morning!

Xelrine! Exploding black hole! Kuiper Belt! Stranded! These words exploded in his mind like supernovas, evaporating his fragile thought processing into atoms, dissipating in the lonely, dark night. He just floated there, dazed, staring at the sun, oh, so far away.

Still not believing what happened, Quroak felt depressed seeing how small the sun looked. And Jupiter, well, he couldn't see Jupiter and its absence affected him more deeply than he could have imagined before. On his home world, Jupiter was always in the sky like a caring guardian where it was a basketball-sized orb with gold, brown and green bands hanging in the sky, shining just as bright as Curon and the other two moons.

There were many myths and legends regarding Jupiter that resonated deep in the Cloudotian soul. These stories all have a common theme; that Jupiter would always lead you on the right path of your life if you just opened your heart and listened. Also, the gentle giant would always guide you home whenever lost. The first tine he visited *Guiding Star*, which is his people's name for Jupiter, he was deeply moved by the majestic giant and like most Cloudotians, felt as if his soul was kissed by God. It was the first time in his life he could not feel the presence of that warm giant and he found it very disconcerting and felt totally alone.

Alone, he thought wearily. No one had ever been this

alone before, this far from home. Waves of cold depression washed through his heart, his soul, freezing his mind, turning his body to ice. The waves were like the surf of the ocean on Earth, where each onslaught eroded more of his life-force, leaving him more and more empty until the emptiness swallowed him whole, submerging him in a sea of numbness.

He kept telling himself he had to do something, but he didn't know what. He felt he should do anything, anything at all just to get himself moving again, but he couldn't find the willpower. He felt like an asteroid floating in the deep darkness with no volition of its own, helpless to the whims of the universe.

His mind struggled to reach the surface of the numb sea, but the cold depths kept reaching up to drag him back to the stygian bottom. Then Xelrine's face with her gorgeous smiling eyes floated into his mind and he clung to her image, using it as a magic lifeboat to help him escape from the grip of the debilitating depths.

After what felt like days, he finally found the mental strength and resolve to move. Though an empty, cold, numbness still gripped his heart, he was now at least able to think and to start taking control of himself. Looking slowly around, he noticed a cluster of asteroids close by, about 2,000 kilometers away.

So he slowly forced himself to head towards the asteroids. He needed to rest and collect his thoughts that were whirling around like the Great Red Spot! He wasn't even sure where he was and needed to get his bearings before just heading towards the sun that was so depressingly small.

When he drifted up to the largest asteroid in the cluster, he collapsed upon the dark, gray, and icy surface and just stared at the tiny sun for what seemed like hours with his mind no longer in a whirl, but frozen on the numbing thought of how far from home he must really be.

He had always felt alone and now, of course, he was really alone! He laid there just feeling waves of depression wash through him and he felt a coldness grip his soul so tight he couldn't remember what warmth felt like. He tried to gather all his inner strength and weave it into a cloak to protect his heart from the cold despair attacking him like the frozen sand storms on Mars. He knew he had a very long and hard journey ahead of him and needed to control his emotions. With his heart thus cloaked, Quroak's mind slowly thawed out and he created a heavy blanket of acceptance of the situation to cover his depression and then stitched together resolve to control his own fate.

CHAPTER 6

"**M**e", I said firmly, withdrawing from Quroak's memories.

"I'm sorry dear readers, but I need a break. It is exhausting experiencing intense emotions. While I'm used to it both because of my own emotions and because of my job, it still takes a lot out of me. And believe me, deep, intense emotions can't be truly described with words so reading about the experience is not the same as actually feeling it."

"But I can tell you that I've never felt more lost, more alone than I do at this moment because I have absorbed Quroak's emotions and it will take some time for them to fade."

"Let me take this opportunity to explain a few things to you. First, to the best of my ability, I'm converting objects and measurements that are alien to you into human terms for your comprehension. For example, when figuring out how far he was from home, Quroak naturally uses terms that mean something to him. To him, an *astronomical unit*, or rather, his term for the concept, is the distance from the sun to Sea of Clouds, not Earth. And he doesn't' even know what a *kilometer* is. Everyone in the Solar System, except humanity, uses *zulats* to measure distance which is extremely accurate, logical and intuitively understood."

"A *zulat* is the distance a Mercurian bloodeagle can travel in the vacuum of space in the time it takes Mercury to travel $1/1,000,000^{th}$ of its orbit around the sun when the planets are perfectly aligned and the bloodeagle is chased by a sunghost. Don't ask. It's from ancient times, but trust me, it is intuitive."

"So anyway, I'm doing all the conversions for you. The same is true for things like time. Obviously, a day, month, year, et cetera is different for each planet, so a day for Quroak is about 1.6 times longer than an Earth day and his year is 2.4 times longer than your year."

"Second, you may be wondering how Quroak can possibly see small asteroids 2,000 kilometers away in the deep darkness of space. Cloudotians' visual range covers more of the electromagnetic spectrum than human eyes where they can see into both the ultraviolet and infrared frequencies and they have excellent night vision like your feline friends. In fact, they got that particular talent from the cats as a gift for . . . whoops, sorry, we're now back into the highly sensitive and classified area again! Please forget I said anything. *For your own safety.*"

"Besides, most objects in space reflect at least some sunlight. Except, of course, the moon around Venus, which absorbs all light like a black hole. What, you never saw Venus's moon? I'll let you figure that out for yourself."

"Also, Cloudotians have the amazing and unique talent of being able to sense the curvature of space caused by celestial objects. In other words, they can detect the gravity well of planets, moons and even small objects such as asteroids and comets."

"Third, if I was you, I would be asking just how fast can Cloudotians travel in space. Well, let's just say that sneaking up on a comet by surfing up through its tail is another favorite pastime for them, and most comets travel around 20,000 kph. Despite their ability to shift their mass to another dimension, their top speed within a planetary atmosphere is very much slower, much to their disappointment."

"Okay. I think I'm ready to re-submerge into Quroak's memories.

CHAPTER 7

So Quroak forced himself up and started exploring this small, rocky and icy planetoid. He quickly discovered signs that this asteroid had been mined in the recent past. Now that he was thinking somewhat clearly again, he realized he must be pretty deep into the Kuiper Belt which his mind was still struggling to accept. But he knew be couldn't be on any asteroid near any of the planets because the sun was so small plus he would have been able to sense such a large gravity well if it was relatively nearby.

No, he was definitely in the Kuiper Belt. And now he had just discovered that someone was mining the Belt! He was dazed by this revelation! He knew his people had never been out this far so it wasn't them. And the indigenous species of *Guiding Star* never left their miniature solar system created by the gas giant because they felt nothing else existed that was worth their attention. None of the other species he knew of had ever been beyond Uranus and certainly no Earthling had ever been beyond their own moon so that left them out.

So that meant some other hitherto unknown civilization existed in the Solar System. He became excited at the thought that he could be the first to meet new sentient beings with obvious intelligence.

All of a sudden, his depressing predicament became an adventure! At least he was going to try to treat it as such to help fight off despair. He imagined dropping an anchor into this calming thought to hold him steady against the emotional storms and started to explore.

The star-speckled night was the only source of illumination, with the starlight clear and sharp on this airless rock the size of a large mountain. He quickly found a huge crater that was obviously created by some kind of high-energy blast, for the dark gray walls were completely smooth. It definitely was not an impact crater caused by the frequent colliding of the asteroids in the Belt.

Walking around the lip of the bowl he discovered a channel that was twenty meters deep and fifteen meters wide. This channel was smooth as glass and ended right at the edge of the crater. Since there didn't seem to be anything else to see here, he decided to follow the channel to see where it began.

While following the channel he came upon many smaller arteries feeding the main canal but he decided not to branch off and continued following the main conduit.

After about two kilometers, the channel led to a shallow spoon-shaped depression with the opening of a cavern at the back of the spoon. As he was about to venture into the cavern, movement caused him to glance up and then violently dive to the ground! A bright purple flash followed by two burnt orange flashes sped across his face signifying danger.

Quickly turning over to see what the danger was, he looked up to see one of the other asteroids in this local cluster pass overhead and on this airless world it looked close enough for him to reach up and touch it, but it was probably a couple of dozen kilometers away. Rising up sheepishly and gingerly brushing off the clinging asteroid dust from his still aching body, he reflected amusingly that at least his reactions weren't dulled by the black hole experience, even if it was to a non-threat.

Entering the cavern boldly, as if making up for his prior show of jumpiness, he was surprised to find a soft bluish light glowing from the rock walls, providing plenty of illumination to see everything clearly without being glaring. The floor was amazingly flat with the walls and ceiling round and smooth. It was also quite empty except for a small pedestal-like structure near the left wall. It seemed to flow up out of the floor, matching the cavern material.

Crossing over to the pedestal, he saw that the slightly convex surface was translucent. He appreciatively caressed the smooth surface and then jerked back, flashed bright purple tinted with yellow in surprise and thought-yelped "Sunghost!" when oddly shaped colored figures flashed into existence floating about half a meter above the pedestal.

He immediately looked around to make sure there was no sunghost lurking around, and then shook his head in disgust at his subconscious superstition. Sunghosts have the nasty habit of appearing out of nowhere, frightening whomever they appeared to, and then giving chase if the startled individual fled. It was once believed that you would conjure up a sunghost just by thinking the word loud enough. He always thought it was funny that his people got into the habit of using the very word they tried to avoid as a curse when startled. He figured it was some kind of masochistic subconscious revenge of some kind.

After ruefully assuring himself he was alone, he realized he must have activated some kind of computer interface. The figures were a combination of squiggly lines and oddly juxtaposed geometric shapes. He could only assume it was some kind of language. He quickly discovered that focusing on a symbol for a couple of seconds caused more data to appear, apparently relating to the mysterious symbol focused upon, but it was totally meaningless to him. After a while he focused on a symbol that looked like:

This caused a spectacular image of the Solar System to appear. Not a diagram, but an actual picture about 10 meters wide and 4 meters high! The sun was in the center with the planets in different positions around their respective orbits. He was surprised to see his own planet, Sea of Clouds, correctly shown. Obviously this species was not fooled by the asteroid belt illusion.

Feeling homesick, he gazed at his world, causing the picture to zoom in so that Sea of Clouds filled the whole image. The image was so clear and close he could make out the cloud cities! Oh how he longed to be surfing the windstorms of home!

Then his heart sank as Xelrine's hazy image came into his mind with her smiling eyes filling him with tender love. He made a quick but heartfelt prayer to *Guiding Star*, asking for her to be real then tried to focus once again at the task at hand.

He noticed a small flashing symbol of progressively smaller circles at the bottom of the image. When he focused on that symbol his homeworld shrunk as if he was flying away from it and the whole solar system was once again displayed.

He quickly looked for and found Pluto and the Kuiper Belt, of which Pluto is a member. He zoomed in on one section of the Kuiper Belt which brought into close focus several planetoids. Quroak wanted to find the specific asteroid he was currently on so he could study the immediate neighborhood. He knew this was a daunting task for the Belt was about 20 AUs wide, containing hundreds of thousands of asteroids and planetoids. Finding one asteroid among so many in such a huge volume of space made looking for a specific grain of sand on a small beach look easy! *Why couldn't they have put a 'you are here' notation on this image?*

He spent most of his time over the next several days searching for his asteroid on the map. Since asteroids this far out don't have proper days as they don't rotate regularly but tumble chaotically during their journey, he had to guess the passage of time.

When he wasn't searching, he took short breaks to sleep but he always dreamed about Xelrine which made him more depressed since he couldn't figure out what had happened regarding her because before she had always seemed real somehow. Now she was just a dream, a desire of what could be if he met the right person. That's assuming, of course, that he made it back home.

Awakening each time after dreaming of her, he sent his mind outward in desperation, hoping he'd be able to sense her, but always to no avail. He would then cling desperately to the wish that the heartlink would be reestablished so that he could at least *hope* that it meant she was real and waiting for him.

After these restless naps, he explored the several tunnels leading off from the main cavern just to keep busy while letting his mind rest from staring at the photographic map for hours on end. The round tunnels with the bluish illumination ran for kilometers deep into the asteroid. The walls, floor and ceiling were smooth as glass and at every quarter kilometer there was a round hole in the ceiling about a half meter in diameter. These holes were only half a meter deep and seemed to connect to a smaller tunnel.

Normally this would have teased his curiosity enough for him to track down the reason for this peculiar layout. However, his usually sharp sense of curiosity was somewhat dulled by the frustration of locating this asteroid on the map and the forever dark circle of depression threatening to swallow him whole.

Then after awakening from an extra long nap, he decided he needed the distraction of figuring out the rhyme and reason of these tunnels in order to help him fight off the encroaching despair.

So he picked a tunnel at random and set off down it, determined to find its end. After a couple of hours, as he brushed one side of the tunnel with the suckers of one arm (he liked the sensation he felt every time he pulled a sucker off the glass-like surface) he felt a vibration through the wall. With his interest now sharpened, he increased the speed of his flight down the circular tunnel.

After another hour passed by, he saw an eerie dark green glow up ahead that for some reason sent chills throughout his arms. The glow seemed to dance wildly like verdant fire along the walls in the otherwise pitch black darkness, as if living flames were reaching out to ensnare him. He slowed his pace cautiously with every nerve on the alert.

Then, after another half hour of approaching the green light slowly, with his imagination running on overdrive, conjuring up monsters of all kinds with the vibrations in the walls getting stronger and stronger, he came upon a spherical mechanical device about six meters in diameter busily eating into the asteroid with a sphere of emerald green light pulverizing the rock into dust, thereby extending the tunnel.

The dancing flames affect was caused by the rock dust roiling in the airless tunnel before it was sucked into the ceiling holes leading to the hidden smaller tunnel. He assumed the dust was being collected via that tunnel in some way. So this asteroid really was being mined by someone but apparently it was fully automated.

He flushed a dark turquoise with excitement as he realized the implications of this discovery. He reasoned the minerals extracted from the asteroid must either be loaded onto an automated ship or was stockpiled to be picked up at some point by whoever had set up this whole operation.

Filling a little giddy at this revelation, he squeezed himself into the nearest ceiling hole. For some reason, whenever he did this kind of thing he always remembered how his de-evolved cousins exiled to Earth amazed humans with their ability to squeeze their bodies into seemingly impossibly small-sized holes, like bottles.

He once saw a video showing a man frantically searching his lab for an escapee who had freed himself through a small gap between the lid and the tank. As the former occupant had been at least ten times bigger than the gap, the man had reacted like the octopus must be part ghost or something. Quroak had laughed when seeing the man's face (and being told what the human's expression meant) and he always recalled that image whenever he was doing his 'ghost' act. Although, it was much easier for him since he could transfer most of his mass, which was *really* ghostlike behavior, unlike his de-evolved brethren.

At the end of the small tunnel he found the mineral dust being blown into a huge cavern, piling up at the far wall. From lingering dust marks on the walls, he deduced that once the cavern was filled, it was then emptied, probably into a freighter ship of some kind to be transported to the owner's home planet. Unfortunately, the cavern was currently only about a tenth full and his best guess was that it would be months before it got full enough for anyone to want to empty it.

Disheartened, he went to the asteroid's sterile surface to see if there were any ships waiting around to transport the raw material but all he found was what he expected: a star-sprinkled black ocean floating above a ragged, dark gray ball of rock.

Eyes brimming with frustrated tears, he floated above the asteroid to let his body absorb needed nutrients from the sun. After staring at the sun wistfully for a couple of hours with his mind drifting like seaweed in ocean currents, he pulled himself together and went below to search one more tunnel that for some reason he sensed was a very short passage.

He quickly found he was correct and discovered the passage ended in a wall of water ice. There was also a small heating device that could be used to melt the rock solid ice into liquefied water he could drink.

The next couple of days he spent solely studying the map with short breaks to the surface. He had to continuously fight his depression to keep his motivation strong enough to continue searching. And the only way he could fight the depression now was by forcing his mind on his task. It was a vicious circle that was slowly driving him mad. His heart was heavy and his emotions were the icy storms of Neptune ripping him apart inside. Performing the simplest action felt as if he was buried in the cold sand dunes of Mars. Though these feelings were not new to him, it was a constant struggle requiring a vast reservoir of mental and emotional energy.

Then he finally located his asteroid on the map. Now that he found his asteroid and focused on it, a big planetoid began blinking in the picture relatively near his current location. He focused on the small world to make the image zoom in to fill the whole viewing area. It was an icy dwarf planet tinged with green and it looked vaguely familiar. With practice from his research, he had learned how to slowly zoom in and out. He slowly zoomed out until the icy world became the size of a *windball*. (Note to reader: a *windball* is a six-dimensional sphere used in a complex game while windstorm surfing. For your purposes, experiencing only three dimensions, think of a bowling ball.) Now he recognized it! It was the planetoid called Quaoar, which is about half the size of Pluto. His people had never seen Quaoar bigger or clearer than the current image so he hadn't recognized it from the closer view.

Quaoar! Now he knew exactly how far from home he really was! The map told him that Quaoar was currently approaching its furthest distance from the sun which put him about two-thirds of the way into the Kuiper Belt. So he was about 45 AUs from the sun, or just over 42 AUs from home! And that was only if he timed his homecoming to be when Sea of Clouds was on this side of the sun, otherwise he would have to go up to an extra six AUs. So, between 42 and 48 AUs to get home.

Although he had guessed where he was before, thinking and knowing turned out to be two totally different things for he immediately turned ice cold inside and the darkness embraced his soul so tight it threatened to merge with him permanently, evaporating his willpower into oblivion.

His mind shut down, all thoughts stopped cold, as he felt his essence shrink until he felt as small as a speck of dust while a part of his consciousness seemed to separate from the rest of himself, feeling like he was floating near the cavern's ceiling, looking down upon himself with detached interest.

He hovered above the pedestal almost perfectly still for what seemed like hours, except for the automatic reflexes that kept him afloat, frozen in mind and soul like the surface of Triton (the coldest place in the Solar System). Abruptly, his consciousness merged whole again, his essence morphed back to the right size and his thoughts escaped their frozen trap, spewing out like an ice geyser erupting on that pinkish ice moon and his hearts suddenly raced as if ignited by a Neptunian lightning bolt.

He forced his mind and hearts to slow down from their frantic pace, stretched his muscles that ached from acting like a statue for so long, and pictured his soul extracting itself from the cold darkness of depression.

He focused on Quaoar making the photo-map zoom in on that planetoid. He was again amazed at the clarity of the picture. Quaoar was a light green hued icy world with cracks running along its surface. The world spun at a very slow rate and . . . what, he could see the sphere rotate? Bright purple tinged with yellow raced across his face from surprise. The sphere rotating seemed to indicate this image was real-time, not just a stored picture as he had thought! This technological achievement really was amazing!

Grasping at anything that would help distract himself from the darkness still hovering over him like a live shadow ready to pounce, he welcomed the quiet excitement filling his mind as he zoomed in for a closer look, focusing on a crack that looked a little too linear.

Suddenly his face lit up dark turquoise from excitement for he saw a small ship fly into the crack! There was either a civilization there or someone was exploring the frozen world! Quroak was willing to bet the flying craft was native to Quaoar because that crevice was just too straight to have occurred naturally. Plus he figured this must be why this world was the only one blinking in the whole image: it was the homeworld of the miners of this asteroid! Quroak now had a destination and he calculated the planetoid to be only about 400,000 kilometers away.

CHAPTER 8

After trying to catch up on his sleep and then giving it up as a lost cause, Quroak left the asteroid and sped to the small frozen world. Though he was excited about what he may discover, he couldn't help but wonder if he shouldn't just head back towards Sea Of Clouds. He figured it would take about twenty years to get home traveling in a straight line. Thinking about that long journey was just too depressing. And postponing for a little while wasn't going to make much difference in a twenty year trip.

However, he wanted to get home as quickly as possible and twenty years was way too long, about twenty years too long as far as he was concerned. Though he kept replaying the incident in his mind for any clues hidden in his subconscious, he just had no idea how the whole thing was even remotely possible. And something told him that he had to get back as soon as possible. He didn't understand why, but he thought it had something to do with Xelrine. It was kind of driving him crazy. *I have to get back so I can continue pretending I have someone in my life? I really have gone where no one has gone before!* That paraphrased quote reminded him of his favorite Earth television program and he wondered what Spock would do in this situation.

He thought-screamed at the universe in total rage and frustration at his unjust and highly unlikely predicament. How could Fate tease him for years with the potential of meeting the girl of his dreams, in more than one way, making him think he was crazy for imagining her with him and then just totally rip apart his reality with the impossibility of an exploding black hole separating him from home in both space and time! He screamed so loud and long it felt like his head was going to explode. With herculean effort, he forced himself to stop and quiet himself. He was emotionally exhausted and drained of willpower. But he forced himself onward. He thought wearily: *I have to get home, if only for my sanity's sake.*

Somehow, he didn't think the cool-minded Vulcan would have reacted the same way.

He usually loved the ebony darkness of space with the sea of stars shining like beacons in the night, promising both warmth and wonders. But now it felt like a sea of black emptiness with the faraway suns cold, indifferent observers, like bored gods who only watch silently while life unfolds before them, totally lacking the capacity for compassion to either intervene or interact with the lower forms of life.

So with only his unwanted thoughts to keep him company, his need to be with Xelrine his driving force and his frayed willpower a tattered cloak against the seemingly hostile elements of the night, he turned his attention to the approaching new world. He did his best to ignore the cold stares of the gods that were mocking him.

Though he was in the Kuiper Belt which consisted of hundreds of thousands of asteroids, the occupied volume of space was so immense that it was easy for him to keep the sun in sight to receive whatever meager warmth and nourishment Sol offered at this distance.

Seeing and sensing so many asteroids made him alternately imagine of a world long destroyed with him flying through the remaining rubble and of a world that never was because the rocks never coalesced into a viable planet creating possibilities for life. Both sent a fresh chill of sadness through his soul as he quietly passed through the graveyard, or unfulfilled nursery as the case may be.

Arriving at the green tinted airless orb a few days later, Quroak noticed how smooth the surface appeared to be. True, there were quite a few cracks running across the globe's surface but otherwise it was icy smooth. Being a part of the Kuiper Belt he expected to see a rough surface heavily cratered from impacts.

Slowly circling the planet, he soon found the narrow canyon into which he saw the ship disappear. Like the rest of the world, the canyon walls were icy gray rock with veins and patches of mint green. Unlike the rest of the world, this huge crack was just a little too straight. At this distance from the sun there was barely the hint of a glow reflecting off the frozen land. He floated down into the crevice where the extremely faint sunlight barely penetrated at all.

The almost total darkness taxed even his superb night vision. After drifting down for about two kilometers, Quroak flipped over to look up to see a faint halo of greenish gray created from the dim sunlight reflected off the icy walls towering over him with a distant small slice of an ebony black ceiling studded with pinpoints of slightly colored lights from faraway stars. Though the canyon was about a hundred meters across, down this far he could feel the presence of the massive walls closing in on him.

Turning over to again face the blackness below, he mused to himself that it was a good thing Cloudotians never suffered claustrophobia. In fact, this phenomenon was never heard of until they encountered the Jovians who are notorious for their fear of closed-in spaces. He figured anyone living in the clouds of such a gigantic planet with no enclosures would naturally feel threatened in a relatively tight space. He knew they always underwent a treatment of hypnosis whenever they traveled in their spaceships, which was rare.

After traveling downward another two kilometers,

Quroak reached the bottom. He hadn't discovered any signs of civilization thus far so he arbitrarily picked a direction and started exploring the length of the crevice. He soon traveled over a spot that seemed slightly different somehow. Everything looked the same but there was a sense of something missing.

He turned around and retraced his flight slowly. He quickly found the place that alerted his senses though he couldn't see anything odd. *Ah ha!* He sensed the mass density of the canyon floor drop to almost nothing right here compared to the rest of the ground. There seemed to be a hundred meter diameter patch of ground where it was hollow!

Upon very close scrutiny he discovered an almost microscopic seam outlining the circular area. He had found the door or portal into which he had seen the spaceship fly into while he was on the mined asteroid. *Now, how to get inside?* He didn't think he could just knock on the door like a neighbor dropping by to borrow a clove of cloudmint. Besides, since there were no clouds on this world, what were the chances of them having cloudmint?

Then he thought, why not? He wouldn't ask for cloudmint of course, but why not just knock friendly like? He wasn't trying to do anything wrong.

Then a few scenarios flashed through his mind in rapid succession, all of them bad. What if the inhabitants were a warrior race who shot first then asked questions?

Or were extreme xenophobes who wouldn't tolerate outsiders poisoning their carefully controlled society and thus would vaporize him with their ray gun? Or they may value their privacy to the extent they'd kill to protect it. Or it may be a civilization of geriatrics who feed off the brains or life-energy of the young to prolong their existence so they can see who gets voted off the island!

Great, just great! That's what I get for leaving myself open to Earth's broadcasts! He knew most of his people carefully shielded their minds from the human's television and radio transmissions which flooded the Solar System, for the constant noise would drive them insane if they didn't protect themselves.

But he had taught himself to filter through the cacophony and select specific frequencies so that he could pick and choose what he wanted to hear and see in his mind. He loved the bumbling antics of Maxwell Smart who always seemed to solve the case, though usually with the unnoticed assistance from 99.

His favorite programs of all were the *Star Trek* series. He enjoyed it because it was one of the few shows where the Earthlings projected a better future for themselves, not a world scarred by war with a decimated population barely surviving in the radioactive rubble. He especially related to the 'aliens' who tried to fit into the human's world, like Spock, Odo and Data. His favorite episode was the first show of *The Next Generation* where Picard rescued a space creature that looked like a 'jellyfish' from Farpoint

Station. Quroak had told his friends about this, how the story was about saving a 𝔰𝔬ℋ𝔰ℓ𝚼𝔸 (the giant small-one), but they weren't amused and they didn't understand why he paid attention to Earth's forms of entertainment, much less enjoy them.

However, he took their scorn in stride for he knew it came from societal embarrassment of an incident the Cloudotians wished they could erase from their history. In the past, the human's transmissions were monitored by the government and many shows were shared with the general population. Then one year, over the course of a few weeks, hundreds of thousands of citizens petitioned the government to take action based on one of these shows, to actually attempt a rescue of a group of people who were stranded and lost to the rest of the Earth. The rescue attempt failed miserably because there was no one to save and this is when Cloudotians realized that most of the transmissions from Earth consisted of fantasies, not real life events. Ever since then, Earth's broadcasts were ignored by most Cloudotians and the name *Gilligan* became a nasty word never to be muttered unless you really wanted to deliberately embarrass and anger someone.

CHAPTER 9

So with ignoring the highly likely possibilities of violent warrior races, ray gun toting xenophobes and life-sucking geriatrics preying on the young, Quroak proceeded with the idea of knocking on their door. He was pretty sure the portal must be too thick for the inhabitants to hear a knock so he searched for a smaller service door. He soon found the thin seam of a two-meter diameter circular door etched in the crevice wall. As he studied the door that looked exactly like the rest of the rocky surface, it suddenly popped inward half a meter and rolled to one side, surprising him so that he jerked backwards.

Flushed a yellowish purple, he gazed into the revealed tunnel which showed a pale jade glow leading into the distance. He didn't know if he had somehow triggered the door to open or he was being invited inside. He hadn't come this far just to turn back so he drifted inside where upon the portal rolled shut.

He tried to determine how to open the door from the inside but to no avail. Since his choices were few, well, actually one, he started to travel down the round tunnel. Since he was almost equally comfortable on a living world and in the vacuum of space, it took him a while to realize that there was an atmosphere here. He vaguely wondered why the atmosphere didn't escape when the portal had opened. He guessed the air was mostly nitrogen and methane which he knew would not adversely affect him.

The tunnel walls were smooth as glass and the pale green glow barely pushed back the curtain of total blackness. Usually he liked the dark, but ever since the whole black hole thing -*Sunghosts, over a week ago!* - he hadn't felt the comfort of wonderfully bright light what with being on the asteroid, traveling through space and now this small world and it certainly wasn't helping to improve his dark mood.

The similarity between this tunnel and the underground passageways at the asteroid seemed to indicate he was right in thinking the same society was responsible for both. The tunnel sloped downward and as he floated along he discovered many smaller passageways leading off on both sides. However, the curious Cloudotian continued going straight until he came upon another round door after about three kilometers. This door, however, actually looked like a door. Actually, it looked like a part of the tunnel wall but you could see an outline indicating that it was in fact, a door. Obviously, there was no need to hide this door.

As soon as he approached the portal, it rolled open to reveal a short corridor. Either the inhabitants weren't worried about uninvited guests or he was expected. Maybe those old folks *were* hungry for his life-force after all!

As he slowly traveled to the end of the hall, he mightily wished Xelrine was with him, even if only in his mind, so that he could be sharing this experience. *Life is about stumbling through it with someone special where you can be each other's lighthouse when you've lost the shores, not all by yourself in the dark stormy seas. Umm, maybe I should start doing poetry when I get back home, that is, if I get back home.*

At the corridor's end, he discovered a huge open space occupied by the strangest and most beautiful city he had ever seen! The city stretched beyond what the eye could see and was made entirely of crystal!

The buildings were incredible structures of spheres, domes, round triangles and wavy rectangles. There were no sharp edges to be seen anywhere. It was like the crystal had been poured into the various shapes. In fact, the structures gave the impression of liquid crystal. He imagined that if the currents of the wind could be seen, it would look like the flowing crystal of this city with its translucent structures softly shimmering in every shade of blue and green imaginable, perfectly blended and flowing like soft breezes. It was truly breathtaking and he just let the pure beauty of it all permeate his soul as he floated just inside the entrance, mesmerized.

The whole city was illuminated by the pale green light

emanating from the stone walls of this inner world and though the ceiling looked to be about one kilometer above the ground and most of the wall was lost in the distance, everywhere was lighted the same with no darkness or shadows to be seen.

Though it wasn't the type of light he was used to, he reveled in it, letting it wash over and through him with its warm caress, enjoying not being in the dark anymore. He had been ignoring how cold he felt externally since being flung to the outer reaches of, well, of everywhere. Oh, how good it felt to be warm again, though it still didn't touch the frigidness created from within, by his emotions.

At first, he thought the crystalline city was empty of life but then he shot twenty meters straight up and turned bright violet with a double burst of dark orange!

By the corridor entrance where he had exited from, were two tall, wide, flat sculptures of alien design. They were made of grayish white crystal with veins of brownish red flowing throughout. They were completely alien shaped to Quroak. (Note to reader: they looked kind of like spearmint leaves.) The top halves had been leaning against the wall. What had startled him was when one of them had suddenly leaned over and gently touched him!

Quroak tried to calm his racing hearts as he floated back to the ground cautiously where he examined the sculpture that clearly was not a sculpture! In turn, the living sculpture twisted this way and that way seemingly to study him as well.

Quroak couldn't decide if this was a plant or an animal but it was alive and he started to feel a tickling in his mind. He sent a friendly thought towards the alien and opened his mind with vague hopes of a response.

The alien did not respond with thoughts but Quroak sensed that the alien seemed satisfied that the Cloudotian posed no threat because it went back to leaning against the wall. The alien seemed to be rubbing the wall, creating gray dust that it then ingested somehow.

After watching the living sculptor trying to slowly consume the cavern wall for a while, Quroak went to explore the city. After all, he did seem to have gotten the seal of approval.

He had barely entered the crystal city via a smooth crimson crystalline path when he encountered another crystalline alien that looked vaguely like a cross between an Earth platypus and a Uranian dragon-cat.

"Me!" I said firmly.

CHAPTER 10

S orry for the interruption but I believe now would be a good time to give you some historical information. Plus I need a break. Though it's perfectly harmless, the immersion process does tend to give you a headache. It's something I'm still trying to fix. I think it has something to do with the time difference involved which the mind has a hard time reconciling.

You see, during a memory immersion you are not actually re-living the experience at the same speed of time that the original memories occurred. In other words, if the original experience occurred over a period of one month, it does not take a month to re-live the same experience during immersion. Re-living a month only takes a few hours in real-time.

So your mind has experienced the passage of a month while your brain and your body know that in reality only a few hours have passed and it's like it causes a short circuit somewhere, causing the headache which can be very intense if you don't take frequent breaks.

Anyway, for those of you unfamiliar with such an exotic creature, an Earth platypus is a squat creature that walks on four legs, has the tail of an Earth beaver, an Earth duck's bill and is a mammal but lays eggs. The platypus is considered to be one of the silliest creatures designed by Nature in the whole Solar System.

Though the whole Solar community laughs at this ineptness of design, there is one organization that quietly laughs the hardest; for a very different reason. This secret group, ELEFANT (Enlightened Losians Enforcement For Alien Non-Tolerance) has been slowing down humanity's progress for centuries by instigating such things as the Spanish Inquisition, the witch trials of the 1600s, the 8-track cassette, pornography, drugs, reality television, and fossil fuels, especially petroleum. Earth would be so far ahead technologically, economically and sociologically if you had only given up your insane reliance on oil and went with natural resources like solar, wind and geothermal.

However, to be fair, you Earthlings are being manipulated. Every time your scientists announce the scarcity of oil, another deposit is miraculously found to last you another ten or twenty years giving your greedy governments and corporations no incentive to look for alternatives. Well, unknown to you, those wonderfully timed unearthed deposits are actually newly created oil lakes! Think about it. Oil is created from the preserved remains of prehistoric zooplankton and algae life. Do you know how small zooplankton and algae are? And you have been using oil at a prodigious rate for about sixty years or so. How could such tiny creatures create so much oil? I've done the calculations and there's no way.

No, in order to retard your advancement, ELEFANT creates these magical lakes of Texas tea whenever it seems you're ready for alternative energy sources. And here is where the innocent platypus comes into the picture. The platypus was *created* by ELEFANT to be their agents on Earth. They determine when a new petroleum field needs to be "discovered", locates the perfect spot for this oil, supervises the creation of this lovely energy source and mischievously leads your greedy corporations to this serendipitous find without them being any the wiser. The icing on the cake was the ridiculous design of the platypus so that Earth would be the laughing stock of the neighborhood! You have to admire genius.

Don't feel too picked upon because ELEFANT is against all alien societies. They tried to interfere with the Cloudotians, the Jovians and every other civilization in the Solar System. How do you think Uranus got knocked onto its side?

By the way, have you ever wondered how the Republican party of the United States got their mascot, the *elephant*? Not a coincidence.

Anyway, the Losians, who make up the secret

ELEFANT organization, are an insectoid species that somehow spawned under the Hellish conditions on Venus. Actually the Losians evolved on Venus millions of years before that planet changed into what it is today. Venus used to be a lot like Earth in that it had oceans, moderate temperatures and yellowish clouds that were like your clouds. Life abounded everywhere with lush jungles and the seas and lakes teeming with all manner of creatures. The greenhouse effect that transformed this luxurious world into your conception of Hell did not occur over night but took millions of years and the Losians were one of several species that managed to adapt to the changing environment where the oceans dried up and the jungles died out.

The Losians are very aggressively competitive in every way but are mostly content to ignore anything beyond the skies of Venus. However, there are always fanatics in every society and these extremists formed ELEFANT and now have their base of operations on the moon I mentioned before that's invisible orbiting their planet. They don't want competition for the Solar System resources and so their goal is simply to stop all technological advancement of alien cultures. I really think I'm revealing way too much information to you.

So anyway, I was only kidding before, I know you know what a platypus is. However, you probably never heard of a Uranian dragon-cat. The dragon-cat is an endangered species from Uranus; to you, the seventh known planet but really the eighth planet from the sun.

They have a long body with a round face that somehow reminds you of an Earth housecat even though it doesn't have a nose or ears, neither of which is really helpful when you live most of your life in space, though they do have whiskers like a cat which allow them to sense the different wavelengths of electromagnetic energy. Instead of legs they have two pairs of flippers and the body ends in a long tail reminiscent of a dragon in your fantasies. However, despite the name, they are one of the most peaceful creatures you will ever meet and one of the most emotionally sensitive.

I actually spend a lot of time visiting these wonderful creatures and try to help them emotionally the best I can. Though they are considered animals, they have the emotional depth and intelligent range of Earth elephants, which are much deeper creatures than you realize. The dragon-cats suffered a tragedy in their recent past and I'm trying to help them recover both emotionally and as a species.

As I said, the Uranian dragon-cat is endangered. Their main diet is icy minerals and they love to feed off the rings surrounding their blue-green gas giant. As a mischievous and cruel prank, ELEFANT had transported a huge herd of these creatures to Jupiter to feed off the Jovian rings. By the time the Jovians realized what was going on, their once spectacular ring system was decimated to what you see today, a wispy shadow of its once beautiful glory that had rivaled Saturn's majestic crown.

In a fit of rage and under the false belief that the dragon-cats had migrated to Jupiter on their own, the Jovians slaughtered most of the herd. It wasn't until it was too late that they discovered the Losians' involvement. I understand they are planning some kind of revenge.

So that's why there are only a few dragon-cats left. For some mysterious reason, they have gotten into the habit of journeying to Oberon, one of the larger Uranus moons. Oberon is heavily cratered and as your scientists have discovered, a lot of the crater floors are dark. That's because the dragon-cats dive into these craters and burrow down through the outer crust of the moon to reach the underground ocean that surrounds the inner core. Dragon-cats can breathe out clouds of acid that dissolves rock so they actually melt their way through the moon. And some dirty ice upwells to the crater floor turning it dark. As far as I know, I'm the only one who knows why the dragon-cats visit Oberon but I'm not ready to reveal the reason at this point.

Okay, sorry for the interruption but I thought it would be helpful to give you some historical perspective. Let's return to Quroak's memories.

CHAPTER 11

Quroak slowly approached the alien that's a crystalline cross between an Earth platypus and a Uranian dragon-cat, with the roundish face, small snout and tail of the dragon-cat, small triangular ears and the squat, upright body and limbs of the platypus but with five prehensile appendages at the end of each arm and leg.

The alien had an exoskeleton that seemed to be of crystal shaded a light blue, like the color of a clear Earth sky on a hot summer day. Within the blue, flowing streaks of the lightest violet enhanced the alien's appearance rather than distract from it. It wore a flowing white and green wavy patterned robe that looked amazingly soft and somewhat out of place both on the hard-bodied alien and in this city of crystal.

The alien waited quietly on the crimson path for the Cloudotian as Quroak wondered how he was going to communicate with this new society. Even using telepathic abilities, it wasn't easy to learn another's language, especially between species from different planets and thus share no common sociological ground whatsoever.

When he reached the entity, Quroak sent the creature warm thoughts. The alien responded with a high pitch screech that Quroak couldn't understand. However, he could see into the entity's mind and was surprised at what he saw. Apparently this society didn't communicate with individual words but with word-pictures that convey ideas! In the creature's mind, Quroak saw the door on the planetoid's surface rolling open that he took to mean "welcome to our city".

Well, this should make things a bit easier, thought Quroak with much relief.

Since Quroak had no linguistic or social reference with this society he didn't know how to signify "thank you". So he just sent a telepathic image of himself at the same time think-saying firmly, "Quroak" to convey his name.

The alien wriggled its sharp ears, pictured itself in its mind and screeched a noise that sounded like two pieces of rusted iron scraping against each other. Quroak took this to be its name and that the wriggling ears indicated it understood what Quroak had told it. Quroak tried to repeat the name several times but the closest he could get was "Eeeecreeech", which the alien graciously accepted.

Eeeecreeech obviously understood the concept of telepathy for he starting picturing images in his mind without verbally speaking to Quroak. Quroak didn't know if Eeeecreeech was a 'he' or not but it was simpler thinking of the friendly alien in terms of gender. The Quaoarian flashed an image of Quroak entering the tunnel leading to the crystal city. He repeated the image but this time showing Quroak coming through the Kuiper Belt before coming to Quaoar. Then again but showing Quroak appearing out of blackness before getting to the Kuiper Belt.

Quroak took this to mean Eeeecreeech was asking him where he came from. So Quroak slowly conveyed the story via images of how he came to be in the crystal city starting with the black hole accident near his home. He ended by showing himself leaving Quaoar but then just floating above the planetoid looking towards the sun. He showed himself starting towards the distant sun, then stopping, returning to Quaoar, then toward the sun again then stopping and returning to Quaoar. He wanted to convey that he was confused on how to get back home.

The Quaoarian wriggled his ears in understanding. Eeeecreeech then turned and started down the path leading into the city. Quroak assumed he was supposed to follow so he drifted alongside his new crystalline friend who clicked softly with each footfall.

Quroak noticed that the city seemed empty and he sent mental images of multiple Eeeecreeech's in the city and then the city empty of all people in order to ask where everyone was. Eeeecreeech indicated that everyone was hiding and that he, Eeeecreeech, was the spokesperson for the population to come out and greet the Cloudotian. At least, that's how Quroak interpreted the images he saw in the Quaoarian's mind.

The city seemed to be aesthetically laid out with crimson paths winding between the flowing buildings. There were gardens everywhere and small parks with a variety of what seemed to be crystal statues that Quroak assumed were plant life based on his experience upon first exiting the tunnel.

Xelrine would love this place. I wish she was here. Then the burst of pain from the hollowness of his heart reminded him that there was no Xelrine, and that he had to get used to the fact that he was alone and probably always would be.

They soon reached the center of the city where there stood in a large, circular open space a small turquoise, sphere-shaped building which they entered to find a single empty room, except for a crystal-like pedestal that seemed to flow up out of the floor like it was a part of the building itself. Quroak realized the pedestal looked like the one he had found on the asteroid that controlled the map of the solar system that had led him here.

Eeeecreeech activated the room-filling map and pointed to their current location. Quroak took control of the map and brought up his home planet, Sea of Clouds, and pointed to it. When Eeeecreeech rescaled the map so that both worlds were visible, it was obvious just how far it was to his planet.

Quroak softly cursed, "Oh sunghost!" Then he

silently prayed to the king of planets, Jupiter, "Oh mighty *Guiding Star*, please lead me from the unlight safely to my home".

The Quaoarian then resized the map again so that Sea of Clouds, Jupiter, Uranus and Neptune slid out of view and he pointed to Pluto. The planetoid Quaoar was at one end of the room with Pluto and Charon all the way on the other side.

Even though Quroak had known intellectually that he was somewhere around 1.6 billion kilometers beyond Pluto, seeing it on the photographic map was devastating as all three of his hearts suddenly felt as heavy as lead. His skin flushed a dark scarlet-emerald as he slowly sank to the floor with his strength evaporating along with his hopes. A terrible premonition hit him like a Saturnian lightning bolt, blasting away all capacity to form coherent thoughts.

Laying on the sea-green crystal floor numb with despair, with pulses of light blue speckled with yellow racing across his ruby and dark emerald bodyscape, Quroak's mind instinctively and desperately reached out to the nearest sentient intelligence; Eeeecreeech's. But that gave him no comfort at all for there he only found confirmation of his premonition.

Due to his emotional state, it took over an hour of telepathic imagery for his mind to absorb and understand that because of fuel constraints of their spaceships, Eeeecreeech's people could only take him as far as Pluto.

By showing Quaoar moving one degree in its orbit, Eeeecreeech made Quroak understand that they couldn't leave until Quaoar was closer to Pluto, which was in about 9 ½ Earth months. And then the trip itself would be another 17 Earth months.

"Sunghost," Quroak cried. "I won't reach Pluto until more than two years from now." Unbidden, his mind numbly did the math and he realized that the trip to Pluto was less than 9% of the total distance he had to go to get home! He went deeper into emotional shock with the thought that it would take more than twenty years to get home!

He felt reality shift somehow as he instantly felt like he had just been dropped into an erupting ice volcano on Triton where the methane ice sucked all the warm life-force from his existence. Though he had never been to the coldest place in the Solar System, he was sure the pinkish moon of Neptune with temperatures 240 Celsius degrees below zero (minus 400 degrees Fahrenheit) could not be as cold as he felt now. The icy numbness would not allow him to think of anything, much less move a muscle, with Xelrine's face frozen in his mind's eye, torturing him with the almost certainty this would be the only way he would ever see her: through his imagined, yet cherished, memories; memories formed from self-delusional fantasies.

In his mind, he felt the universe crack open and all of reality drain into the resulting rift of pure darkness with all starlight slipping over the edge into oblivion. He vaguely noticed through the numbness that had absorbed his very being, a blackness shutting out his awareness like hazy, obsidian curtains closing in all around him until all that was left was a tiny opening through which shined Xelrine's beautiful, smiling bronze eyes with her graceful arms flowing behind her as she floated above the mint green clouds of their homeworld. Then he was lost in the universal rift and all reality ceased to exist for him, and he found he didn't have the strength to really care.

CHAPTER 12

I would like to point something out about memories. Memories are not photographs of events. They are not perfect recordings of what transpired in a person's life, but are highly subjective to the one creating the memories and also when remembering them. If six people witness the same event, you will hear six different stories, even if they were interviewed right after the event. Some of the stories will differ only slightly, but some will be as if entirely different events were witnessed. This is because everyone sees things from their own perspective; their own history, prejudices, current level of awareness and emotional state.

It only gets worse as time goes by. It may seem to be a paradox but it is true that while memories are strengthened every time they are relived, whether mentally or verbally, they are also *changed* every time they are revisited, though usually only slightly. However, over time, those minor changes may add up to significant changes. Research has shown that memories are very malleable and usually change based on what the person is feeling at the time the memories are relived.

Also, people don't always hear what is being said to them because they are either focusing on something else altogether or they are *interpreting* what is being said to fit into their own perception of reality. If one habitually tries to manipulate others via word games, they will not recognize a truly honest and straightforward person, who means what they say, nothing more and nothing less, but will instead assume there are hidden meanings behind every word and will act accordingly. So the memories of most conversations between the manipulative, suspicious person (suspicious because these types of people tend to believe everyone is like them) and the honest person will be quite different.

Everything that happens to a person can become a permanent memory and sometimes the fact that something actually happened or not can be lost. For instance, I had a patient that believed he could float on air. He was human which don't have that capability, but he remembered floating down the stairs, out of his house and down the street. It turned out it was just something he had dreamed once but it felt so real and natural to him that he didn't even question the validity of this memory until a couple of years later. He didn't try to fly by jumping off buildings or anything like that, but he had just accepted that he had floated on air that one time and thought nothing of it. So if a dream is real enough, powerful enough, it can become a memory as if it was something that occurred during our waking life.

Now of course, some people do have photographic memories or can faithfully play back every pitch and tone heard in a symphony, but most don't have perfect recall. Most people store and recall memories based on their individual character and how they assimilate and filter information. For some, taste is the operative sense where they can recall minute details surrounding an event that involved eating. They can remember conversations, what everyone was wearing, give a detailed description of the surroundings, et cetera.

For others, it is seeing, hearing or any of the other senses that drives what they remember and how much. However, a lot of memories are just remembered based on the person's emotional engagement at the time. In fact, there is one factor that increases the likelihood of more details being remembered in any memory: emotional intensity. The more intense the emotion or feeling at the time of the event, the more details that will be remembered later on. Things like the color of the sky, the smell of the leaves, the taste of a meal, the curve of a smile, the melody of a song that was playing in the background that was barely noticed at the time.

All of this explains why when reliving Quroak's memories, some events are described with more details than others and why different types of details are remembered for each event. Since Quroak is an emotional being, the details of his memories correlate with the intensity of his feelings at the time.

So, speaking of Quroak, let's jump back into his life.

CHAPTER 13

The next thing Quroak was aware of was his fourth arm twitching slightly. He tried to stop the spasms by grabbing the arm with his seventh arm but he couldn't move, at least, not on purpose.

Then he became aware of a cold hardness pressing up against the whole length of his body. He quickly forgot about that as the inner Triton-cold ice entrapping his heart and soul swept into his awareness like an Arctic blizzard whipping ice particles through a broken forest of icebergs on Earth and the shock almost pushed him into the welcome haven of unconsciousness again. But he was denied this route of escape, for though he teetered on the brink for a while, and indeed wished for it, he reluctantly pulled himself back to full consciousness, albeit slowly.

When he finally opened his eyes, he saw that he was in a small room with the sapphire walls and ceiling flowing in graceful curves, enhanced by waves of light green tumbling through the blue. In fact, the walls and ceiling were really one, with the only flat surface being the floor. There was a wavy shaped rectangular opening on the wall opposite him which served as a window.

He thought he could hear the whisper of flowing water but he couldn't discern its source or even ascertain it was real and not his imagination.

He discovered he was lying on a low slab of nearly transparent reddish crystal standing on six curvy legs. Otherwise, the room was empty except for the city's ubiquitous pale green light. He was also alone.

With herculean effort against the mountainous weight of icebergs crushing his emotions and willpower, he slowly raised himself from the bench. At least his body was responding to his commands now, though he felt like he was trying to move through the dense atmosphere of Venus without the ability to transfer his mass. As he listened to the complaints of his aching body, he wondered if the Quaoarians even knew of the concept *softness*.

He slowly fought his way to the window and from his height of what seemed to be about twelve meters, looked out upon the city. The first thing he noticed was all the Quaoarians out and about. Dozens of people were walking on the crimson paths that wound throughout the city or running and playing in the parks participating in what seemed to be different types of games or sports. He saw a lot of pairs together, which he assumed were couples, making him think of Xelrine.

He quickly squashed that flight of thought and admired the curves of the beautiful buildings. With the flowing buildings, the many small parks shared by many small animals, which he hadn't noticed before, and the people and the river-like crimson paths seeming to slowly wind through the city, it all created a feeling of peace and harmony. And something about the soft, sea green light gave a certain kind of warmth to the whole scene. Not *warmth* as in heat, but as in coziness.

With this thought giving him comfort and the whole picturesque scene giving him a small amount of peace inside, he sighed and turned back to face the room where he saw a arched doorway which he had missed noticing before.

As he floated towards the doorway, he couldn't help thinking about his pet Qat, hoping someone would remember to feed it. (Note to reader: Qat is a dimenhopper, which slightly resembles a rainbow colored ghost of an Earth seahorse with feathers. The dimenhopper is named such because this creature hops between dimensions at will but is somehow permanently tied to each dimension. A dimenhopper is usually very docile and cuddly but when it becomes very hungry it transforms into a vile-tempered monster capable of creating profound chaos throughout the entire time-space continuum: kind of like a restless teenager.)

Exiting from his room, Quroak found himself in a larger circular room where the walls flowed in shades of dark blue and violet, reminding him of star-exploded swept gaseous nebulas he had seen through telescopes. There were five other doorways gracefully leading to other rooms, presumably like the one he had just vacated. He saw a ramp circling along the wall leading down to the level beneath this one.

The room was empty except in the center where several art sculptures seemed to flow up from the floor gracefully, encircling a small pool of clear water that was fed by a sheet of water falling from an opening in the ceiling. The waterfall made only the softest of sounds making him wonder how the Quaoarians were able to dampen the sound so effectively in an empty, marble-like room where the noise should have been deafeningly.

While staring at the waterfall, trying to let his mind float on the whisper softly echoing around him in an impromptu form of meditation, he heard a quiet, sharp, rhythmic clacking sound from the ramp. He turned to see a Quaoarian approaching.

Quroak only realized it was Eeeecreeech when he felt the familiarity of the Quaoarian's mind. The young Cloudotian felt a little embarrassed that he didn't recognize Eeeecreeech by sight alone. Though it was true, he reminded himself, that he had only seen one Quaoarian up close so he had no way of knowing the commonality among the species and the relatively slight differences of individuals.

While Eeeecreeech approached, he touched his head

with both hands and then reached out to Quroak which the Cloudotian took to mean "Hello" so Quroak replied in kind with his first and third arms. Quroak also assumed the gesture was an invitation to see into the other's mind for communication so he reached out telepathically as well and found the Quaoarian's mind to be open.

In Eeeecreeech's mind he saw an image of himself crumbled on the map room's floor in distress when he had realized how long it would take just to get to Pluto and then an image of himself as he looked now. After flipping back and forth between these two images quickly a few times, Quroak realized Eeeecreeech was asking him "How do you feel?"

Not wanting to burden the Quaoarian with his despair, he simply responded with the 'now' image with a sun shining in the sky and his arms spread to welcome the sunlight to signify he was better. Besides, without knowing the Quaoarians better, he didn't really know how to convey emotions with images that would make Eeeecreeech understand. He just hoped Eeeecreeech understood him this time.

Eeeecreeech then flashed a series of images through his mind showing what had transpired in the past few days. Apparently Quroak had fallen into a catatonic state of depression in the map room, having collapsed on the floor. The Quaoarian had tried to rouse him but with no success and so had carried him to the room in which Quroak had awoken. Over the next few days, Eeeecreeech had watched over him and tried to help but didn't know what to do. Another Quaoarian had visited, made a cursory examination but ultimately told Eeeecreeech there was nothing he (she?) could do. Quroak assumed this individual was a physician. So they had just waited, hoping Quroak would soon awaken.

Quroak didn't know how to say thank you in Quaoarian so he conveyed in his own language by entwining his second and fifth arms together.

Eeeecreeech then slowly took Quroak on a tour of the crystal city with all its wonders, apparently hoping it would take the Cloudotian's mind off his predicament for a while. He indicated to Quroak that all was his to explore and enjoy and that this was his home for now.

"Me!" I said firmly.

For the interests of time, I will summarize the next two years of Quroak's life. I have lived through his memories and created another manuscript about his time with the Quaoarians for my exobiologist, geologist, archeologist and other 'ist' colleagues of mine for their scientific value. Though those two years were interesting to Quroak, he was basically waiting to start his journey home. Or rather, his first part of the journey home, for he had no idea what he would do once he reached Pluto.

So Quroak spent the next 9½ months living on Quaoar learning about its people and their culture. At first, Quroak enjoyed the newness of his surroundings and discovering everything he could about the Quaoarians but he soon became 'stir crazy', I believe that's the phrase you humans use, and impatient with his situation. He spent a lot of time exploring the neighborhood in the Kuiper Belt but became bored with that since most asteroids are pretty much alike.

However after the sixth month, Quroak started to feel calmer inside. The Quaoarians were a deliberate and patient people. They did nothing in a hurry and thought long before making any decision and once a decision was finally made, they took even longer making plans before taking action of any kind. Half of each Quaoarian day was spent deciding the menu for their meal. Fortunately, they only eat once a day!

Before you decide to laugh at this thought and make some kind of judgment regarding their time management skills, you should realize that Quaoarians have very long life spans; up to six years. Sorry, I forgot to translate for you. That's six *Quaoarian years*. One year on Quaoar is 285 Earth years so that converts to up to about 1,710 of your years. So I think you can understand why they may be a little laid back and not feel the need to rush into anything. Okay, *a lot* laid back!

Anyway, eventually Quroak adapted to this slow pace of life. But it was something more than the Quaoarians' sedate pace that calmed Quroak inside. They had a simple philosophy by which they lived their lives. When trying to explain their way of thinking, they showed Quroak mind-pictures of Quaoarians quietly working on asteroids while the asteroids were tumbling chaotically within the Belt and being bombarded by asteroid rain or colliding with neighbors. The Quaoarians would take the necessary precautions and actions to avoid harm but they accepted the random events calmly. The Quaoarians related that this calm demeanor underlies their culture's philosophy, which translates to *chaos is*. They believe that the universe is randomness, or chaos, and the only reasonable thing to do is just accept it and deal with it.

Quroak figured that with their extraordinary long life spans, the Quaoarians could just wait out any problems and saw no reason to worry or get upset about anything. But even with his relatively short life span, Quroak did find merit in this way of dealing with life and so changed it slightly to be; *accept what is*. Since he couldn't do anything about his current situation, he was wasting his energy and time by being upset about what he couldn't control. So he *accepted what was* and spent his remaining time on Quaoar trying to create peace within himself by practicing patience and finding the beauty and good in everything that surrounded him. He soon realized that it was not easy to maintain this attitude but he kept practicing, hoping it would take considerably less than 1,700 years to master!

He made a herculean effort to practice this as much as possible, especially since he still felt that odd emptiness caused by Xelrine's absence. Though he kept reminding himself that she was never real, that he had never actually met anyone even remotely like her, he still felt a deep, cold loneliness from . . . well, from the change of the way it felt imagining her before he crossed paths with the micro black hole and after. He knew something fundamentally had changed, he just didn't know what and he had to try everything he could to not let despair and depression overwhelm him; like practice *accept what is*.

Quroak had plenty of opportunity to test this new philosophy during the seventeen-month trip from Quaoar to Pluto because there was really nothing to do or see. Eeeecreeech did not accompany him on the trip to Pluto, not liking to travel far from home. Though Quroak knew two of the six Quaoarians on the rather small and cramped ship, he hadn't really spent much time with them on their homeworld.

The Quaoarians like to play a game on trips between Quaoar and Pluto. I mean, they play *one* game, *not* the same game over and over again. Just one seventeen-month long game! It's actually an Earth game that they had discovered floating around Pluto about fifty years ago. Have you heard of the game Monopoly? In the interest of my cultural studies of humanity, I have played it a few times and it's as good a way as any to kill an hour or two. However, can you imagine playing a seventeen-month game of Monopoly? I mean, you already own Park Place and you land on Board Walk. How long does it take to decide to buy it and build? Would you believe two weeks?

With his newly adopted *accept what is* philosophy as a shield against the mind-numbing boredom, Quroak managed to reach Pluto without throwing himself into the ship's nuclear reactor core. But then something amazing and, in his eyes, wonderful occurred giving him a new understanding that lifted his spirits considerably.

CHAPTER 14

U pon reaching the icy planet, the Quaoarians immediately turned around for Quaoar, not liking being so far from home. Quroak certainly understood how they felt so he simply thanked them, said goodbye and started to explore Pluto and its moons.

He was gratified to see that the sun appeared to be a little bit bigger than it had from Quaoar, although not by much. But it did mean he was that much closer to home. Now he just needed to find a way to cross the ebony ocean to the next safe harbor: Neptune.

He calculated that he had just traveled about four AUs (about 598,400,000 kilometers) to get to Pluto. From looking at the Quaoarian solar map, he knew Neptune was currently around nine AUs from Pluto.

While his people were comfortable in space, they could only travel so far without shelter from that harsh environment. Taking a trip to Jupiter was fine but that was only two AUs from Sea Of Clouds. So he definitely needed to find a way to reach the Neptunian system. So, trying not to let his situation emotionally freeze him into immobility, he set out to explore Pluto.

Besides, after being cooped up in that cramped ship for over seventeen months, it felt great to stretch his arms and be out in the open again.

He spent a few days exploring the light coppery planet but Pluto revealed no surprises, being just as it appeared, a lifeless icy ball with small mountains and craters dotting the surface.

Being on the outermost planet seemed kind of surreal to him with the small sun so far away, shining like a tiny beacon providing the barest of glows around Pluto as the light reflected off its icy surface. From what he remembered from Astronomy class, he believed that Pluto must be near its furthest point from the sun in its orbit, for the atmosphere was gone, having frozen and fallen to the ground. It felt strange to be on a planet and to have the horizon be space itself with stars shining steadily, with no atmosphere to make them sparkle. Standing on an asteroid was one thing, but . . .

Floating a meter above the surface in the absolute silence in the dark night made him shiver inside as he felt he was truly in the middle of nowhere, like he was on a rogue planet that had been flung from its parent sun, lost in interstellar space.

He left the planet to check out the smaller moons,

Nix, Hydra and a third satellite yet undiscovered by humans. All of these rocky moons proved uninteresting, at least to him.

However, it was while exploring a huge ice cave on Charon, Pluto's largest moon, that Quroak found something totally unexpected. The cavern was so immense it must have spread under the surface of the entire moon. The cavern was artificially created, for the walls, ceiling and floor were not of indigenous rock or ice but of some kind of material that felt like softened gold but with a light bronze color.

As Quroak floated through the cave, lights of a pale orange activated from a source he could not identify. He soon realized the light was coming from the air itself and he guessed it was being powered from the bioelectricity of his body or something. As soon this thought crossed his mind, he suddenly realized that there actually was *air* here even though there was none on the moon's surface. But he soon forgot about all of this as he soaked in what the light revealed.

Sprawled across the floor was a city with the buildings constructed of the same soft gold-like material. The buildings spread as far as he could see into the cavern. The structures were tiered up to six levels high with elegant terraces at each level. Some of the buildings were connected at the top level via transparent enclosed bridges that spiraled in crazy designs. Quroak looked up towards the ceiling that was at least a kilometer above and flashed a bright yellow-tinged purple in surprise. The city was also *on* the ceiling with those buildings reaching downward!

He couldn't help but wonder who built this place but he had to admire their use of space. To build the city on the ceiling was pure genius in his eyes. He imagined being in one of those buildings above and thought it would be pretty weird having the 'top' of the building connected to the ground (ceiling) instead of the bottom.

He floated upward to investigate the upside down city and received an even bigger surprise. When he was halfway there, he suddenly felt completely weightless. When he continued, he felt gravity pulling him upward! So though he had started going *up* to the city on what had originally been the ceiling of the cavern, he was now going *down* to get there and the city he had just left was now *above* him. So, he reasoned, because of the way the gravity worked, the buildings on each side would work the same in terms of up and down. For ease of reference, Quroak decided to call the city he had just left Hansel and the one he was approaching Gretel.

(Note to readers: Your fairy tale called Hansel & Gretel is considered by many Cloudotians the perfect story representing the morality of the human race where children are dumped in a carnivorous forest to fend for themselves or be gleefully eaten by wicked stepmothers who emulate and bow down to black widow spiders as their gods and lay waiting in their lairs made of gingerbread and gumdrops. Most Cloudotians don't actually believe this but it has become their little joke to call anything that's baffling, unfathomable, immoral or just plain crazy as the 'Hansel & Gretel Syndrome.' The Cloudotians sometimes have a weird sense of humor.)

Anyway, Quroak explored a small portion of both cities and found them abandoned, empty of all life. Though everything was immaculate, he sensed that this place was very old, at least thousands of years. He quickly discovered that some of the buildings were completely solid with no entrances at all. Other buildings had some levels solid and others hollow. And all the hollow spaces were empty, devoid of furniture, even the buildings that were entirely hollow. The only exception was the frequent hollow, opaque tubes that spiraled between levels and buildings.

Sensing something intangible, Quroak flew to the line between Hansel and Gretel where gravity was zero to see both cities from the same height. From this vantage point he saw that there was a pattern to the layout of the buildings that was mirrored in both cities.

He flew at this height for a long time, staying in between of the cities, confirming both that the mirror image continued and that the cities seemed to extend all the way around the interior of the moon.

He was just reaching the conclusion that the mirrored pattern seemed to lead to a focal point located in the zero-gravity plane a few kilometers away, when he suddenly realized how tired he was. He hadn't rested at all since reaching Pluto, what, four days ago, being anxious in finding a way on his next leg of his journey home. So he floated down to Hansel, searched for and found a near frozen stream of water that barely flowed between some buildings and quenched his thirst. He then picked out a two level structure at random and folded himself on the second story floor.

Thinking of the enormity of this place and what it must have taken to build it, he fell asleep dreaming of the underground cities.

He awoke dreaming of an argument between two Quaoarians on whether or not one could build a house on Reading Railroad. He thought-groaned to himself, remembering that three day long heated debate on the trip to Pluto and how he had wished he could *will* himself into a coma for the duration of the journey.

Except for a slight headache brought on by that painful memory, Quroak felt well rested. He decided to check out the focal point he had perceived before resting. As the young Cloudotian approached this focal point, he got the impression that the structures were not just buildings but also integrated components of a machine of some kind. It reminded him of the inside of a computer. He thought this might explain the strange nature of the buildings if they were really circuits, relays or other such computer-related things.

At first, there didn't appear to be anything at the focal point but as he approached, a spherical opening, a portal about twenty four meters in diameter appeared out of nowhere.

Through this portal, he could see a spiral galaxy hanging in the velvet ebony of space! It was like he was floating a million light-years above the galaxy so he could see the whole thing. It was absolutely stunning with its milky white arms glittering with white diamonds accompanied by light blue and green clouds of stellar nurseries and the bronze lanes spiraling outward from the pearly white center. After being mesmerized for a long time, Quroak noticed a smaller window beside the portal with images flowing through it.

He floated up to the image-maker and froze as he realized what was being shown, for it appeared to be a historical review of the civilization that built this place! These people, who vaguely resembled Earth geckos with golden hair and luxuriously feathered wings on their backs, did not originate in this solar system but from another system that orbited a blue giant.

Right now the images showed a horrific interplanetary war that, based on the evolution of weapons, warships and defenses, seemed to have occurred over several centuries. All resources seemed to be drained into this unstoppable conflict, leaving nothing left for the growth of their civilization in terms of medicine or scientific advancement other than for warfare.

Then Quroak shot backwards flushing the palest blue, horrified, when the window suddenly flared up when one of the planets suddenly exploded into huge chunks flying away in every direction! He didn't see the weapon used to cause such a catastrophic event but it left him mentally reeling and emotionally shocked.

Before he was able to regain his balance, the other five inhabitable planets and sixteen colonized moons exploded in quick succession, annihilating the populations on all those worlds.

Aghast, Quroak watched as the solar system instantly became a graveyard of planets and moons. The few thousand people that survived, having been on ships, formed an uneasy alliance, horrified at what they had just done. They soon left the destroyed planetary system in a few dozen barely useable spacecraft and wandered the cosmos for years, lost in the unfathomable grief and remorse over their civilization's blind hatred leading to the devastation of their species and home.

Then slowly, out of grief grew a seed of determination that sprouted into a vision and then full-grown into a purpose that was not to be denied.

They started to investigate solar systems in search of the raw materials needed to fulfill their newborn purpose. They also wanted an uninhabited system, for they wanted to be alone.

They soon came across our Solar System, decided the Oort Cloud and the Kuiper Belt met their requirements and landed on Charon, which at the time was not a moon of Pluto but just another free roving object in the Kuiper

Belt. The huge array of linked underground caverns and the asteroid's mineral content suited their needs perfectly.

In fact, their first action was to nudge Pluto away from the center of the Kuiper Belt into its current highly elliptical orbit and moved Charon into orbit around Pluto to create a more stable environment, minimizing the impacts from the other Kuiper denizens. They had intended on Pluto's orbit to be more circular but there was a minor accident with one of the ships pushing the newly created planet, causing the loss of the spacecraft and for Pluto to cross Neptune's orbit around its journey around the sun.

Over the next 200 Charonian years (about 50,000 Earth years) the survivors created the means to fulfill their new vision. They created this cavern and the city-sized machine that eventually opened this portal. They also created the tools they would need to accomplish their upcoming task; to fulfill their destiny. By manipulating their DNA they evolved themselves into a higher life-form, with the least of their newly created characteristics being immortality.

They then used the portal to find a newborn galaxy and then once found, as a gateway to that infant galaxy to finally begin following their new path: to be the guardians of this awakening galaxy!

They wanted to do some good after the travesty caused by their own species. So they started from scratch with a new galaxy where life was just starting to form. They became the benevolent gods of the entire galaxy, protecting and guiding each sentient species on thousands of planets to exist peacefully as they evolved into civilizations. They called themselves the *Guardians of One*, meaning they were protecting a single peace for the entire galaxy. They had begun living this purpose, this destiny over two billion years ago! Then the image-maker went blank.

The images shown had all been real, at least as far as Quroak could tell, except for what happened after the aliens went through the portal to the infant galaxy. After that, the images had been artificially created with one of the Guardians-to-be enacting out their intentions, showing what their purpose was.

Then the last images shown were of this Solar System, apparently so that anyone seeing these images could deduce the approximate time these events took place by comparing the images to the current condition of the planets and moons gracefully sweeping around Sol.

So this image-window was a historical log for anyone who chanced across it to understand both the events and the motivations propelling this ancient civilization's actions and to explain the purpose of this moon-size machine.

Quroak's mind was numb, unable to comprehend the true enormity of the unfathomable responsibility these aliens had assumed out of their grief and remorse born out of the ashes of their civilization's annihilation. Their sense of purpose drove them for tens of thousands of years just in preparation of what they felt had to be done to make amends for their species' inexplicable destructive hatred, allowing them to accomplish incredible achievements and scientific advancements that would smack of pure magic to every other civilization Quroak had ever heard of. And their unwavering belief in a specific destiny gave them the strength and patience to stay on a path that was before previously inconceivable to their species even on a planetary scale: peace. But they took on the responsibility of creating and ensuring peace for an entire galaxy!

There was no way to tell if they had succeeded or not. If they really had become benevolent gods or had let their violent tendency arise once again to engulf an unsuspecting galaxy in horrific destruction.

Actually, there may be one way to find out how that galaxy evolved, Quroak thought soberly. For there it was, floating silently but invitingly in the portal which appeared to be still functioning, at least superficially.

It seemed to him that he could just float through the portal and instantaneously arrive at some safe haven within that huge whirlpool of gleaming stars. Indeed, that gentle maelstrom of light seemed to be calling to him, urging him to dive into its bright, magical sea of warmth. He found the swirling sea of brightness against the infinite ocean of night to be mesmerizing. He actually found himself drifting closer to the portal before he shook off the hypnotic spell.

After some heavy contemplation and totally overawed

by the whole thing, Quroak continued to explore the cavern-machine. He had no desire to enter the gateway to the galaxy under the *Guardians of One's* protection.

Besides there was no way of really knowing if it still worked after the past two billion years except by actually going through and he wasn't feeling that lucky. With his luck he'd end up a billion light-years in inter-galactic space with no hope of reaching anywhere in a thousand of his lifetimes except maybe a rogue brown dwarf where he could at least live out his existence with a companion where they shared something in common: both being failures. A brown dwarf being a star *that never was*, not having enough of what it takes to become a sun. And of course, Quroak would have failed in getting home. With that gloomy thought, he flew away from the portal.

After a while, he found what seemed to be an observatory of some kind. He didn't understand how it functioned for it just looked like a box to him but it was showing him images of the Solar System. By accident he brushed against the front panel and the top of the box changed to show that the instrument was tracking every object in the Oort cloud and Kuiper Belt with the Plutonian system clearly highlighted.

He was in luck for he discovered that a very fast moving comet was approaching Pluto and would be traveling past Neptune's vicinity on its elliptical orbit around the sun. He estimated he had about four months before the comet arrived near Pluto, so he made himself at home and decided to spend his time trying to study the machine and search for more historical logs left by the amazing race that had created this place.

CHAPTER 15

One night, after thinking all day about the *Guardians of One's* sense of purpose, the young Cloudotian had a dream. The dream seemed very familiar, very warm, like coming home after a long sojourn. Then he realized it was a dream that he had once cherished but had long forgotten, having been worn away by the trials and tribulations of life. But apparently it had remained flickering in his heart like a candle protected from the strong winds.

In his dream, he was totally free like the eastern warm breezes on Sea of Clouds that are unpredictable but always welcomed. He felt a sense of completeness, at peace and one with the universe where he was understood, accepted and safe. He sensed this dream was not really about a place, a location, but about a *state of being*. Where joy is the warmth of sunshine, passion the air he breathed and love what he lived every moment. This is what his heart longed for and why it secretly and diligently protected this dream, this hope, out of the belief that there is more in life then simply existing. Quroak deeply felt this was his destiny and a new sense of purpose permeated throughout his soul.

That same day, something totally amazing happened to him, lifting his spirits even further and renewing a hope he thought had been obliterated by the explosion of the black hole.

It was while he was gazing through the portal at the swirling galactic jewel of the night. He was mesmerized by the pale blues and greens dotting the white galactic arms, trying to image all the stars being born in these regions.

"Lovely, isn't it?" The words whispered softly in his mind.

"It's incredibly breathtaking", he answered. "It reminds me of . . ."

Then he snapped out of his reverie, shocked to realize someone was communicating with him! Then he felt it; the warm, sweet, familiar caress in his mind that he had missed so much and thought was lost to him forever. It was her! It was Xelrine! He hearts stopped and his mind went blank, for a long moment not daring to believe while a cold chill ran through his body from emotional shock even as his suckers flexed with his skin tingling with excitement.

Then tentatively, "Xelrine?"

"Yes, Quroak, it is me".

He suddenly felt weak as relief roared through him like a tidal wave. Then his main heart started racing so hard it felt like it was trying to jump out through his beak. He first flushed turquoise from the flood of love and affection racing through his being and then flushed much darker from excitement as he realized he wasn't totally alone!

His eyes filled with tears and a sharp pain crashed through his heart like lightning splitting him in two with one half writhing in agony as if he had been cut open by the jagged electric bolt allowing all the trapped pain inside to pour out to be truly recognized instead of desperately buried and ignored while the other half laughed with pure joy and relief that the cold darkness had finally been ignited into light and warmth.

He clung to the joy as if it were flotsam keeping him afloat in stormy seas with the pain like an anchor trying to drag him under. He willed himself to close down the pain of loneliness and focus on the light, on her warm caress in his yearning mind.

He was starting to win with the joy making him lighter and he began to feel so ridiculously happy that he . . .

Then it all crashed down upon him. *This wasn't real!*, his mind lamented. *You're going crazy! Again.* The word *crazy* echoed through his mind with the booming sound of doom, bouncing around in the stark emptiness where hope had just flamed to life again, only to be extinguished by cold reality.

"Feel my presence, Quroak". Though the words whispered in his mind, he was too upset to pay attention.

The sudden whiplash of emotions left him drained as he struggled to understand what was going on. His head hurt and his heart was bursting with pain yet felt coldly empty and very, very heavy.

He was vacillating between ignoring the voice in his head (that warm, soft, inviting voice that he would give anything for it to be real) figuring he was becoming schizophrenic and firmly embracing these conversations as a way to keep both his sanity (?) and hope. He wasn't sure how far he would get towards reaching his homeworld without the hope of having someone to go home to driving him on.

Then her whispered thought finally made it through to his sluggish mind: *feel my presence*. What does that mean? He was here inside Charon completely alone. How could he feel her presence? Then he did feel *something*. At first, it was vague, like something was different but he couldn't . . . no, wait, it was deep inside of him. A soft warmth with a familiar tingling sensation was filling his heart. *The heartlink*!

Then he knew for sure, Xelrine *was* real. He didn't understand how the heartlink could have been created when he had never met her, but he sure wasn't going to question it anymore. She was real. He truly wasn't alone now. Positively giddy with joy, he swooped through the cavern doing loops, figure eights and steep dives all the while laughing uncontrollably.

"Xelrine!" he thought-shouted, "I've missed you so much! Welcome back!"

"I've missed you, too."

Having expended his sudden burst of boyish energy, Quroak floated back down to the portal.

"Though I desperately hoped, I didn't think you were real. Then when I was blasted out to the boondocks and couldn't hear or feel you anymore, I was sure you were an illusion, evaporated by the stress of my situation. And now you are here again. How? Why did you leave? These past two years have been awful for me!" Quroak's thoughts tumbled out in an excited rush.

He relished the feel of her thoughts softly flowing through his mind as she answered, "I lost you. I've been reaching out to you all this time but couldn't find you. Where were you?"

Quroak opened the door to his memories from the time he ran across the black hole to now, allowing her to see directly his experiences since it was a much faster way to communicate than thought-conversation.

Almost instantly, she gasped, "Oh *Guiding Star*, I'm sorry! How horrible! Are you okay? "

"I'm okay now that you are back," he answered quietly; still not sure he wasn't dreaming all of this.

"I guess you were too far away before and that's why I lost you. But now that you're closer, I can be with you again."

He knew he was being selfish, but he wished she was

actually was with him, in person, just so that he knew for sure she *was* a person and not a make-believe companion or lost ghost. Then he reminded himself that he wasn't going to question her reality anymore. He supposed that he could be insane enough to imagine the heartlink sensation, but he believed that was not even possible to fake. *So just go with it*, he commanded himself. *Accept what is*. He couldn't help laughing to himself: *even insanity?*

So while imaging Xelrine was with him, Quroak left the portal and flew towards the cavern exit to the surface.

Since he had just shared all of his memories directly with her, she didn't have any questions regarding his experiences; however, she was excited about the Quaoarians.

"That was a great job you did in tracking down the Quaoarians. You're lucky they are friendly and helped you get this far," Xelrine thought in wonder.

"Yes, I was lucky in that, at least." Quroak replied as he reached Charon's airless surface. "Though, that Monopoly game on the trip was pretty torturous! I still haven't recovered from it!"

"You poor dear!" she laughed softly. "I'm sure the worst is over now."

He couldn't help but laugh at that, thinking how much he had missed her.

He hadn't been having much luck understanding the workings of the cavern-machine and so decided to give it up as a hopeless task. The *Guardians of One's* technology was just so far advanced that it was pure magic to him. In fact, it was so far advanced, it was only because of the history log he found by the portal that he even knew there *was* advanced technology here.

So while he and Xelrine discussed the impossibility of an exploding black hole and how far he was from home, he decided to explore the neighborhood more closely since he still had about a month before the comet reached Pluto's vicinity.

On the moon Nix, he discovered a very small spacecraft, roughly the size and shape of an Earth American football. He had missed this on his cursory survey of the smaller moons upon first arriving here.

The spacecraft was in a small dark crater and seemed to be intact; at least, the hull didn't appear to be damaged. Xelrine was excited to actually share in a discovery as it happened, instead of via his memories.

"Wow, they must really be tiny creatures to fit in that small spaceship. Are you sure it's a spaceship?" she asked skeptically.

"Yes, look at the three legs holding it a few centimeters off the crater floor. What else could it be but a spacecraft? I don't think it was created to travel on this moon."

There was no way to know how long it had been there or if it was still operational. So he looked around for its owners, knowing they wouldn't be easy to find for they must be very small creatures indeed.

In a nearby flat plain pocked with craters and covered with a thin layer of some kind of ice, he came across a colony of ice-worms. They were about half a meter in length, very flat and totally featureless with no visible means of seeing, hearing, or apparently receive any type of signals from the electromagnetic spectrum, though he supposed they must be able to somehow.

When he heard a booming "Welcome!" in his mind, he knew they not only were aware of his presence, but were sentient and, obviously, telepathic.

"Greetings and open arms to you", Quroak thought-replied with the traditional Cloudotian greeting when meeting someone new.

"And to you" they replied in synchronous harmony, apparently understanding his meaning that he comes in peace, despite having no arms themselves.

"Is that your ship over yonder?" he asked though he was pretty sure it couldn't be. They obviously didn't have the physical dexterity to control ships, though he supposed if they had telekinetic abilities, it was possible. However, they were much too large to fit into this particular vessel.

"No, it does not belong to us, friend," they replied as one.

Curious, he had to ask, "If you don't mind my asking, are you individuals telepathically linked together speaking in agreement or are you all parts of one creature?"

"We are all parts of one mind" they answered somewhat puzzled. "Are you not part of a larger one?"

"Well, I am a part of a society, but I'm an individual with my own thoughts," Quroak thought-said slowly. "Though we communicate directly with our thoughts, we are each alone to think and do as we please and we usually close off our minds so that we can be alone with our own thoughts. And rarely do we act as a whole because everyone has their own opinion."

"This seems inconceivable to us," they replied sounding mystified.

"What do you call yourselves? My species is called Cloudotian and my name is Quroak."

"We are Kulan. It sounds like you live a lonely existence if you live in the silence of your own thoughts. How do you bear not being one of many all sharing one thought, one purpose?"

Hiding his thoughts of Xelrine, he replied "Yes, it does get lonely sometimes. However, it is how we evolved. It's the only way we know."

"We can understand that part since we don't know of any other way than the way we are as well," the Kulan replied.

"Do you know the origins of the spacecraft? Or how long it has been here?

"We do not know from whence it came," stated the Kulan. "However, it has been here for two in-swings."

Quroak hazarded a guess as to what 'in-swing' meant

in this context. Pluto and its moons follow a highly elliptical orbit around the sun where it swings in closer to Sol than Neptune and then crosses the blue giant's path again to return deeper into the Kuiper Belt. The difference in distance to the sun is about three billion kilometers and takes about 248 Earth years for one cycle. So the spacecraft had been there at least 500 Earth years.

"What about its crew?" Xelrine asked.

After a long pause, Quroak realized the Kulan could not hear Xelrine in his mind so he asked, "So you have not seen the spacecraft's owners?"

The Kulan answered in their strange multi-voice way, "No, we have never seen the crew of this ship. We change our mind about this mystery every couple months. We currently speculate that the ship was left here as an emergency lifeboat for explorers of their kind who might have need of it in case their ship has a catastrophic failure or accident. We don't really know anything about it."

"I guess that is possible," Quroak mused.

"We are curious about your 'aloneness' of mind. May we inquiry more into this?" asked the Kulan.

"Sure, I have plenty of time." Quroak laughed as he settled on the cold, rocky crater floor, piling up his arms into a pillow for his head.

CHAPTER 16

The four months waiting for the comet passed quickly for Quroak as he spent time with the Kulan and studying the cavern-machine of the *Guardians of One* on Charon. However, what really helped was having conversations with Xelrine again. He was so happy to have her back. For now, it was okay that she may be a figment of his imagination created from loneliness: for now. He would have to do something about it, though, when he got home, though he didn't really know what.

For now, though, he enjoyed her company in his mind and they spent a lot of time just lounging around on the airless moons looking up into the dark ocean filled with thousands of bright lights adrift in the absolute silence. Sometimes they would stare wistfully at Sol, so small and so far away.

As the comet approached, Quroak knew he had to be ready, for this comet traveled about six times faster than most comets, about 120,000 kph. He would only have one chance to rendezvous with the hurtling comet, for if he missed this opportunity he could never catch it.

Though he knew this was the only way to get to Neptune and thus closer to home, he wasn't really looking forward to the trip. He calculated it was going to take over 16 Earth months for the comet to reach the vicinity of that giant blue planet. Sixteen months riding on an ice ball streaking through the empty night! Sixteen mind-numbing months of complete, unbroken monotonous boredom! Really, what is there to do on a ball of ice? It wasn't like he could hop off to explore anything then hop back on. If he got off the comet, it was gone and he would be stranded, and then dead.

"Come on, Quroak, you wouldn't be dead!" Xelrine scolded him. "Lost. Beyond hope, maybe. But not dead. At least, not right away."

"Oh thanks, that really cheers me up!" he said sarcastically, realizing she was trying to do just that.

She laughed. "I bet those nine tortuous months playing monopoly with the Quaoarians are looking pretty good to you right about now."

He couldn't help but laugh at that, relaxing a little. Realizing that this was not going to be easy, he set about trying to find anything that would help him.

He studied the alien spherical spacecraft as best as he could but didn't get anywhere because he couldn't figure out how to open the hatch. In fact, he couldn't even find the hatch. There were no visible engines or propulsion system on the exterior that he could determine. He didn't understand how this was possible, but he admitted he wasn't an engineer and neither, apparently was Xelrine for she could offer no advice. He didn't want to break it open for maybe the owners would really come back one day with a desperate need of their craft. So giving it up as a lost cause, he continued searching the caverns on Charon.

Halfway around the moon from the entrance into the cavern, he finally came across one section that was apparently reserved for supplies. This storage area was huge, running a few kilometers in length but seemed to be very organized with everything neatly in place. There were things there in every shape and size imaginable and most of it was completely beyond his grasp as to its function or purpose.

However, after hunting around he found two things he was looking for: a tiny guidance-control computer module and chemical explosives. Or rather, he found the chemicals necessary to create a controlled explosion from a formula he remembered from his Chemistry classes. As for the rest, he found items he had no clue as to their function and shaped them into what he needed using a construction lab he found adjacent to the storage area.

After much trial and error and with Xelrine's advice, her creativity surprising him, he had an explosion-driven, computer-guided grapple-like device that he was going to use to hook a ride on the comet as it shot past.

He was none too soon, for the comet was due to pass his way tomorrow. In fact, he could see the comet now, a small, dirty, white ball that was getting larger every time he looked at. Of course, it had no tail, not being close enough to the sun for its surface ice to melt.

So he went to talk to the Kulan one last time. He had already explained to them what he was going to attempt.

"I just wanted to say what a pleasure it was to meet you," Quroak said sincerely.

"For us, as well. Though we knew other life-forms existed due to the abandoned spacecraft, we had never met another sentient being before." The Kulan paused in contemplation. "And we had never imagined the concept of individuality. It is still a concept we can't fully comprehend but at least now we know it exists."

"Well, you are unique in my experience too," he thought-said with a warm feeling.

Then he gave the traditional Cloudotian parting, "May *Guiding Star* always be with you, leading you into the light."

Though the Kulan had never seen Jupiter, because of their prior conversations, they recognized the well-being the Cloudotian was wishing upon them. "And Good Darkness to you, our friend. May you soon fly your green skies once more."

So Quroak flew about 800,000 kilometers away from Pluto to a spot the comet would pass in a few hours. He wanted to get there in advance because this ice wanderer of the deep night was his only hope of getting closer to home.

As he floated in the empty night, he tried to carry on a light-hearted conversation with Xelrine but he couldn't really remember what they were talking about as his nerves were strung too tight. He tried to think positively to reduce his anxiety for he knew he couldn't make a mistake here. He had one chance and one chance only. If he blew this chance . . .

He tried not to watch the comet as it got closer and closer, fearing it would stress him out more. But he couldn't pull his eyes away from it. It was a huge, imperfectly round gray ball of ice and rocks splashed with craters and riddled with fault lines. At least, from his perspective, it looked huge. But it was probably only about a kilometer in diameter. However, as it raced towards his position, he couldn't shake the impression that a moon was about to run him down, freezing him on the spot with fear with his hearts pounding furiously and every muscle drawn tight.

Even though he had known the comet was streaking through the dark at 120,000 kph, he hadn't been viscerally prepared for the sheer blinding speed. He snapped himself out of his spell, removed himself from the comet's path by about twenty meters (the size and closeness of the hurtling mountain-size boulder made it feel like only twenty centimeters), turned, reduced his mass to almost nothing except his arms (all of which were tied to the harpoon gun) and fired his makeshift harpoon, all in one motion *before* the comet reached him.

As it was, he was almost too late for the comet moved so quickly the harpoon hit the trailing end of the ice ball. If it hadn't been computer-guided, he would have missed it completely. But the harpoon struck the ball of ice with enough force to bury itself a couple of meters where it immediately opened into a metallic alloyed grapple-hook strong enough to stay embedded under the comet's surface.

When the harpoon fired, he was first flung *away* from the comet due to the *for every action there's an equal and opposite reaction* maxim caused by the explosion and then he shot forward as the harpooned comet shot past, dragging him along, as if he had just 'caught' a fish that outweighed him by a factor of a million.

He was thankful the comet didn't have much of a tail to speak of for him to contend with as the harpoon gun reeled him towards the comet's surface. Just as he finished that thought, three of his arms were struck by tiny ice particles streaming off the tumbling comet and such was their velocity, they went completely through his arms causing him to thought-groan in agony.

Thank *Guiding Star* that he had tied his arms to the harpoon; otherwise, he would have lost his grip right then and there. He just wished he had thought of creating a shield.

However, he quickly reached the cold surface without further incident where he sagged to the ground, weak from relief. A rush of euphoria flooded through him as he impulsively hugged the rocky ice, fervently thanking *Guiding Star* for this gift; and then himself for not messing up.

"We made it!!" he thought-screamed joyously.

"I never had any doubt in you" whispered Xelrine warmly.

"Thanks, but that was too close for my comfort" he exclaimed, suddenly weary as his adrenaline dropped off abruptly, as if a value had been turned shut.

After staring at the unblinking stars which didn't seem to move at all though he was shooting through the night at 120,000 kph, he released his arms from the harpoon gun by the simple method of reducing their mass until he was free of the restraints. He wiped away the globules of blue blood clinging to his puncture wounds, saw how small and clean the holes were and decided he should heal pretty quickly with no lasting problems. Right now though, those three arms hurt like tiny flames were racing up and down those appendages causing his suckers to be really sensitive to the touch.

He quickly explored the leeward side of the hurtling comet, being careful not to expose himself to the solar wind slamming into the shooting star as it rushed inward. It was just a lumpy, uninteresting, grayish white sphere of icy rock. Unfortunately, this unremarkable ice-rock was going to be his home for the next sixteen months.

He found a sizeable crack which he deepened and widened with the harpoon gun into a small cave for himself.

The next sixteen months were one continuous blur to him where he spent long periods of time staring into the empty dark night haunted by silent distant lights from the past, creating interesting stories to pass the time, meditating, talking with Xelrine, roaming the comet and sleeping as much as possible. He even tried imagining he was playing Monopoly with the Quaoarians in his mind but it just became too much for him to bear after there was a heated argument over how many hotels he could build on Reading Railroad. Though he figured the imaginary game took at least six months, he really had no way of keeping track of time on the comet for there was no night and day cycle to help him. Xelrine was marking the passage of time for him but since he wasn't totally convinced she was real (though he was taking her word for it) he didn't really know how much time was passing.

Besides, he was so bored, all he knew was that it seemed he was on that comet forever, with Neptune a pale blue marble floating in a tranquil sea of darkness beckoning his ice-ship to make safe harbor after a long journey.

With agonizing slowness, Neptune grew in size until a few eternities later, it dominated the night with its blue light promising a haven for weary travelers with the Great Dark Spot flowing across the surface like a dark eye searching the cosmos for ship-wrecked survivors in the cold unforgiving sea.

The azure glow slowly penetrated Quroak's boredom-induced stupor to fully re-awaken his awareness, for he had slipped into a kind of dreamy state of consciousness somewhere during the long journey. He made a mental note to send a suggestion to Earth's American General Surgeon to start putting messages warning of this type of thing on their Monopoly games.

CHAPTER 17

The gas giant hung in the obsidian darkness, a jewel of the night against the backdrop of tiny white diamonds, with bands of cobalt blue circling the southern hemisphere while wisps of white floated upon the currents of azure, indigo and royal blues that dominated the globe with white cyclones racing past their much bigger, ultramarine cousins, the Great Dark Spot and the Small Dark Spot, all given a majestic quality as the planet floated serenely in the center of a glittering, reddish icy pond created by its rings.

Quroak was very much entranced by this sight and was unbelievably gratified for the azure light reaching out to him. He had been in total darkness now for about twenty months, ever since he had been dropped off by the Quaoarians at Pluto, and he was quiet tired of it and missed light more than he realized. While he had been able to sustain himself from the ices on the comet,

Cloudotians get a lot of their sustenance from light of which he had been lacking. *Well, Charon did have that pale orange light*, he reminded himself. *So okay, it's only been about sixteen months but that's still a long time.*

He needed to get into that light to replenish his strength. Plus after being so inactive for so long, he looked forward to surfing the currents of Neptune which he knew has the strongest winds in the whole Solar System with storms ripping across the skies at 2,100 kph.

Just before the speeding comet reached its closest point to the Neptunian system, Quroak floated off the back of the comet. He instantly regretted not thinking this through better. His ride was currently bursting through a cloud of ice particles causing turbulence in the comet's wake, buffeting him uncontrollably. He quickly dematerialized, yet his momentum from the comet's velocity carried him at a speed of 120,000 kph, much too fast for him to gain control.

He wished he had the skills of the Ancients who could reduce their mass to zero where he would have lost all momentum. At least, so he thought. As it was, he could only decrease his mass to about twenty percent which seemed to have slowed him down but only marginally.

He knew he had to find a balance to make himself solid enough to slow down from resistance but not too solid to fatally injure himself from the impacts of ice and dust particles. With a quick prayer to *Guiding Star,* he spread his arms, though keeping the ends furled, to open his mantle as wide as possible to act like a sail against the out-flowing solar wind to slow himself down. He constantly had to change his density in an effort to find that balance where he would instinctively dematerialize more after each agonizing hit from an ice or dust particle that felt like it was a jet-propelled spear.

After what he guessed was half a day, with his head pounding from the continuous effort and his body aching from the strain and the bombardment, his velocity finally decreased where he could take control of his flight and he slipped out of the comet's wake and came to a stop.

Wearily he looked back at Neptune which he had passed hours ago and realized it was going to take him days to reach. Drained and exhausted, he hung there, not being able to move, barely able to keep his eyes open.

Then he felt Xelrine's sweet caress tinged with anxiety, "Are you okay?"

Unexpected relief flooded though him as he heard her for the first time since departing the comet's surface, for his concentration on gaining control had been total, not leaving any room for anything else, not even communicating with Xelrine. He barely managed to reply "Yes, I'm fine" before he passed out.

Upon awakening, he was confused as to where he was. He felt lost in a stygian sea of darkness with a blue beacon beckoning him towards safety but he had no body with which to move towards that haven.

Then he heard vaguely in the distance, "Quroak, I'm here. Come to me."

The thoughts felt familiar so he forced his way towards the voice, not understanding how he was doing it. But the voice kept calling out to him and seemed to be getting closer and clearer. Finally he swam up out of the stygian sea to find himself in his body which was floating in a slightly less dark ocean of night.

"Xelrine?" he reached out.

"I'm here. You've been out for two days now. Are you feeling better?"

Stretching his muscles, he discovered he could move with only a dull ache accompanying each movement. "Yes, much better".

"Though I wished I had thought about how to get off that stupid iceball before getting on it in the first place," he thought ruefully.

"Well, you are going through a lot and you can't think of everything. But I'm sorry I didn't think of it for you." He could feel regret flavoring her thoughts.

While they rehashed his experiences both while on the comet and departing that temporary home, Quroak steered for the Neptunian system. It took him about a week to reach Nereid, one of Neptune's outer moons. He found Nereid to be pretty unremarkable and quickly flew inward to Triton, Neptune's largest satellite.

He remembered that Triton is supposedly the coldest place in the Solar System and though he had just spent 16 months numb with boredom on an ice ball, he couldn't muster up enough curiosity to stay more than a couple of days at an even colder place. All things considered, he wouldn't mind a swim in Io's lava flows right about now. He did, however, dive into an erupting ice volcano just for the novelty and the bragging rights of being the only one to do so, though he didn't know if he would ever find anyone to boast to, except Xelrine, who may only be his imagination anyway.

Ever since reaching the Neptunian system, he had felt a subtle emotional pull towards the blue giant that dominated Triton's sky. He couldn't understand what it was or even how to describe it to Xelrine, but it was as if he was being hypnotically pulled towards the azure planet. Thus far he had been able to resist the siren call, but now he found it much more compelling so he left the pinkish moon and decided to skip the other dozen or so satellites and headed directly for Neptune.

"Can you feel the attraction towards Neptune? It seems to be on an emotional level that echoes silently with a dire need to be explored," Quroak tried to explain.

"Yes, I can feel the call in your mind," she replied with awe. "What can be doing that?"

"I don't know." As he approached Neptune, he first skated around a portion of the thin blue-shadowed rings circling the gas giant before continuing to the planet itself. Upon entering the atmosphere he felt his soul was being caressed by some kind of emotional energy, like a soft breeze. He didn't know how to describe it but it sent a chill through him.

Quroak had once visited on Curon (one of the moons of his home planet) the sacred Ascendancy Crater where the glow-bats went at the end of their current level of existence to ascend to the next plane of life. This involved a rich and complex ritual in which the ascenders and the whole community participated. The glow-bats guard this sacred place carefully and as far as he knew, Quroak was the only one the glow-bats had allowed to visit the Crater or even let known about its existence. While at the Crater, he had sensed the emotional vibrations within the crater's walls and floor imprinted by the intense energy created by the emotional rituals and celebrations.

What he sensed now while traveling through Neptune's clouds was not the same but similar in that he felt an emotional presence. He was also feeling a heaviness of the heart that he could not explain. Though he always did feel a little sad when thinking of the glow-bats because it reminded him of their ancestral cousins who lived on Earth. He knew the Earth bats were actively trying to save life on that planet but they were misunderstood, generally feared and unjustly vilified by the humans. But he didn't think that fully accounted for the heaviness in his heart now.

As he dived into the upper atmosphere, he luxuriated in the relative warmth radiated from the planet. It was by no means the soothing warmth of Sea Of Clouds, but it was much less colder than any place he'd been since leaving the Quaoarians about 21 months ago. He tried to absorb as much as the heat as he could, though he knew he wasn't really going to be able to thaw out. He had pretty much taken feeling frozen as a given.

While avoiding storms as much as possible because he still didn't feel at full strength, he soon came upon a dense cloud formation about the size of Earth's moon. Within the cobalt cloud, he discovered a colony of creatures that vaguely resembled the ♊♓♌♈♑ (the giant small-one) on Sea of Clouds but they had a light blue beak and four sets of talons. These Neptunian jellyfish were harvesting methane ice crystals from the cloud. He couldn't imagine what the creatures could want the methane ice for.

As he watched them, hidden from view, he immediately felt there was something oddly different about these creatures but he couldn't quite place how right away. He sensed a hollowness within them. Then it slowly dawned on him that there was an *absence* regarding these Neptunians. Then it hit him. They had *no emotions*! This was the first species he had ever met or even heard of that was truly emotionless. He knew of species that felt different kinds of emotions unknown to others and other species that completely hid them, but these Neptunian creatures had *no* emotions whatsoever.

"Xelrine, how is this possible. What kind of environmental conditions would inspire this evolutional choice by Nature?"

"Hmmm, I don't know. I don't see how this would increase their chances of survival," she replied thoughtfully.

"Yea, I don't understand the benefit of being without emotions on the species level. Most creatures wouldn't survive without emotions like fear."

"It does seem strange," she mused.

The Neptunian jellyfish seemed to prefer their solitude, as a group that is, so Quroak left them alone to continue exploring the immense blue ocean of clouds that was Neptune. He found the cloud formations and swirling currents to be wondrously beautiful but he also felt colder inside the longer he explored. He had the feeling that he was not alone but . . .

"Xelrine, did you see that?" he suddenly thought-gasped.

"What?"

"I thought I saw, uh, well, I don't know exactly what. It was like a slight rippling in the clouds that can't be explained by the winds. Then it was gone."

The next moment he dodged wildly to one side as a small white cyclone flew past him at a speed he hadn't believed was possible. The strong pull created by its blinding rotation almost sucked him into the crazy storm before he had the chance to dematerialize. He didn't feel quite ready to surf one of those babies yet.

It whirled around so fast and traveled the thick blue sky so rapidly, it reminded him of an Earth nature show he once saw with a creature called the 'Tasmanian Devil'. His people had been fascinated with that creature and had secretly searched for it on Earth, but it was nowhere to be found. Neither was its pal, the six foot talking bunny. They finally assumed they must have gone extinct, like so many other wonderful animals on that hazardous planet.

As he dove deeper into the clouds, he noticed that he felt stronger, more energized than he had for a very long time. He saw that his wounds were healing very rapidly, much faster than normal. In fact, he swore he could see the punctures close up and his flesh reseal itself as he watched.

"Wow!" he thought. "There must be something about this planet that affects Cloudotian physiology".

"Maybe it's the intense blue light," hazarded Xelrine. "And the fact that most of the red light is absorbed by this air. I think I heard somewhere that too much energy in the red spectrum negatively affects our immune system. Maybe, the opposite boasts our immune system."

"Yea, maybe," Quroak replied distractedly, thinking he just saw another mysterious ripple in the swirling clouds.

As he continued downward, he kept seeing the vague ripplings that never materialized into anything solid but were occurring with more frequency.

He flexed his muscles as he dove and swooped with enthusiasm at being in clouds again, riding the winds with abandon. This was where he felt most comfortable, not stuck on asteroids or comets, or even planets or moons with no substantial atmospheres. And the deeper he dove the warmer it was. Though it was still pretty cold, compared to the frigidness he had been exposed to, this was a sauna where he soaked up the warmth with relish.

He felt something massive far above him, looked up and was astounded to see a large cyclone passing above. He had never seen the bottom side of a cyclone before where he was untouched by its winds. He stared up at the inverted cone of pure wind that both tore open the blue clouds and sucked them into its raging hunger. Then the storm passed and the clouds rushed in to fill the vacuum left behind and suddenly it was raining methane ice.

The ice crystals fell fast, much faster than expected as if they were metal being attracted by a super-magnet. It was so unexpected that an ice crystal went right through his seventh arm causing him to cry out in agony. He quickly reduced his mass as much as possible and scooted out of the downpour with drops of floating blue blood marking his path.

As soon as he escaped the crystal rainstorm, he examined his arm and was surprised to see it almost healed already. *This is amazing! If we could recreate these conditions at a hospital . . . I have to get home to let scientists know about this miraculous light.*

But first I have to find a way home. Though he didn't expect to find anything on Neptune to achieve this goal, the relative warmth and freedom of the skies was too enticing for him to leave right now so he continued exploring the wonderful wind-sculpted clouds which were in more shades of blue than he had known existed.

He soon realized that though his body was now completely healed, whereas before he had felt energized, now he was really fatigued, very tired. For some reason, he felt drained as if he had been in a sustained, highly charged emotional state for a very long period of time.

He was rapidly losing his curiosity and energy for exploration as he just started to let himself sink deeper into Neptune's windy atmosphere which was turning a darker blue as he fell. Also, Neptune's gravity, which is the second strongest in the Solar System, was pulling him down faster and he was starting to feel a crushing weight, not only against his body by the tightening grip of the planet, but also within by some unknown force.

Down this far from the outer layer of the atmosphere, though there were strong winds pushing the heavy mass of clouds, there didn't seem to be any storms, for which he was grateful because he didn't think he could avoid them if any suddenly appeared out of the dark blueness.

Instead of his mind flowing freely, each thought now had to struggle for completeness, like it was trying to pass through semi-frozen slush before fully forming into existence. He felt lost in his own mind, with a dark heaviness slowly squeezing out the light of reasoning and recognition.

"Xelrine, I feel really weird," he thought-murmured.

"I feel like I have no strength to do anything, like I just got intensely depressed out of the blue." Then he managed to add weakly, "No pun intended."

"What do you think is happening?" she asked nervously.

Paradoxically, he felt a huge emptiness inside while he was also filled with such intense emotional pain that he thought he was dying from sheer agony. The agony quickly overwhelmed him until he felt numbness throughout his core.

After a few moments, her question sunk down into his hazy, slow moving mind and he responded wearily, "Don't know."

"Quroak!" she shouted in his mind. "You've got to get out of there!"

With his head hanging limply, he continued to drift downward, his arms unresponsive and flapping in the wind. The insane depression was a crushing weight, making even the simplest kind of action, whether emotionally or physically, a Herculean feat beyond his capabilities. He was emotionally exhausted where he couldn't feel anything except a numb emptiness eating away his existence.

A heavy darkness weighed upon him, suffocating the light and life out of him. He could no longer tell if he was actually awake or asleep in a bad dream. His mind struggled to lift the veil of blackness that completely shrouded him.

"What?"

"Go up! Quroak, go up!" she screamed frantically.

He opened his eyes, which he hadn't even realized were closed, and found himself surrounded by the ghostly ripplings. Though he didn't know how he knew, he knew they were creatures of some kind.

As he tried to think about what that loud voice in his head had shouted, he continued to sink downward with his emotional energy leaking from him like air from a punctured balloon.

The ripplings circled him, flitting in and out of existence with just a fleeting parting of the azure clouds marking their passage, though he still wondered if they were a figment of his exhausted mind as he slipped towards unconsciousness.

His heart was heavier than a mountain, which would have to be moved before he could feel anything again beyond numbness and emptiness. He had no energy whatsoever in order to have any kind of interest in anything.

Somewhere from far away, he barely heard, "Go up. They're killing you. Go Up."

The voice was so sweet, yet so earnest. It sounded like an angel to his sluggish mind, as if he was dying and the angel was here to collect his soul. He felt so drained, so very tired that he knew it must be true, he must be dying because he no longer had the strength to live. *I have to go to the angel. I have to save my soul.*

As his strength drained from him like rain from a cloud, he focused his mind on this last task; reaching the angel so he could finally find eternal rest. With his eyes closed to block out all distractions, he slowly struggled towards where he thought the angel was. After what felt like an eternity, the heavy clouds in his mind parted slightly for just an instant, just enough for him to hear the sweetness of the angel's voice again.

"Quroak! You have to go up! These are emotional vampires! Go up!" cried the angel.

Then the ocean-heavy fog clamped shut again, leaving his mind in a cold darkness where the pressure crushed his will. *Emotional vampires*, he thought distantly, as if it originated from another galaxy. Though he couldn't muster the strength to really care all that much, it slowly dawned on him that the invisible creatures must be draining the emotional energy from deep inside him.

What did she say? Oh, yes, go up. He couldn't remember why he should go up. He didn't really *want* to go up. In fact, he didn't *want* to do anything except give in to the overwhelming desire that was consuming his entire being; sleep. *Oh Guiding Star, sleep is my paradise now.* He didn't know anymore what he had been struggling for, or against, but if he could just lie in the serene arms of Vermist, the goddess of eternal rest, he would be at peace.

Though this thought resonated truth in his weary soul and he longed for this sleep like nothing before, somewhere deep in his mind, a mantra started softly: *Go up. Go up. Go up.*

He became aware that he was again being drawn deeper into the heart of Neptune and though that's where he wanted to go with all his heart, some instinct deep inside made him listen to the mantra: *Go up.*

With great effort, he slowly tore open a tiny hole in the heavy, dense cloak of indifference that shrouded his mind. *Go up.*

He walled off the overwhelming desire for sleep using the very thing that caused his soul to beg for rest: exhaustion, telling himself he didn't have the energy to fuel such a demanding desire as sleep. *Go up.*

He searched his heart for any remaining tiny sparks of hope, any glowing embers representing dreams still sought so that he could stoke them into flames to push back the dark coldness inside and regain the surface of the sea of depression before the insatiable vortex finished pulling him down into the inescapable depths. *Go up.*

He fought against his sluggish muscles, demanding them to respond to his commands even though he felt he was trying to flow through solid rock. *Go up.*

He opened his mantle as wide as possible to act like an airbrake, like a parachute. He flared his suckers as much as possible to increase air resistance. *Go up.*

With concentrated effort, he finally slowed then stopped his descent towards the azure darkness reaching up for him from below. *Go up.*

This major victory fanned his tiny flames of hope as he gathered the remnants of his strength and struggled upward. Now that he was more focused, he felt the hunger of the vampires feeding on his emotions, trying to drain every last bit of energy from his heart, licking eagerly at the flames of hope burning deep within him. But he was determined to not let them snuff out the slowly growing fire, somehow knowing if they succeeded, his will to survive would go up in smoke. *Go up.*

He fought with all of his inner strength, summoning up every ounce of willpower to struggle upward through the thick clouds and away from these horrible creatures. At the same time, inside his heart, he was fighting his way upward out of the stygian darkness of the whirlpool that was hungrily dragging him down to the bottomless depths of depression.

Though his flesh felt the warmth of Neptune's core from below, he felt totally frozen inside. From past experience, he knew very well that though everyone thought Hell was hot, emotional Hell was a frozen wasteland where the frigid surface of Triton was like the furnace of Venus in comparison.

On both fronts, physically in Neptune's clouds and internally against the vortex, he gained some altitude but then his will faltered for just a split second under a concerted attack by dozens of the creatures desperate to keep their prey from escaping. Their attack was so intense that it momentarily broke through all of his mental and emotional defenses, laying bare the very core of his being for them to feast upon. The effort it took for him to shore up his defenses again, even minimally, used up all of his remaining strength, as he starting to fall again, trapped within the vampires' unseen yet overpowering snare.

His waning willpower forced him to fight on, but he was beyond exhaustion as his body became weaker and weaker with the planet's grip dragging him down deeper. He struggled to remember what he was supposed to be doing. He was supposed to be going somewhere but that knowledge eluded him as he fought to stay conscious. He couldn't tell if his eyes were closed or if the sky had turned totally dark. He wasn't even sure the blackness wasn't just his consciousness slipping away.

The whirlpool inside now was in total control, bringing him faster to that wasteland. His heart was filled with icy winds that both numbed him and filled him with agony as ice daggers ripped through him.

Then when he thought it was over, he suddenly heard the angel's voice again, but this time it was clear. "Quroak, I am here with you. You must go up. Come to me. Come home."

The familiar sweetness of that voice's warm and gentle caress stirred the love in his heart that was still clinging to its existence with desperation. However, it was the word *home* that reached deep inside him, discovering the flicker in his heart that was the dream of finding his home. Once found, the sound of that voice lovingly coached that flicker into a flame to create a glimmer of strength deep inside him. He desperately took that small flame of desire and carefully fanned it into a beacon of hope and kept feeding it till it became a raging fire of defiance and while burning up this last reservoir of strength, slowly fought upwards through both the clouds and the vortex.

He felt the invisible creatures attack even more fiercely as they felt him slowly but determinedly slip from their snare. With their increased intensity, the inner whirlpool swirled faster, tightening its grip against his desperate swim upwards.

But with each successful struggle upwards, the sweet and loving voice of the angel became clearer through both his muddled mind and suppressed heart. "Come to me. Come home."

After what seemed an agonizing eternity, he finally escaped the whirlpool and reached the surface of the sea of depression. Now, he only felt intensely depressed, not the all-consuming agonizing despair of hopelessness. Now, he only felt very cold, not the glacial frigidness of Triton's ice volcano. Now, he only felt numbness of exhaustion, not the paralyzing numbness of agony.

This major victory strengthened his resolve, giving him the emotional strength to fuel his willpower to override his physical weakness and exhaustion, renewing his fight against both the emotional vampires and Neptune's grip.

"Quroak, come home. Come to me," thought-whispered the angel.

He opened his eyes to see there were fewer ripplings around him and the sky was a lighter shade of azure. With his last ounce of strength, he shot up through the remaining kilometers of clouds until he finally escaped the vampire's hold by reaching the safety of space above Neptune's atmosphere.

He immediately collapsed in upon himself and struggled to stay awake as a few hours later his momentum carried him to the ruddy rings where he allowed himself to fall unconscious.

"Me!" I said weakly, yet firmly as I slumped over the library interface, falling asleep.

CHAPTER 18

I t turned out that I had slept for two days in that library kiosk. I'd forgotten the library was going to be closed for two days to celebrate a planetary holiday. Otherwise, someone would have found me earlier and awoken me. As it was, I awoke on my own when the twin suns shone their glorious and unique lights through the window.

You may wonder why the sunlights didn't stir me on the previous two days. A two-day double eclipse was occurring which is why there was a holiday because this rare event only happens every 204 of our years where both suns are eclipsed by the strange and complicated dance involving six of our moons with such beauty and perfection you would think the whole thing was choreographed by an artistic god. I was around for the last one and it was truly glorious and something I will remember for all time. I'm really sorry I missed it this time around.

However, living Quroak's memory of escaping those

vampires of Neptune really drained me emotionally and sent me into the deepest of depressions. Over time, I've purposely created some self-defense mechanisms where I've set triggers via self-hypnosis in the event of certain situations in order to protect my psyche. As happened in this case, when I'm exposed to depression or emotional pain of such intensity that I'm in danger of losing myself, an overpowering desire for sleep is triggered where my psyche can reassert itself while I slumber. All of my triggers are specifically set to go off only when the situation is due to my living another's memories.

Of course, these defenses are *not* triggered when the pain is truly my own for I prefer to deal with problems head on instead of hiding or ignoring them.

As an emocologist, naturally I have done a lot of research into the cause and effect of emotions, especially in how these intangible yet very powerful forces drive all creatures. Well, most creatures, anyways. I know of only one higher life-form (species above insects) that has no emotions whatsoever.

But I have also studied intensively what occurs in the *absence* of emotions. I don't mean unemotional people who don't feel strongly, but rather individuals who have *no* emotions whatsoever due to brain damage where the region responsible for emotions is destroyed and the capacity to feel anything at all is gone.

It is not as simple as the Neptunian vampires were just sucking all the joy from Quroak's heart. No, they were siphoning off all the energy that emotions create. Creatures that evolved with emotions can't survive long without their emotions or without the energy emotions create. It's not just that emotions create the quality of one's life, but they also generate the drive to live, to survive. Even if you don't feel particularly emotional, it doesn't mean you're not driven by them. It's the energy generated by emotions that creates your *will* and without willpower you are numb, frozen, and powerless to perform even the simplest, most basic everyday tasks that must be accomplished to live, much less achieve any dreams. In fact you wouldn't even have dreams, not just fantasies, but those dreams that drive one to create something to better the quality of life, such as irrigation, industry, music, art, et cetera.

But more than that, you can't function at all without emotions. You may be able to survive for awhile, but only with someone to take care of you every minute of your life. Experience with individuals with damage to the emotional centers of the brain has shown that emotions drive decision making, any kind of decision. Even when you think you're making a choice solely intellectually, it is actually based on your emotions. What brand to buy, what to eat, *whether* to eat or not, what to wear, which side of the street to walk on, it's all based on your feelings. People with their emotional centers destroyed are simply incapable of making any decisions on their won.

The species I mentioned before that has no emotions

had evolved with other mechanisms to replace the function of emotions. The *Weznian nightsnow* are so alien that the very concept of their existence would be impossible for you to imagine so we will leave that for another time.

Now you are probably wondering about the Neptunian jellyfish that Quroak had discovered mining methane clathrate high up in the vivid blue clouds. On the surface, it certainly seems obvious that they evolved without emotions to save their species from the planet's emotion vampires; what we call *emovamps* for short.

There are other species' on Neptune who do have emotions but they developed other ways to defend themselves against the emovamps.

I have spent a lot of time at Neptune studying both the emovamps and the *wraiths*, which Quroak referred to as Neptunian jellyfish. These wraiths are not what they appear to be in that they are not true sentient beings.

They are actually clones of individuals of the true species, *shadowcaster*. The name shadowcaster is a misnomer. When the relationship between the wraiths and shadowcasters was first discovered, it was originally thought the wraiths were mere shadows, albeit with substance, of their originators and the name stuck even after the truth was discovered.

The shadowcasters live in the water-ammonia ocean that encircles the planet's core far beneath the clouds. They are extremely emotional, thereby very delicious to the emovamps. Since the shadowcaster have no real predators in their natural habitat, the hot dense ocean, their numbers exploded well beyond the available food supply. The source of their food actually originates high up in the clouds but doesn't become edible till it falls into the ocean where it is transformed into their food.

So somewhere in their ancient past, the shadowcasters tried to control the fall-rate by traveling up into the clouds, but they were always instantly assailed by the insatiable emovamps, succumbing to the emotion-sucking attacks.

Nature's evolutionary answer to this dilemma was to give the shadowcasters the ability to instantly create *empty* replicas of themselves. The replicas are *empty* in the sense that they have no emotions, no will and actually no true thoughts of their own. So on an emotional, sentience and consciousness level, there's nothing there, which is why we call them wraiths.

The clones are *programmed* to do only one thing; harvest the seeds of the shadowcasters' food. The replicas harvest the methane ice, which is simply methane trapped within water ice crystals, from the glacial cloud formations high up in the atmosphere.

They bring the methane ice, safely past the emovamps, down to their originators in the ocean where the water ice crystals melt, thereby freeing the methane inside and the extremely high temperature and pressure conditions of the ocean causes the methane to decompose into diamond crystals, upon which the shadowcasters feed.

I discovered this shadowcaster-wraith relationship

decades ago quite serendipitously during an expedition to the Neptune Ocean, classifying the myriad of life-forms existing there when by chance I happened to see a shadowcaster create the replica of itself, the wraith. I was quite surprised and so followed the wraith and so discovered its function. Once a wraith's task is completed, the shadowcaster reabsorbs the wraith back into itself.

I have sufficient mental shields and defenses that the emovamps never affect me so it wasn't until I relived Quroak's memories that I truly understood the complete emotional devastation they cause and how dangerous they are to most species.

CHAPTER 19

Quroak's next memory is of waking up, safely embraced within the ruddy ice rings crowning Neptune. When he opened his eyes, he saw the vivid azure light of the giant planet reflecting off the ring's ice particles creating a mysterious looking, yet lovely, show of sapphire and dull ruby sparkles dancing in the blue infused night.

His mind was really woozy and it took him awhile to fully become aware of his surroundings. He felt a little down, a soft sadness he couldn't quite place as for the reason. He found his body curled up in a ball and he felt cramped all over. With effort he unfurled his arms and stretched his sore muscles among the ice crystals.

His thoughts finally started to flow again and he wondered, "What happened?"

"Welcome back, darling," a sweet thought-whisper caressed his mind.

"Xelrine? What's going on?" he asked vaguely. He felt like he was trying to awaken from a century long sleep.

"You've been asleep for three weeks. I've been waiting for you."

"*Three weeks?*"

"Yes, you needed time to recover. You came so close to dying down there. It took you so long to escape. I thought I had lost you. I'm so glad you woke up. I was going crazy hoping, praying, reaching out to you, and trying to help you get away from that awful planet and those horrible monsters! Then you did, but you collapsed. I was starting to get frantic thinking you would never wake up again. Never be there to talk to. Never be there when I needed you. But you did. But it's been so long! I've missed you terribly!" Her thoughts tumbled into his mind so fast he wasn't sure he got it all in his current hazy state.

"What do you mean I almost died? What. . ." Then it all came back to him like a flash of lightning. The events that almost claimed his life deep within the blue clouds crashed into his consciousness and the memory of the vampires draining his life away was so vivid he instinctively curled up into a ball again.

But he immediately realized these were just memories and that he had recovered his emotional strength and willpower. However, he couldn't prevent a sharp coldness from running through him as these memories flooded through his mind.

"Well, this explains why the jellyfish evolved with no emotions," he murmured thoughtfully.

"Yes. How are you feeling, Quroak?"

"I'm tired, but emotionally sound," he replied slowly. As he thought of his experience, he realized that the 'angel' who had helped him by penetrating his hopeless despair, shining light through the heavy darkness woven by the vampire's attacks and leading him from both their snare and the depths of Neptune itself, had been Xelrine.

"Xelrine, you saved my life," he thought quickly. "I'm forever in your debt. How can I ever repay you?"

"I know you will," Xelrine thought-whispered softly. "You were quite amazing. You are the strongest person I know. Anyone else would have died for sure. I just gave you a little help, which everyone needs sometimes."

"Please don't underestimate what you did, Xelrine." Quroak said emphatically. "I would not have survived if your sweet voice hadn't caressed my mind, giving me both the incentive and the strength to fight harder. You really did save my life and I'm grateful to you."

When Xelrine didn't respond, he continued, "There's no way I can describe how it felt being attacked by those invisible emotion-suckers. But you were in my mind so you know how it was. You know what I was going through. Thank you."

"You're welcome. I'm glad I was able to help you in some way. I really did miss talking with you all those. . ."

Xelrine broke off her thought, rather hesitantly, it seemed to Quroak.

"What is it, Xelrine?" As he was finally becoming more aware of his surroundings, he noticed the stars looked a little different. They seemed off somehow, like they were in the wrong positions. "Uh, Xelrine, there's something odd going on here. I know it sounds crazy but the stars seem out of place."

Xelrine took her time in answering. When she did, her thought-reply was slow and felt shaded with turquoise streaked with light yellow, which conveyed caring warmth yet with tentativeness like she didn't want to upset him.

"Quroak, when you were ensnared by the vampires and you were fighting for your life, I know you were in such agony that you lost track of time. I don't know how to say this except to just say it." Yet, she still hesitated. Then, "It took you three years to escape them. Three years for you to finally climb out of the depths of Neptune."

Shock hit him like a meteorite out of the blue. His mantle closed instantly, pulling his arms tightly around him, his head drooped with his skin blushing a dark ruby-emerald. His eyes bulged wide with Neptune's soft blue light reflecting off their blank expression. His mind went blank with his main heart racing uncontrollably while the other two hearts seemed to have stopped, paralyzed.

Time seemed to have stopped. *Time.* The word echoed around in his mind, bouncing off the hard walls of disbelief. Then one weird bounce seemed to have been against a sharp corner, splitting that thought wide open to create two other words: *three years*.

After a long pause, he finally managed, "Three years? Are you tickling my arm?"

"No, I wouldn't tease you. That's what I mean by you being strong. Having the strength to fight continuously for three years, and survive!"

"But it, it, just seems so, so, inconceivable," he stammered out. "I, I just don't know what to think."

Then a flood of thoughts rushed out as he unfurled himself in a flash and started zipping in and out of Neptune's rings in his sudden agitation. "I lost three years of my life without even knowing it. I fought for *three years*? And I was amazed when you told me I had slept for three *weeks*. No wonder I slept that long. I'm surprised I didn't sleep for three *years* after that ordeal. Oh, *Guiding Star*! Oh, sunghost! Three years!"

Quroak suddenly fell quiet and floated to a stop, exhausted from just thinking about it.

"Quroak, are you okay?" asked Xelrine anxiously.

"Yea, I'm okay. It's just a lot to take in. I'm really tired," he replied wearily.

"Maybe you should go to sleep."

"I just slept for three weeks. I'll sleep later. Right now, I just want to get out of here. I've given enough of my life to this place."

As he glanced around trying to decide what to do next, the reality of those three years sank in and he found he was a little amazed at himself for having such inner strength to fight so long. He knew he couldn't have done it without Xelrine's help but still, how many would have survived even with help? *I deserve to feel a little proud of myself.*

"So how have you been for the past three years, Xelrine?"

"I've really missed you and I was so scared for you. I was with you whenever I could."

She sounded so apologetic that he had to comfort her. "Xelrine, I understand. Believe me; you helped me more than you know. Besides, you have your own life to live. I really appreciate you spending as much time talking with me as you do." He knew when she wasn't with him that she was working or spending time with family and friends.

He wished he was home, but more than that, he really wished, yearned, to be with her. He silently cursed the universe for his situation.

"Xelrine, please tell me what's been going on with you for the past three years."

So she told him about her life for the past few years and while he listened, he couldn't help but feel depressed that he was not sharing every event with her. He so wanted to share life with someone, both the everyday mundane routine and the curveballs that life throws at you. He was very careful in not letting her know that she was making him feel lonelier with the news of her life and her stories of adventures or mishaps that occurred to her.

When she began telling him general news of their homeworld, while ignoring both his mind's and body's requests for sleep, he turned his attention to continuing his journey home.

"Xelrine, the next milestone home is Uranus. I think that's about 1.7 billion kilometers away. Of course, it could be a lot further if Neptune and Uranus are on opposite sides of the sun."

"Well, you've made it this far. How far did you go to get here from where you started, Quaoar?"

"My best guess is around 3.6 billion."

As usual, she offered up the positive side of the situation. "See, you've already come twice the distance as it is to Uranus."

"True, but that was with the help of the Quaoarians, who had a spacecraft, and a faster than usual comet that just happened to be going my way," he pointed out. "You don't happen to have a spaceship or comet you can send my way, do you?"

"Sorry, but my ship is in the shop for repairs. The heat is on the fritz again."

"Yea, the last thing I need right now is a ship without heat," he laughed, thinking of his trip on the frozen comet.

"But really, if I don't find something to help me, it would take me at least ten years to get to Uranus on my own. But that's not really an option anyway. You know about Quipit, right?"

She thought-sighed dejectedly, "Yea, I know about Quipit."

Most Cloudotians knew about Quipit, having been warned by their parents when first venturing into the hostile environment of space. The longest any Cloudotian had survived in the middle of space was six years but the poor guy, Quipit, was never the same afterwards, for he suffered from space dementia where he thought he was a star. Not a star as in celebrity, but a star as in the sun.

Quipit insisted that he was providing all the light and warmth for Sea of Clouds and couldn't be on the planet for he was too hot and was about to go supernova because he had no more hydrogen to burn. The strange thing was is that he escaped from the hospital, flew into orbit around Sea of Clouds and soon exploded! In that instant, the poor guy was a second sun in the sky, shining as bright as Sol and then in a flash he was gone. In an amusing tribute to the human race's fascination with celebrities, the Cloudotians named this dementia the *Hollywood syndrome*.

Quroak had heard of others lasting up to eight years in space but they had all been sheltered by comets or asteroids, which he didn't have handy right now. As he felt he had already set enough records for now, being the first to surf a black hole, being the first Cloudotian going beyond Jupiter (and much, much further), having discovered more new species than anyone else, the first to dive into an erupting ice volcano, Quroak didn't really feel like trying to break the record for being the longest in open space. He didn't want to finally make it home just to go supernova!

As he was about to leave the shelter of the rings, his memory was suddenly tickled by the sight of one of the shepherd moons a few kilometers ahead of him.

"Hey Xelrine, did you ever hear about the rumor of Neptune and Uranus being connected somehow?"

After a long pause, she replied slowly, "No, I don't think so. What do you mean *connected*?"

"I don't really know. I don't think anyone does but a few decades ago some planetary scientist posed a hypothesis. I really don't remember the details or what it was really about. But I think it had something to do with the rings around Uranus."

"Sorry, never heard about it."

"Hmmm, I'm going to check out that shepherd moon up ahead."

"What's a shepherd moon?" she asked, not really knowing much about astronomy.

"A shepherd moon is a moon that maintains a planetary ring's shape with the influence of its gravitational pull. All ring systems have them. In fact, have several of them"

"Oh, I get it. It's like one of those nature shows on Earth showing a shepherd dog keeping the herd of those white fluffy animals together, right?"

"Yes, the shepherd moon keeps the ring's formation intact."

As he flew towards the tiny moon, Galatea, Quroak's eyes were continuously drawn to the azure glow of Neptune. At home, he had always watched Neptune through a telescope his father had built for him, fascinated by the blue color of the planet with its reddish rings and the moon with the ice volcanoes. He had imagined wonderful creatures living in the clouds and the terrible windstorms said to tear around the giant globe. Now he felt cheated, having had his childhood fantasies shattered by the horrific vampires.

Vampires. ELEFANT. For some reason, thinking of the terrible creatures of Neptune made him think of the Venusian fanatical sect that is widely known for being vicious in its cruelty. His eyes turned back to the ice rings he was currently skating above.

Dragon-cats. Rings. Then he slowly recalled what had been speculated but never proven. Based on how quickly the dragon-cats had diminished the Jovian rings, everyone had wondered how the rings around Uranus could still possibly exist, since obviously the ring-grazing animals were voracious eaters.

"Hey Xelrine, I think I remember something here. Have you heard about the mystery of Uranus's rings?"

"Sorry, no. Really, Quroak, did you study astronomy or something? How do you know so much about this stuff?" she queried.

"Oh, I just do a lot of reading, that's all. But please tell me that you have heard about the Jupiter Massacre?"

"Massacre? At Jupiter? When?"

He couldn't believe it. He thought everyone knew about that.

"A while back, ELEFANT had lured the dragon-cats to the Jovian system where they happily grazed upon the rings crowning the king of planets. At that time, Jupiter's rings rivaled Saturn's rings in beauty and almost in size as well. Those rings were amazing! This was way before my time so I didn't see them personally, but I did see holographs of them. The Jovians had tinted the rings with intricate patterns of color that magically changed with each orbital dance of Io, Ganymede, and Europa. Out of rage of having their artwork destroyed, the Jovians decimated the dragon-cat population before realizing it was the cruel work of ELEFANT. The Jovians, feeling deep remorse, then led the remaining innocent dragon-cats back to their home around the green orb of Uranus. Only a few hundred of these magnificent creatures survived the Jovians' rage-induced massacre. The dragon-cats are a very sensitive species and half of the survivors died out of grief."

"How terrible!" thought-exclaimed Xelrine. "Did the Venusians get what was coming to them?" she asked angrily.

"No, not yet, anyway." He twisted his first, second and seventh arms in anguish. He always felt both grief and anger whenever thinking about this. He wanted to get past this.

"The point is, the dragon-cats proved they have a huge appetite by what they did to Jupiter's rings in so short a time. The mystery here is that the rings around Uranus still exist though they should have been finished off a long time ago by these creatures."

"Hmmm, I think I see what you mean," Xelrine replied thoughtfully. "Are there any theories?"

He untwisted his arms as he arrived at Galatea, where he floated above its dark gray surface. This tiny moon was irregularly shaped and was thought to have been created by coalescing rubble after the destruction of an earlier version of the moon when Neptune captured Triton as a satellite.

"Well," he said, "I know it sounds crazy, but there is a theory that says the Uranians had built a way to replenish the rings on a continuous basis to feed the grazing dragon-cats. The moon Ophelia, one of the shepherd moons around Uranus, seems to spew a disproportionate amount of material into the ring system than can be readily explained. As the theory goes, the tiny moon must be getting the ice, rock and dust it feeds the rings from some external source."

"And they think the Neptunian system is that source?" Xelrine asked excitedly.

"Yes. But remember, it's only a theory. There's no proof whatsoever," he cautioned.

"Yea, but you have to search for that connection if it exists."

"I will. But I need to rest first. I feel wiped out from what you told me. Three years, I just can't believe it." So with that, he floated down to Galatea's surface, found a small crevice into which he slipped into and immediately fell asleep.

After sleeping for about half a day, he awoke when the ground shook slightly from the impact of several iceballs slamming into the surface near his resting place. He felt well rested as he stretched his arms.

After saying hello to Xelrine, he started to explore the immense territory ruled by the blue giant. He always wondered what Xelrine was doing when not talking to him but he was afraid to ask too many questions. He just didn't want to hear an answer that proved, or even hinted, that she wasn't real but just a figment of his stressed out mind.

He eventually came upon the outermost moon orbiting at the extreme edge of Neptune's gravitational hold. He knew that no other civilization in the Solar community except the Cloudotians had yet discovered this moon, which the Cloudotians call *Asteroid-Catcher. Well, maybe the Quaoarians knew about this place*, he thought. Neptune is near the Kuiper Belt and this moon was known for being constantly bombarded by the meteoroids and asteroids of the Belt, hence the moon's name.

As he approached Asteroid-Catcher, Quroak saw six asteroids, each about a couple of kilometers in size, slam into the moon. But there was something odd about the collisions. Usually when a moon or planet is hit by a meteorite, rocks, dust and ice are ejected into space from the explosive impact of the collision. However, here there was no material erupted and that just didn't fit the laws of physics. His current angle of view did not allow him to see the actual impacted area.

When Quroak reached Asteroid-Catcher, he found no evidence of any recent impacts. There were plenty of craters but they were all pretty old, probably thousands of years old. Flying around the small moon he noticed a couple of peculiar things. First, moons this small were usually irregularly shaped, whereas this one was a perfect sphere, even with all the craters dimpling its surface. Secondly, the gravity well of the moon felt much deeper, much more intense than such a small object should create. The gravity pull was more like that of a small black hole than a moon.

Curious, Quroak flew to the surface to land. But there was nothing solid to land on! He kept going right through the moon! The boundary of where he was before and where he was now was extremely thin and he suddenly found himself floating above a gigantic hole in space!

"Xelrine," he thought-shouted, "you are not going to believe this!"

"What is it? Why are you so excited?"

"Asteroid-Catcher is not a real moon! It's a hologram! Highly sophisticated, too. It looks like a moon and it orbits Neptune like a moon but it's just a high-tech illusion."

"Now, who would do that?" she wondered.

"It must have been the Uranians," he answered as he gazed into the space hole.

"You know, I can't see the bottom. This must be a tunnel of some kind through the fabric of space itself," he said hopefully.

The opening of the tunnel was the width of the fake moon, about sixty kilometers. The tunnel's curved walls seemed to consist of nothing solid but were delineated by swirling, twisting lines of lights shining in purples and into the ultraviolet end of the spectrum.

Before he had a chance to explore further, he suddenly sensed a massive object approaching fast. So he quickly flashed to the nearest wall to get out of the way and just as he reached the curved wall, which he realized was pure energy making his flesh crawl, an asteroid about the size of a small island flew through the holographic moon and down into the tunnel.

Looking back, Quroak had no idea what made him do it, but on impulse he leaped onto the asteroid as it flashed past him on its way deeper into the tunnel of light. He hurriedly searched for and found a small crater on the backside of the dark asteroid to use as shelter.

Curling up into the smallest ball possible, he looked up out of the crater, watching the shades of purple and ultraviolet lights swirl and twist in crazy patterns along the circular walls of energy with the space within the tunnel almost purely back with just a hint of purple shading the ebony.

He didn't know how but the asteroid suddenly accelerated greatly until the swirling lights of the tunnel were too painful to watch and he had to close his eyes.

All of a sudden the asteroid lurched and he felt shockingly strong vibrations flow through the crater's walls. The asteroid shook so hard it felt like it was being torn asunder. He shot out of the crater. He turned towards the front and saw that the asteroid was being torn apart into pebble- and rock-sized chucks!

He couldn't see what was causing the destruction, whether machine or some fantastical monster but it was very eerie seeing the asteroid destroyed with no roaring sound accompanying the obliteration. It was utterly quiet, as it usually is in the darkness of space.

He quickly transferred most of his mass to another dimension and squeezed the rest of himself into the smallest mass possible so that he wouldn't become pebblized himself!

He barely accomplished this when he suddenly found himself ejected out of the light tunnel into space (thankfully still in one piece) along with the pulverized asteroid. As momentum carried him along with the stream of newly created pebbles and rocks, he looked ahead and saw that he was about to join a ring system.

Looking around, he turned the brightest purple splotched with dark ruby-emerald in unbelieving astonishment, for right before him, hanging in the darkness was a ringed, glowing, pale green giant of a planet knocked on its side: Uranus!

Apparently, Xelrine felt the shock of his mind for she asked, "Quroak, what is it? What happened?"

After a moment of numbing shock, he finally managed to thought-whisper, "You're not going to believe this."

After waiting a few moments for him to continue, she asked "Well?"

"Uh, I'm at Uranus."

If the sun had suddenly turned into a Venusian toadfly and melted away half of Mercury with its acidic, yet sweet tasting, saliva, Quroak could not have been more surprised than he was right now.

"Xelrine, I've just traveled over 1.7 billion kilometers in, what, a few minutes!" he said disbelievingly. "It should have taken *years* to reach Uranus from Neptune!"

Still stunned, he looked back at where he had just been shot out of the tunnel and saw Ophelia, a moon of Uranus. *Another holographic moon!*

"So, it is true," Xelrine exclaimed excitedly. "The Uranians had connected Neptune with Uranus. This tunnel is the connection!"

"Yes. The two planets are connected via this unbelievable tunnel that goes through, I don't know what to say. *Through* space? *Under* space? *Outside* of space? Anyway, it somehow eliminated the vast distance of *normal* space between the two planets."

He slowly stretched out his arms which had reflexively

curled up in his astonishment. "It is this physics- defying tunnel that continuously feeds the Uranian rings and thereby the dragon-cats."

"So," Xelrine said thoughtfully, "the Neptunian end attracts asteroids from the Kuiper Belt into the tunnel with its dense gravity well. So the asteroids actually *fall* into the tunnel, right?"

"Right," he answered, rather proud that she was grasping a better understanding of physics.

"Though I didn't see it, the Uranians had also created some kind of monster device at the Uranian end to chew up all matter coming through into the right size chunks so that the asteroids *add* to the rings instead of destroying them."

"Xelrine, think about this for a second. *How far advanced are the Uranians over us in physics and engineering to pull off something like this*? They actually created a tunnel outside of normal space, or underneath the space-time fabric of reality, as it were, between Asteroid-Catcher and Ophelia."

With this thought, they were both stunned into silence.

Chapter 20

While Quroak couldn't explain how it was possible, he was grateful for the quick trip to Uranus. Out of respect for both their amazing achievements and for the tragedy that had occurred here about three hundred years ago, he gazed at the green sphere in awed silence.

It was the Venusian ELEFANT sect that had knocked the giant planet onto its side. No one knows what the fanatic's intentions were, but it was widely believed to have been a cruel prank gone horribly wrong. The details of what happened are not known. In fact, no one even had a general idea of how this tragedy occurred. After all, how do you tip a planet over?

All anyone knows is that no Uranian has been heard of since, though it's widely believed that their civilization still thrives. The Uranians are the ultimate pacifists and so would never retaliate against the Losians. So it was a common understanding, though never proven, that the

Uranians were quietly living their lives, either shielding themselves from detection here in the Solar System, or around another star.

Not for the first time, Quroak marveled at how each planet was unique with its own characteristics. Before the whole micro-black-hole-explosion fiasco, he had only seen Sea of Clouds, Mars and Jupiter with his own eyes. He had seen the other planets via telescopes but it wasn't the same.

Since he had been flung to the far corners of the Solar System, he had seen Pluto, Neptune and now, Uranus up close, plus the planetoid Quaoar. Out of these, Neptune was by far the most dynamic and to him, the most beautiful with its breathtaking brilliant azure light, white and dark storms racing through the upper blue clouds streaked with white, all crowned by glistening ruddy ice rings and accompanied by the volcanic ice-erupting satellite, Triton.

And here was Uranus, also unique from the other three gas giants. Besides traveling with both its poles and rings traveling perpendicular to the plane of the Solar System, it was also different in its very blandness. It was pale green with very little differentiations in its cloud covered surface. No storms were visible at all. He wondered if this was the Uranians' doing. Anyone who can create a trans-spatial tunnel between Uranus and Neptune just to feed their ring system and thus the dragon-cats surely had the capability to transform their home planet anyway they wanted. At least, so he reasoned.

Though he wanted to explore the planet itself for clues into the mystery of the Uranians (not much was really known about them), he decided to check out the Uranian system first.

He had barely gotten started, having only briefly scanned four tiny moons, when he noticed a small herd of dragon-cats heading towards Oberon, the second largest moon around Uranus. He remembered it was a mystery as to why the creatures visited this seemingly unremarkable moon, so he decided to discreetly follow the group.

As soon as the herd arrived at the icy moon, they proceeded directly to a large mountain where halfway down the slope was a small opening into which the whole group disappeared.

He quickly trailed them into the cave to discover a smooth round tunnel leading sharply downward. The tunnel was completely dark except for traces of infrared left from the body heat of the dragon-cats as they passed. He trailed the tips of his arms along the walls and was surprised to find them almost perfectly smooth. *So this tunnel was not naturally made. The dragon-cats must have carved it out before with their acid.*

As he descended through the infrared tinged darkness, he realized the tunnel bored straight down past the moon's surface towards the center. The herd up ahead gave no sign that they knew they were being followed as they dropped downward in silence. After traveling what he guessed to be about 160 kilometers, Quroak abruptly entered a cold liquid. Tasting it, he realized it was water!

The water was very, very cold, absorbing so much of the dragon-cats' body heat, the infrared trail dissipated like mist falling on the sun so that the darkness was complete and seemed to press in around him like a living thing.

He was able to keep track of the dragon-cats by sound for it seemed that they were singing and their voices seemed to create beauty and joy; at least, that's what the soft gong-vibrating sound inspired in his heart.

Swimming through the stygian darkness, he now realized why dragon-cats had flippers; to swim in water. He had always wondered about those flippers since obviously they weren't all that useful in the emptiness of space. He also figured they must be using their whiskers that sense the electromagnetic spectrum to guide them to wherever they were heading.

After traveling at a steep angle downward for what he guessed was several kilometers, he realized that this was not just an underground pool of water but must really be an underground ocean encircling the core of the moon. *I'm certainly making a lot of discoveries from this disaster.*

As they continued downward, he was pleasantly surprised to find that the water temperature kept rising. In fact, the water was no longer icy cold now but only mildly cold. *Maybe the core is still volcanically active*, he wondered.

Though he had first passed it off to his imagination being over-stimulated by the extreme darkness, he realized it really was getting lighter and lighter and he was beginning to see shades of blue.

Also, he began to see flashes of light in all colors of the spectrum. Some would come and go in a blink; others pulsed like a pulsar while still others vibrated like a strummed guitar string. As he went deeper down he even saw greenish light that seemed to sweep through the dark sea like a lighthouse beam. He then saw the source of these strange yet beautiful lights; animals!

As life on his own ocean world, Sea of Clouds, never evolved bioluminescence, Quroak was mesmerized by the splendor swimming all around him.

Up till now, he had been alone in his thoughts, but now he wanted to share these wonders with Xelrine.

"Xelrine?"

After a long moment, "Yes, I'm here, Quroak. What's up?"

He paused, always a little stunned by how the caress of her thoughts in his mind made his body tingle all over and sent all of his heart's racing a little faster. No matter how often they shared thoughts, he was always somehow unprepared for how she made him feel.

Recovering, he said, "I wish you could see this. I'm in an underground ocean of Oberon and there are animals here that I can't really describe because it's dark and they only appear as flashes of light."

"Light? How is that possible? Oh wait, I think Earth has some strange undersea creatures that can make light," she replied.

"I don't remember that. Anyway, it really is beautiful."

"How did you find this ocean?" she asked.

"I followed a group of dragon-cats from space down to Oberon then through a tunnel to this ocean."

"Wow! You know, I'm sorry you are so far from home, but you are seeing a lot of things that no other Cloudotian has ever seen."

"Yea, I know. It is exciting but it's also pretty lonely." Then because he didn't want her feelings hurt, he quickly amended, "I mean, it's been great having you to talk to and you certainly helped me to survive those vampires, but it's not quite the same."

"I know. I really want you to get home so we can meet and be together. I feel so close to you. Much closer than I've been to anyone before."

Quroak stopped swimming in surprise with his flesh turning turquoise streaked with sea-green from affection and love pouring from his heart and happiness from hearing her say this. He suddenly felt giddy and wanted to laugh and sing but he was afraid she wouldn't understand, so he simply said, "I feel the same way and I can't wait to meet you!"

He was afraid to tell her that he loved her, for how can he love someone he had never met before? But he knew he did, he loved her deeply and with an intensity he felt must be hidden, at least for now, otherwise he might scare her away. *Oh great, now I'm worried about scaring away someone that will probably turn out to be my own imagination!*

But aloud in his mind where she could hear, he said, "I've never felt this close to anyone before and I feel like I could talk to you about anything."

"Me, too," she quietly whispered. "I also know that just as you say I helped you at Neptune, you will help me in the future."

"What?" he said somewhat bewildered. "How can you know this? Is there something wrong?" This was the second time she had hinted at this. The first was after he escaped Neptune and she had said she knew he would repay his debt to her.

"No, I'm okay. But I don't want to talk about it just now."

Confused, but happy about what she had said before and that she seemed to believe they will meet in the future, he changed the subject and tried to describe what he was seeing and experiencing as he continued diving deeper into the ocean where the dragon-cats were now far ahead of him.

After swimming a kilometer or so below the flashing animals, the water became quite tepid and he felt like he was in heaven as the warmth seeped into his cold muscles. He couldn't remember the last time he had been this warm but it was on his own world and that was years ago. *Oh Sunghost, it's been seven years!*

But before that thought turned into a heavy anchor pulling him down through the cold darkness of depression into the abysmal depths, he quickly concentrated on what Xelrine had said and lost himself in the warmth of the ocean that was permeating his body: *it felt so great.*

At this depth, the water was a light blue-green with a halo of oranges and reds shining from below. Down here there was much more animal life in all shapes and sizes.

There was also plenty of plant life where huge fields floated upside down with animals darting among the stalks and leaves. Big upside down forests decorated with flashes of exotic creatures drifted on the currents where the tree-like plants reached towards the bottom of the ocean, not upwards.

After a while, the ocean bottom came into sight. Here the water was very warm and it was as bright as a summer night on Sea of Clouds where both moons were full with the watchful bright gaze of the *Guiding Star*, Jupiter, shining.

There were many thermal vents along the ocean floor from which spewed out clouds of silt and steam in a fiery red halo that quickly dissipated into a blue glow, permeating upward a few kilometers to feed the upside down floating islands of plant life reaching down for the precious nourishment. The light and heat were coming from Oberon's core via the life-giving vents.

Upon reaching the silt-covered floor, the dragon-cats swam toward a large mountain looming in the distance.

As he followed them discreetly, Quroak continued to describe to Xelrine everything he saw, without much success he suspected. So he opened up that part of his mind allowing her to see through his eyes where upon she gasped with awe and joy at the beauty surrounding him.

When near the mountain, the herd suddenly disappeared in many miniature whirlpools of silt pulled from the floor by the creatures' abrupt increase in speed. Surprised, Quroak approached the mountain cautiously. He soon discovered that the mountain was really a honeycomb of small caves. It was into these chambers that the dragon-cats had vanished.

At the sight of the honeycombed mountain the dragon-cats had stopped singing and now they were very quiet, as if silently communing with this surreal place.

Not wanting to disturb the dragon-cats in the privacy of their caves, he waited patiently while scouting out the area and talking with Xelrine. He explored a floating island forest as it drifted by and was amazed at all the animal life living within.

According to Xelrine, a few days later (Quroak couldn't judge the passage of time since there was no day/night cycle within the moon's interior) some of the dragon-cats appeared from their small caves.

"I think I might as well show myself and see what happens," he told Xelrine.

"Be careful," she warned.

"They've never been known to be dangerous." He

hoped that was really true as he left a small drifting colony of tall plants and revealed himself to the dragon-cats.

He approached slowly to give them time to evaluate him. He felt they were very sensitive creatures and hoped they would sense that he was gentle and sensitive himself and know he would not harm them. He didn't know what they actually sensed in him but at least they didn't seem to be alarmed by his presence.

Reaching out with his mind, Quroak sensed they had intelligence on par with the Earth dolphins or dimenhoppers from his home planet. Drifting down to the honeycombed mountain, he approached to within three meters of a slightly smaller individual whom he sensed was a female.

Her whiskers were rigid though she seemed to be calm as she watched him approach. He had never been close enough to see individual characteristics before and as there was a male (he couldn't tell by the body but by the flavor of his mind) nearby, he could do some comparisons.

She was a little smaller with a shorter tail. In fact, now he noticed that the tail actually ended in three small prehensile appendages. Their eyes were big and round with vertical pupils, his were dark blue and hers a dark purple. Their hairless bodies were mostly black with white and ultraviolet stripes on their faces and flippers, though the patterns were different between his and hers. Their small snouts ended in mouths filled with rows of flat, pointless teeth. The male was missing all the teeth on the left side and his face was scarred, indicating something violent had happened in the past.

She made a kind of mewling sound which he could not understand so Quroak did his best to send warm thoughts of greetings to her.

"They don't seem nervous by my presence," he thought to Xelrine. "They seem calm and I think she's trying to communicate with me."

"Any idea what she's saying?"

"No, but I sense it's friendly. Maybe she's saying 'hello'. But there's something wrong here. I'm sensing an inner turmoil from them that I can't quite understand."

"What do you mean?" she asked.

"I'm not sure. It's hard to describe with words." So instead of trying to describe it, he sent her the feeling itself for her to experience.

(Note to reader: as best as I can describe it, it was a kind of deep sadness flavored with a quiet desperation that was blanketed with a forced calm, quietness and serenity as if trying to hide the desperate sadness. But underneath all of that, there was some other layer of emotion that was struggling to survive against the overwhelming sadness. It was this layer that Quroak couldn't quite define.)

"Oh *Guiding Star,* that's . . . that's really . . . wow, I don't know what to say. I feel bad for them," Xelrine murmured.

"Yea, me too," he agreed.

As he tried to understand what he felt from them, the

female looked him straight in the eye, waved her tail at him and then slowly backed into a cave.

"I'm not sure, but I think she just invited me into her cave," he told Xelrine.

"What are you going to do?"

"I'll accept, of course," as he swam slowly towards the cave.

To double check his interpretation of the female, Quroak looked over at the male dragon-cat to see if he was making any threatening moves but the male just glanced at the young Cloudotian then swam away towards some floating plants. So Quroak entered the honeycomb cell after the female.

The cell was roughly oval shaped with the length running about twelve meters from the entrance to the rear and the width being about eight meters with the ceiling only about four meters above the floor. All the surfaces were rough except for the left half of the floor which was oddly smooth and when he looked more closely, he noticed it wasn't exactly solid either but instead finely granular as if it was a big hole filled with sand.

The water was quite warm and had a reddish glow from the tiny thermal vent at the very rear of the cave from which hot billows of cloudy water spewed. *That explains the floor; it's covered with silt*, he realized.

The dragon-cat drifted to the back of the cave which held the only real object in the chamber: an orange silky web strung from the ceiling above the thermal vent.

Cradled within the web were dozens of small orange-speckled green eggs.

Quite a few eggs were cracked open and within each he could see tiny dragon-cats that hadn't survived. The female slowly removed a broken egg from the web with her prehensile tail, held it over the spewing vent for a moment with her eyes closed while touching the tiny baby's chest and then tenderly buried it in the silt-covered area of the floor.

Throughout, he sensed a great sadness within her, but it was buried deep as if she didn't want the gloom darkening her heart to radiate outward to poison the chamber's atmosphere somehow. No, outward she projected calm and peace.

He sensed that there were hundreds of hatchlings that hadn't survived buried in that small graveyard.

Watching the female to make sure he wouldn't cause offense, Quroak slowly and solemnly approached the web, picked up a ruined egg and mimicked her actions. He also made sure to mentally send waves of peaceful energy towards the undamaged eggs while burying his own less than happy feelings deep within.

Seeing that she accepted his help, he continued to help her lay these unfulfilled souls to rest. Each egg he picked up made his heart heavier, his puckers close tighter and his skin blush an Earth summer-sky blue freckled with yellow as realization sank in.

After the last was buried, he sent her warm thoughts

and quietly left the chamber that was both a nursery and a graveyard.

After relating what had occurred to Xelrine, he thought-whispered softly, "Now it all makes sense."

"What does?"

"Well, now we know why the dragon-cats visit Oberon. That honeycombed mountain is their nursery. There are only a few hundred of them left and they are desperately trying to bring their species back from the brink of extinction."

"Yes, that seems obvious, but I have the feeling that you meant something else," she perceptively encouraged.

"My sense is that the dragon-cats are very sensitive creatures, even before they hatch. I can feel the intense sadness and desperation within the adults. It's like boiling magna deep inside a restless volcano ready to erupt. Yet they still force an emotional air of tranquility when around the eggs to mask the underlying despair."

"So you think they are trying to protect the unhatched babies from the negative emotions which may cause them harm?" she asked thoughtfully.

"Yes. Even when a large number of eggs produce dead babies, the adults still force that external calmness while caring for the surviving eggs, though they are hurting inside. And now I know what the underlying emotion is: hope."

"Yes, I see that now," agreed Xelrine. "Despite the conditions, setbacks and heartaches, the dragon-cats are driven by intense hope that they can create a thriving population again to have a safe and free tomorrow."

"I could not have said it any better." Quroak was deeply touched by their situation, by their hope that was like a living creature with its own needs and dreams. He was especially honored that they had shared the very core of their survival as a species with him.

Quroak sent the dragon-cats waves of life-force energy consisting of warmth, affection and good wishes, then left the honeycombed mountain, the underground ocean, and then finally Oberon to leave them in peace.

CHAPTER 21

Quroak spent the next couple of weeks exploring Uranus and its moons. He and Xelrine spent a lot of time discussing both the *Guardians of One* and the dragon-cats. They both avoided discussing or even bringing up even indirectly anything about the Neptunian vampires as that was still a very painful subject for him.

Uranus turned out to be a very beautiful planet where the pale green cloud surface hid a world of intricate wind patterns that swirled with colors in every shade of green and blue where Pluto-sized pockets of atmosphere was totally devoid of clouds and the skies were a translucent, shimmering emerald-green. The blue-green ocean was warm at the poles but was covered with ice hidden under a heavy green mist at the equator.

However, the planet was a disappointment in that there was no evidence that any civilization had ever existed there. There was plenty of life in the ocean but no signs of sentient intelligence.

As Quroak left the planet, Xelrine asked him, "So what did you find?"

"What do you mean?" he wondered.

"Ever since you reached Pluto, you've been telling me everything. Describing everything you see and feel. But on Uranus, you haven't said anything at all," she answered. "So what did you find?"

So he told her about the clouds, the ocean and the huge pockets of cloudless areas.

"That's it?" she asked. "Then why were you there so long?"

"Huh? It was only a few hours"

"*A few hours?* You were there for almost two weeks!" Xelrine exclaimed.

"No, that can't be. It was only a few hours," he insisted, though somewhat distractedly.

"I'm telling you, Quroak, you haven't spoken to me in two weeks, ever since you entered Uranus' atmosphere. I was starting to get worried because I couldn't reach you for some reason."

"Hmm, that's odd," he said, with no interest at all.

"Quroak, what's going on?"

"Nothing."

"You disappear for two weeks then return with no explanation! There's something wrong here." Xelrine thoughts were colored with anxiety.

"Nothing happened. I went down, explored the planet, there was nothing to see and so I left. I don't know why you're getting so excited," he said. "I'm going to explore the moons again in case I missed something."

Xelrine tried to continue the conversation but he held so little interest in the mystery of the missing time that she gave up.

"Me," I said firmly.

After living through this particular event, I decided to dig deeper into this mystery. Since Xelrine insisted that two weeks had passed while Quroak only remembered a passage of a few hours, I was sure something was wrong. Obviously, I knew Quroak was telling the truth, at least as he knew it. And I had no reason to believe that Xelrine was lying. So I studied Quroak's brain waves during this time period.

By the very nature of the process, when memories are downloaded into the library, the brain activity is captured as well. By studying the differences in his brain waves before he dove into Uranus' atmosphere and during his time there, I realized that his memories had been tampered with. The whole two week period he was on Uranus was wiped out in his mind and replaced with benign memories of the planet's atmospheric and oceanic geography that reflected a passage of only a few hours.

Since it is not likely that this was caused by a natural phenomenon but artificially induced, I sent a team to Uranus to investigate. However, everyone in the team experienced the same missing time (though they didn't know there was a time gap) and shared the same general memories of the planet's topography.

Interestingly enough, they also all had attitudes of disinterest when made aware of the time difference between what they remembered and reality. They simply shrugged it off and had no desire whatsoever to even discuss it, much less think about it. Just like Quroak.

The only theory that makes sense to me is that the Uranians are doing this to protect themselves. I don't know if this means they are still on their homeworld or they don't want anyone to recognize clues to their current whereabouts or technology. However, it is obvious that they rewire the visitor's brain to not only create specific benign memories that mean nothing, but also to stay away from the subject of any time discrepancies noted by others.

In truth, I have not delved into this too deeply, wishing to honor the Uranian's desire for privacy. Nor have I discussed this with Quroak.

Now let's slip back into Quroak's shoes, so to speak, though since Cloudotians don't wear shoes, that's a pretty bad analogy.

As he approached the wispy rings around the jade planet, he reflected on his next step. He was pretty sure the next planet sunward, Saturn, was currently on the other side of the sun. This meant that the next planetary system he would have to reach on his way home was

Jupiter. But *Guiding Star* was over two billion kilometers away and would take more than eleven years to traverse without assistance.

Since he had no desire to momentarily light up the Solar System with his luminous self in a blaze of *Hollywood syndrome* glory, he needed to find a way to reach Jupiter safely. So he decided to stay with his original plan of re-exploring the moons.

It was while approaching Umbriel, the third largest satellite around Uranus that he found a small spacecraft orbiting the moon. The ship was triangular with two smaller trapezoids on either side of the main body like unfolded wings of a bird in flight. The whole ship was artistically rendered in burnt orange, pale reds and bronzes. That and the avian-shaped design immediately identified the ship as Jovian.

"Xelrine, a ship! And they're Jovian," he thought-shouted excitedly.

"Great, maybe you can hitch a ride."

With a surge of hope, he rushed to Umbriel. When he reached the spaceship he noticed some dim lights on the moon's surface near its equator so he headed down. At Wunda, a large crater ringed with bright methane ice that was created when Uranus was tipped over by ELEFANT, Quroak found a couple of Jovians in their brightly colored spacesuits digging in the regolith. They seemed to be collecting methane ice, dust and crushed rocks.

He once again marveled at the diversity of life. He

would have thought that similar conditions would create similar biological designs. But that wasn't the case for the gas planets in the Solar System where the environmental conditions, while not identical, were similar.

The Jovian's spacesuits, being just energy fields holding back the harsh conditions of space, didn't hide their avian nature with their thin cylindrical bodies sporting two pairs of wings, one pair small with the other pair much larger, which he knew changed colors instinctively to blend in with the environment. Right now their wings were dark gray, matching the moon's somber color. However, unlike birds on Earth, Jovians had nebulous bodies that seemed more gelatinous than solid.

Quroak didn't know how the Jovians were able to move about on the moon's surface since there was no atmosphere to 'push' their wings against and their two thin, meter long tentacles which ended in spade-shaped pads weren't built for walking.

One Jovian was using a couple of small shovels to scoop up the regolith into spherical containers while the other was using some kind of scanning device, picking out the areas for the other to dig.

Some instinct made them look up as Quroak approached from above, revealing their snouted faces covered with fine bronzed fur with their intelligent golden eyes reflecting curiosity but no alarm as he landed near them.

Since Umbriel had no atmosphere and sound doesn't travel in the vacuum of space, he couldn't talk to the

Jovians. And he knew that Jovians were offended if Cloudotians used telepathy to read their minds during communication.

However, he knew their written language, which oddly enough was different from their spoken tongue, so he started to write in the regolith using a sharp edged rock he found nearby to communicate with them. Slowly, using as much brevity as possible, they swapped stories.

The Jovians conveyed that the external sensors on their ship malfunctioned and as a result their ship collided with a small asteroid, damaging a number of systems, including communications and navigation. Without communications to call for help, navigation to steer them safely home and sensors to avoid objects, they were stranded here unless they could do repairs. So they were here on Umbriel collecting raw material to be refined on their ship in an attempt to make reparations.

I can get you home, Quroak wrote. *With my Cloudotian ability to sense gravity wells, I will be your navigator plus your sensors to warn of any dangerous objects.*

One of the Jovians excitedly scribbled *soft winds*, meaning 'wonderful'.

So Quroak joined them as the Jovians climbed into the small egg-shaped vehicle that he hadn't noticed before a few meters away and they flew up to the ship in orbit.

CHAPTER 22

As they approached the ship, Quroak was reminded of a story his father had once told his younger brother. The family was sharing the evening meal watching the sunset from the top of the highest clouds. His brother was only a couple of years old and had just started to really learn about the dynamics of controlled flight. While moving about came instinctively to his people when first hatched, the dynamics had to be taught in order to be applied to meet situations that came up in today's world.

The story was actually similar to the current situation, which is why he thought of it, where a Jovian ship was stranded on Earth's moon. It was during the early period of spaceflight for the Jovians and their ships weren't adequately shielded and this one was caught out in the open during a cycle of intense sunspot activity and their ship's electronics were fried, leaving them without navigation, communications, sensors, et cetera. In fact the only thing that functioned was the engine.

After a week of frustrated repair work that failed, the Jovians started to really worry about their chances of getting home. But then a wandering Cloudotian who had been exploring Earth's oceans found them and offered to guide them home.

At this point, Quroak's brother, Kosod, had naively blurted out, "But Dad, why didn't they just look out the windows to find Jupiter and to miss asteroids?"

"Well, my little ball of arms," his father said affectionately, "that does seem like the obvious solution, doesn't it?" His father always had the patience of *Guiding Star* and looked for any situation in which to teach and to make his children think. "But I think if we flew out of the clouds a little, the light may reveal a more complicated reality than anticipated."

Then he asked, "First, how big is space?"

"Huge!" Kosod excitedly thought-shouted, waving his arms all about. Of course, he had never been outside of Cloud of Sea's atmosphere before, just repeating what everyone told him.

"It's much bigger than that," his father laughed, "which you will find out when I take you to *Guiding Star* in a couple of years. However, since Jupiter is big, the biggest planet around Sol, and shines very bright, I will grant you that it is easily seen from Earth and so the Jovians could find their way home. However, at that distance, Jupiter is barely more than a pinprick of light and it would be very hard to keep that pinprick centered in your window without controls keeping you in a straight line. But, let's accept that it is possible, okay?"

"Okay," Kosod answered, confused as to where this was going.

"Now, how about avoiding objects like moons and asteroids? You think just looking out the window will solve that?"

"Yea, sure. If you see something ahead, turn the ship and miss it," Kosod said simply.

"Let me ask you this, then. Are most things in space stationary?"

"What is 'stay in airy'?"

"*Stationary* means not moving," Quroak had piped in.

"I guess so," Kosod said hesitantly.

So his father proceeded to tell his brother that nothing in space is stationary but is usually traveling anywhere from thousands to millions of kilometers per hour. Using pieces of their dinner for illustration purposes, he showed Kosod how a comet or its debris traveling at 20,000 kph could 'appear' out of nowhere and be on a collision course even when the object is not in front of the ship and thus why sensors are critical for a safe journey. That a ship needs enough advance warning to change its trajectory in time.

Quroak wasn't sure how much Kosod understood, for his father had been using desert for his illustration and his brother just seemed to follow the food with a hungry look.

However, Kosod did say, "Okay, I see. It would be really dangerous."

"But let's just say that the whole ship was one big window so the Jovians could see everywhere at once. Also, that their eyesight allows them to see far, far away into the night so they could see danger in time to avoid it. Or that they have our ability to sense gravity wells and so again, avoid oncoming objects." His father paused then said, "Now, do you think they could get home just by looking out the window without navigation or sensors?"

As the purple rays of the sun slowly slid below the horizon leaving radiant rays of dark greenish violet blazing across the encroaching dome of night, Kosod pondered for a moment, scrunching his face in exaggerated thought.

Kosod apparently felt a trap had been set for him but he saw no way out for he said, "I don't see why not."

Quroak remembered his father turned to him and asked, "Quroak?"

He playfully swatted his brother behind the head as he replied, "Jovian ships don't *have* windows, squirt!"

"Oh. Who ever heard of a ship without windows? That's crazy!" Kosod complained, "How would I know that?"

"You don't have any experience with aliens so you wouldn't know." As Quroak started to give a smug look, his father continued, "However, you did make assumptions. You assumed that the Jovian ships had windows just because our ships have them. You need to try to not assume anything. It will get you in trouble one day."

With a dejected look, Kosod replied, "Okay, I'll try." But then with the emotional elasticity that only the extreme young or the emotionally unstable seem to have, he perked right up and asked excitedly, "But why *don't* they have windows on their ships?"

"Well son, the Jovians don't have windows on their ships because they abolished windows a very, very long time ago. You won't find a single window on Jupiter or in anything the Jovians created."

"No windows? Why?"

"Because Jovians are terrified of windows!" father said giving his thoughts a feeling of creepiness. Quroak remembered their father had timed this story perfectly for the sun had disappeared, neither moon had appeared yet and the family had sunk lower allowing a bank of clouds to blanket out the stars so that it was very dark with just wisps of light green floating by like wandering ghosts.

"Who could be scared of a window?" Kosod scoffed.

"Things aren't always as they seem, Kosod. When a Jovian looks through a window, he doesn't just see what's on the other side but also sees the horrible monsters that are trapped within *all* windows that no one else can see."

"Monsters?" his brother whispered with eyes wide open, curling his small arms into a ball.

"According to the Jovian legends, each window is a gateway to another dimension that is inhabited by unspeakably hideous creatures that are completely savage with no morals at all who do nothing but fight insanely and devour each other. The Jovians believe that if you look too long into a window, one of the creatures will notice you and pull you into their frightening dimension."

His father had kept the creepiness factor in his thought patterns throughout so that Quroak thought Kosod's eyes were going to explode, becoming so wide as he subconsciously searched the darkness for any wandering, lost window.

"So that is why you will not find a single window on any Jovian spacecraft, home or anything that they construct," his father concluded.

The docking of the small vehicle to its mother ship brought Quroak back to the present. The ship was bigger on the inside than he thought possible based on the exterior. However, upon reflection it made sense once he saw the layout which was designed so that the Jovians would have room to spread their wings.

There were no true corridors but just big open rooms joined together in a line creating an arrow-straight flightway, so to speak. Likewise, in the main body of the ship, there weren't multiple decks, but just one open height with computer consoles lining the walls from top to bottom since the Jovians found it easy to hover in place.

The Jovians quickly led him to the front of the ship where the circular command center was located. He was surprised to find that the Jovians had already set up a computer console for him where he could enter information quickly into the system which would be shared by everyone else on the ship immediately. With his role as the navigator and warning system, he needed to be able to disseminate information quickly for it to be reacted upon in a timely fashion by the ship's crew.

CHAPTER 23

The next four months were a blur to Quroak as the strain of constantly looking out for asteroids, comet debris and other hazards, all of which have insignificantly small gravity wells that taxed his ability to sense them, exhausted him, draining his energy and dulling his senses, which made him concentrate all the harder. Plus keeping the ship, the *Red Winds,* pointing at Jupiter was not as easy as he had originally thought it would be as the spacecraft kept drifting off course. He had no downtime to relax and reenergize or to socialize with most of the Jovians.

The boredom was overwhelming. By the time the third month inched by, he was longing for a Monopoly game with the Quaoarians.

The constant strain of vigilance was wearing him done, including his defenses and depression started to seep in through the cracks as it usually did when he was pushed to his limits. Since arriving at Uranus, he had been pretty good at keeping depression at bay by distracting himself and talking with Xelrine. But now that exhaustion was a dark cloud upon his soul, depression was pouring rain into his heart and the monotony and stress of his tasks had melted away whatever umbrella he had created for protection. He felt the all too familiar iciness take hold as his defenses and shields melted away.

He communicated with Xelrine as much as possible; however, he really wished he was with her. So as a consequence, even on a ship filled with about a dozen Jovians, he was feeling pretty lonely.

The only thing that kept him going was the thought of getting home to Sea of Clouds so he could track down Xelrine. He wanted to see her so much that it hurt. His heart was aching to see her smiling eyes and his body ached to hold her tight and never let go.

After the first month, the youngest Jovian on the ship, Roton, seemed to have taken pity on Quroak because she started conversations with him and began to spend most of her free time with him to keep him company. Roton was a medical doctor and had joined the trip to study the psychological affect on Jovians of being cooped up in a confined space for a long period of time. They had been traveling in this ship for about two years now and Jovians were much more comfortable in wide open spaces.

Most of what he and Roton discussed never really sank into his tired brain. He mostly remembered Roton doing most of the talking, mostly about problems in her life he vaguely recalled, with him doing the 'good listener' routine. Beyond that, he couldn't really remember anything about their conversations. However, her company did make it slightly easier for him to endure the monotonous trip.

During the fourth month, Xelrine called out to him weakly, "*Guiding Star.*"

"Xelrine?" he tiredly answered. His mind was so foggy and slow from exhaustion that he wasn't sure he had heard her correctly. In fact, he wasn't even sure his mind wasn't playing tricks on him.

"Please help me. *Guiding Star.*"

The phrase 'help me' penetrated his mind like lightning through clouds, awakening him from his stress-induced stupor. All of his senses jumped to an alertness he hadn't felt in months.

"Xelrine, what is it? Are you alright?" he frantically called out.

"*Guiding Star.* I need you. Quroak, help me," he heard faintly.

"Xelrine! What's wrong?" But there was no answer. "Xelrine, talk to me. Where are you? What's happened?"

His anxiety melted away his exhaustion as if it had never existed as worry flooded his body with adrenaline. With his hearts racing, he kept reaching out to her with his mind but to no avail.

He still felt her warm presence via the heartlink so he knew she was still alive. He had finally decided that she must be real and not a figment of his imagination. He had come to that conclusion by the simple reasoning that if she was not real, was not waiting for him after his seven plus years of black-hole-induced exile, was not there to comfort him after everything he had endured, especially the three years of torture with the life-force sucking vampires, then the overwhelming disappointment would kill him.

To find out she wasn't real would create a wave of despair rolling through his being. To find she was an imagined dream would energize the quiet wave of darkness into an ever growing wave of destruction moving faster and faster. To find she was just a hoped-for-love would transform that tidal wave into an unstoppable tsunami against the shores of his heart which would be utterly destroyed under the wave's onslaught and he would drown in the darkness.

So, she simply had to be real. And since the heartlink was strong, in fact, it had been growing stronger the closer he approached Jupiter, he knew she was alive. Now, he prayed she was also unharmed.

He urged the Jovians to increase the ship's speed to its maximum. However, the damaged ship was already moving as fast as possible.

An agonizing week later, it actually felt like a year in his worried state, he guided the ship to the Jovian spaceport located on Ganymede, Jupiter's largest moon. All week long he had tried to communicate with Xelrine but with no luck. He kept replaying her last words in his mind trying to understand what happened. She needed help, that much was obvious. And she had said *Guiding Star* several times. At first, he had thought she was simply beseeching *Guiding Star* for help, which all Cloudotians did subconsciously when in trouble or in need of guidance. However, he now believed she was telling him that she was at *Guiding Star,* at Jupiter when trouble befell her.

After landing, he quickly departed the ship among a flurry of 'thank yous' which consisted of the Jovians flapping their smaller wings. But once he was in the spaceport he realized he didn't really know where to begin searching. He wished the heartlink could be used for triangulation to guide him but it didn't work that way. All he could tell by the strength of what he felt via the heartlink was that she was probably within the Jovian system. While that narrowed it down to this corner of the Solar System, it consisted of a gas giant big enough to swallow around 1,300 Earths. It also constituted the more than sixty moons, two of which were the same size or bigger than the planet Mercury. That was a pretty big corner to search he thought wearily.

As he was trying to decide what to do, Roton suddenly flew up to him with another Jovian close in her wake.

"Quroak, something terrible has happened!" she said urgently. "You said your friend's name is Xelrine, right?"

"What? Yes, Xelrine. What about her?" He didn't remember mentioning her, but since she had been the uppermost thing in his mind most of the trip, he supposed he shouldn't be surprised he spoke about her.

"Quroak, this is my cousin, Zwane. His lifemate is friends with Xelrine. But they're gone! They are both gone!" she screeched frantically.

Quroak looked over at the young male Jovian who seemed filled with anxiety as he didn't seem able to float in one place, flittering about their small group nervously.

Zwane dramatically announced, "They've been kidnapped! About two weeks ago!"

That's when Xelrine called out to me! Quroak blushed a dark turquoise with excitement, hoping Zwane could give him a lead into finding her.

"Can we go somewhere and talk in private?" Zwane asked quickly.

Feeling the icy tendrils of fear grip his heart, Quroak followed Zwane and Roton to a nearby outdoor eatery that was nearly empty of customers where they picked a secluded booth.

His surroundings barely registered on his consciousness as his entire being was laser-focused on Zwane. "What happened?" he demanded.

"About a month ago, Zola, my lifemate, attended a medical cultural exchange conference held here on Ganymede. That's when she met Xelrine and they immediately took a liking to each other. They spent the next two weeks with Zola showing the sights on our homeworld to Xelrine. I met her a few times and she's really great. She talked about you and was excited that you would arrive soon on the *Red Winds*."

"Wait, what, Xelrine was here? She didn't tell me that." Quroak exclaimed.

"She wanted to surprise you," Zwane said.

Wow! His heart swelled with emotion, really touched that she had come all this way to do that. He knew she had never left Sea of Clouds before due to her fears so for her to come way out to Jupiter for him really meant a lot. But looked what happened on her first journey offworld. His skin flushed a dark blue with light orange stripes showing the sudden guilt crashing through him. *Sunghosts! This is my fault. She would not have been out here if weren't for me.*

"Then two weeks ago, when they were on a guided tour of the Orange Wonder, they vanished! No one else on the tour saw what happened. Zola and Xelrine had drifted behind to admire the eye while the rest of the group went ahead and they were not seen again." Zwane flapped his smaller wings with anxiety.

As Quroak let this sink in, the image of Orange Wonder floated through his mind. It was a centuries old storm that was unique in that it was about ninety kilometers below Jupiter's cloudtops and thus was not visible from space like every other of Jupiter's big storms. *So they must have been taken while in the eye of the storm.*

"What has been done about it?" he asked Zwane.

"I got the local authorities involved but they didn't find any clues or witnesses and have pretty much given up saying they have nothing to go on. I did some investigating myself and found that about twenty other people have disappeared over the last four weeks. "

"Twenty people! And the authorities are doing nothing about it? I don't get it."

Zwane sighed heavily, which for Jovians comes out as a low whistle. "I think politics is in involved here where they are more interested in keeping things quiet so as to not scare away visitors than they are in trying to stop the abductions."

Great, just great. Since Cloudotians had no sense of greed in terms of possessions, power or fame, there weren't really politics on his homeworld. But he did understand the concept from studying both Earth's and Jovian history.

He was wondering what Zwane was going to do next, hoping he wasn't ready to give up yet when Zwane's next statement made Quroak think he was going to be on his own searching for Xelrine.

"I'm dying."

CHAPTER 24

"You're dying?" gasped Quroak, giving his new Jovian acquaintance a horrified look while his skin turned a greenish purple, reflecting his inner turmoil.

"Yes, I will soon dissolve into nothingness," replied the Jovian in his whispery voice that was characteristic of all Jovians. Jovians always speak softly but have the amazing ability to pitch their tone such that they can be heard at any distance they wish, even through the constant sizzling of lightning and roaring thunder reverberating throughout Jupiter's clouds.

Jovians did not like the imagined intrusion into their thoughts, so while they tolerated Cloudotians sending thoughts to their minds, especially since Cloudotians could not speak audibly, Jovians always replied out loud and expected Cloudotians to listen to their words and not read their thoughts.

Quroak respected the Jovian's desires and never looked

into their minds, even though he could easily have focused his attention to what they wanted him to 'see' and nothing else, but he didn't think they could be convinced of that. However, it was frustrating having to use spoken language because it was a very slow way of passing information. This whole conversation would have taken only a few seconds if it were held strictly via telepathy.

"What do you mean: *nothingness*?" he inquired.

Zwane answered quite simply, "When my life is over, I will dissolve into the clouds. My essence will be reabsorbed into the world from which I was created and will be recycled into the essence of someone waiting to exist."

Quroak studied the nebulous body of the Jovian that seemed more gelatinous than solid and guessed he understood why Zwane's body would dissolve. After digesting the Jovian's words, he asked, "But *why* are you dying?"

The Jovian hesitated, glanced at his cousin Roton, and then slowly said, "We don't usually like to talk about this with offworlders. However, I'm hoping you will be able to assist me so I will tell you. But I would like you to give me your oath that you will not repeat this to anyone."

Quroak said earnestly, "If I can help you in any way, count on me. And I will not repeat anything you say."

Zwane waved his tentacles in thanks. "We Jovians have a unique physiological makeup. When we are late adolescents, we are compelled to find a lifemate by our intense emotions which are partially driven by biological processes we don't fully understand. Once we find our lifemate, we bond and become physiologically bound to each other. Our body chemistries adjust to each other. If you have ever noticed, Jovians are very affectionate towards each other, always touching and caressing. We don't just do this out of what humans call *love*. We also do it because we literally can't survive without our lifemate's touch."

Zwane paused for a moment, as if to collect his thoughts before continuing. "The loving caress from a lifemate gives us healing energy for our body, sending soothing vibrations for our heart and soul. If we don't feel the caress of our *lover*, as the humans would say, a chemical imbalance occurs and slowly destroys our body from the inside out. And our intense sense of love, of intimacy, ensures that we do touch and caress each other frequently as if it were a need, which indeed it is, both emotionally and physiologically."

(Note to reader: Quroak did not know how to hide this memory so it was downloaded along with the rest. So in keeping with the spirit of his promise to Zwane to not reveal this matter that is intensely private to the Jovians, I have put a hypnotic suggestion in the above text to make you forget all about it in the very near future. And don't think that just by *knowing* about the hypnotic suggestion you will be able to nullify it. You won't, you'll forget.)

Quroak just stared quietly at Zwane and Roton as a few people entered the outside café.

The spaceport was located in a shallow, ancient, dark crater with the rough walls reaching up to the dark sky which was tinted with the merest hint of blue from its thin oxygen atmosphere scattering the faint sunlight.

Jupiter majestically dominated the sky with a small arc of its rings visible and he could see several white cyclones whip across *Guiding Star's* banded surface. He also saw fiery Io float above Jupiter and because of the planet's bands, seemed to be floating in a brown and white ocean. Under any other conditions it would have been breathtaking, but their current conversation made it all feel surreal.

Then he inquired "But what happens when one of you dies?"

The Jovian answered quietly while making sure no other customers were near them, "If the lifemate dies while touching the other, then the survivor has about a year to find another lifemate before succumbing to the *softra*, the chemistry imbalance. This is only possible because in the last breath of life, a part of a person's essence is passed to the survivor. If one can't hold the dying lifemate, then one will be destroyed by the *softra* in about one month. The same is true if both are alive yet separated."

The Cloudotian dreaded asking the next question, but he forced it out: "Since Zola was kidnapped two weeks ago, you only have half a month to live?"

Zwane's sea green eyes clouded over like a dark pink cloud obscuring a perfect sunrise over the sands of Mars. "Yes." Then with the most profound sadness drowning his voice, "The same is true for Zola."

"My Seas!" declared Quroak. "But who and why would anyone do this?"

"I don't know *why*, but I think I do know *who*. I have reason to believe it is the Losian sect, ELEFANT that is behind all of this," Zwane said angrily.

"ELEFANT?" asked Quroak. Then he quickly said, "Sunghost, this does sound like something they would do!"

"Yes," chimed in Roton, who had been quietly listening to the conversation, "remember they lured those Uranian dragon-cats over to devastate the glorious rings that crowned our planet! Since then, ELEFANT has tried all sorts of ways to hurt us."

Quroak brought his gaze back to Zwane's eyes as he thought-asked, "Besides this fitting their style, do you have any other reason for suspecting ELEFANT?" He heartedly hoped there was no other reason because he really didn't want to contemplate what they were doing to Xelrine.

Zwane folded his tentacles atop each other that represented a Jovian shrug, "One of their ships was seen in the area about three weeks ago. It has to be them."

Quroak was inclined to agree. It was always bad news when one of their ships was spotted. *Sunghost!* The thought of Xelrine in their claws made his blood boil and he blushed a bright sapphire blue with dark green rings, indicating his deep anger.

The Jovians looked at him, puzzled, since they had never seen these colors displayed by any Cloudotian before, having the reputation of not angering easily.

"This *softra*, how are you feeling now? What are you going to do?"

Jovians are acknowledged as possessing the most expressive eyes of any species in the Solar System and Zwane's eyes right now showed a depth of love and determination that could never be expressed adequately with words. The energy of his emotions was like the physical force of a typhoon blowing across the seas of Sea of Clouds, and Quroak actually backed away a little from Zwane by the sheer intensity.

Zwane's voice swam in emotion as he said, "My heart is drowning. The memory of Zola's touch is haunting me and if I close my eyes I can feel her sweet caress and I can feel her softness under my tender touch. My body screams for her and aches as if being crushed by the weight of Ganymede. Yet my body also feels like it will explode like the volcanoes on Io from the pressure of controlling my emotions that are completely out of control. My eyes long to drink in the light of her smile and my ears yearn to hear the lovely melody of her voice. My mind is a whirlwind of incoherent thoughts that are drowned out by the agonized howling of my love. I need to love Zola like the sun needs to shine or a fish needs to swim."

The passionate Jovian paused to calm down, and then continued more slowly, "I need to find her. Not just for my life, for I'm nothing without Zola and can't imagine life without her. But I need to find her to save her from the *softra*, even if it means to die in her arms to give her that year to survive so she can find another lifemate so that she can live out her life to the fullest."

Quroak was so emotionally moved my Zwane's passion and love plus feeling pretty anxious himself to be actively searching for Xelrine that all he could say was, "Where do we start?"

Zwane glanced at Roton for a moment then gazed intently at Quroak as a Jovian ship lifted off with barely a whisper half a kilometer away from them. The other customers left the eatery, apparently to find a better viewpoint to watch the spacecraft as it left Ganymede, leaving the three of them alone again.

"I believe Zola is being held in the center of the Little Red Storm."

"The Little Red Storm? But isn't that just another one of your planet-sized artworks?" Quroak asked.

Again Zwane glanced at Roton who quietly said, "Yes, we did create it, just like the artstorm the humans call the Great Red Spot. However, something went wrong. The Planetary Art Institute keeps this under wraps from the general population to avoid embarrassment and public outcry, but the artstorm is out of control."

"What? You mean you actually control the Great Red Spot?" The thought amazed Quroak.

"Well, no, not really. When we create the seed for an artstorm, it is done with care and such precision that we know how big it will grow into and the velocity of its winds and how fast it will travel around the planet's surface. And we have a fairly good idea how long the artwork will last. But once it is formed, no, we can't control it per se, though over time we can make it slowly dissipate."

"So what happened with the Little Red Storm?"

Waving her smaller wings in agitation, Roton explained, "The Institute wanted to create a smaller version of the Great Red Spot as a contrast to the larger artstorm. I don't know what that means exactly, but that was the idea. So they created the seed for the storm and let it go. At first, everything went as planned. The new artwork was smaller with slower winds and traveled the planet at a leisurely pace. But then about two months ago, it suddenly changed dramatically."

"In what way?" he asked when she paused.

"The new storm is still much smaller than its brother, though it has grown by absorbing several white cyclones. It was designed with wind speeds of about 300 kph. But it quickly surpassed the Great Red Spot which spins around at 400 kph and is now whipping up to 620 kph and is still increasing! And nobody knows why. Possible sabotage has been mentioned but not seriously investigated since no one can imagine how that is even possible. It's completely out of control."

After pondering this for a few moments while the two Jovians looked at him expectantly, Quroak finally asked, "And you think Xelrine, Zola and the others are being held in the center of this out of control storm. Why?"

Zwane gazed at him with such intense anger in his

eyes Quroak felt he was being attacked with laser beams. "We have never, never had a storm go berserk before. Control was lost about two months ago. The kidnappings started about a month ago. And ELEFANT has been seen in the Jovian system. This is too much of a coincidence for me. And whenever anything out of the ordinary occurs and those foul Venusians are around, you know they have to be the cause of it all."

"I get all that, but why do you think they are in the Little Red Storm?" Quroak persisted.

"It's a hunch I have. I can't think of any other place they could be hiding and I have to believe they sabotaged the artstorm for a reason." Zwane silently pointed out a bronze-colored glowmouse scurrying in the café's garden. Glowmice were rarely seen and it was considered a good omen for upcoming ventures when one was spotted.

Quroak thought about what Zwane had said. Even though he was told there didn't seem to be evidence of foul play regarding the artstorm, when you put all three events together, the kidnappings, the out of control storm and the ELEFANT sighting, it all added up to Zwane's hunch, though he had no idea *why* the Venusians were doing this.

Before he could say anything, Zwane interrupted tentatively with, "I was hoping you could help me in another way. Besides accompanying me."

"Anything I can do," Quroak answered, wondering what was coming next.

"The winds of the Red Storm are extremely fierce.

No Jovian has ever attempted to enter winds even close to 620 kph before, simply by the fact that they never existed before. I know Cloudotians have the ability to shift their mass to other dimensions so as to not be totally affected by things in this dimension. I've heard a rumor that Cloudotians can shift the mass, at least partially, of anything or *anyone* they hold in their arms as well. If this is true, I was hoping you could do this for me and take me at least part way into the Storm."

Quroak turned a bright silver blue from despair as he said slowly with deep regret, "It is true that we can do that for anything we wear and for small objects we may be holding, but most of us can't do that with anything alive. Only the oldest elders have that capability and they never leave Sea of Clouds. Even if they did, they couldn't get here in time, I'm afraid. I really wish I could help you, but I just don't have that ability. But, of course, I'm coming with you and will help you in any way possible."

Zwane smiled sadly at Quroak, who was visibly crestfallen, and said, "That's okay. I knew it was a long shot. I think we need to leave as soon as possible."

"Of course. I'm ready now."

With that, they left the café in a rush to try to catch the next shuttle to Jupiter. Glancing back at the small glowmouse, Quroak fervently hoped the legend was true because they were going to need all the luck they could find if they were going to succeed.

CHAPTER 25

Quroak spent the whole day and a half trip from Ganymede to Jupiter sleeping. He was still very tired from the strain of guiding the Jovian ship from the Uranian system to Ganymede and he didn't think he was going to get much rest in the near future.

Upon reaching the floating, open structure of the shuttle station in the northern hemisphere , Roton reached out to both Quroak and Zwane with her tentacles, giving them both a squeeze and said quietly with her eyes expressing great warmth and concern, "May the winds be gentle and the rings bright."

Quroak understood this was the Jovian equivalent of the human expression, 'good luck'. "Thank you. I hope to see you soon and be able to introduce you to Xelrine." *Actually, I hope to meet Xelrine myself. If she's hurt in any way* . . . But he couldn't afford to think about that, otherwise it would affect his ability to find and rescue her.

He was going to need a clear head and couldn't waste his energy on distracting emotions like worry. Anger he could and would use but worry would just sap his strength. So instead, he imagined her smiling eyes in his mind to help give his emotional energy focus.

Zwane didn't verbalize anything when he gave his cousin a hug goodbye, letting his eyes express everything that needed to be said.

The Little Red Storm was on the other side of the gigantic planet and even with the cyclone racing towards them, it took Quroak and Zwane five days to reach it while only resting a few hours each day.

Even after being on the giant planets Neptune and Uranus, Quroak still wasn't used to the scale of Jupiter. To reach the Red Storm as quickly as possible, they hadn't stayed on the cloudtops to skim the uppermost surface of the gas giant, but had instead dived down below the colorful ammonia cloud layers of muted browns, reds and oranges, below the layer of water clouds where lightning reigned with huge, planet-blasting bolts scorching the sky, and down into the clear, twilight sky of mostly hydrogen gas where they flew above the sea of liquid hydrogen that surrounded the planet's core.

This greatly reduced the distance they had to cover but it still took five days. *Five days. I can circle Sea of Clouds in a half day!* He just couldn't grasp the size of *Guiding Star*. On the way they had seen planet-sized storms high above them that took hours for them to pass. At the top of the cyclones, some bigger than his homeworld and could easily swallow Mercury or Mars without noticing, the winds swirled at around 250 kph, but down here where the narrowing funnels extended, the air whipped around at 400 kph. They didn't have time to go around these windstorms so they just flew straight threw them as both Cloudotians and Jovians are quite adept at handling high winds, though these wind velocities were taxing Zwane's abilities.

If he wasn't so anxious about Xelrine, he would have enjoyed the beautiful yet surreal twilight surrounding with the colorful mass of clouds weighing down from above and the choppy dark ocean below with the scattered Pluto-sized wind funnels seemingly anchoring the two together.

He thought he could understand why Jovians were uncomfortable in closed spaces, after millions of years of evolution of such openness that essentially seemed to go on forever. But, in his mind at least, he thought it could have gone the other way where Jovians would have felt lost in such vast openness and would have craved the comfort and safety of an enclosed area, like that of an Earth cat that loves boxes or anything that creates the feeling of a small personal cave.

They saw plenty of wildlife during the past five days with flaming orange cloudhawks diving in and out of storms hunting their prey and gargantuan shapes moving in the seas below.

Five days. Though Zwane hadn't said anything, Quroak knew the Jovian only had a little over a week before the softra destroyed him. As for himself, he kept reaching out with his mind, trying to contact Xelrine. The heartlink told him she was alive but he needed to know that she was unharmed. He needed to talk to her. He silently cursed the universe for having sent him to the edge of the Solar System from where it took him over seven years to return where he thought he would finally meet Xelrine, who was quite literally the woman of his dreams, only to have her snatched away by a sadistic Venusian sect before he even had a chance to lay eyes on her.

Even though the sky was gloomy, they were able to see the funnel of the Little Red Storm from a day away because it was so huge. Even though the Red Storm was half the size of the Great Red Spot, the Red Storm was still larger than the planet Earth.

From a few hours away, they could feel the whole atmosphere move swiftly as one huge mass due to the suction created by the furious cyclone. They were no longer *flying* towards the storm but were being *pulled* towards it. And it was no longer a funnel to them but a solid wall of raging wind that stretched in all directions, except behind them, as far as the eye could see.

Zwane glanced anxiously towards Quroak, "I thought experience with the Great Red would prepare me for this, but now I'm not so sure."

"Don't worry, I'll help you," reassured Quroak,

confident in his ability to reduce his mass and thus be less affected by the racing winds.

Thinking about it for a moment, Quroak said, "However, I do think it would be best if we entered the twister from the top instead of fighting our way through the solid wall of the funnel."

The Jovian agreed so they flew upward in as straight a line as possible, though it was really at an angle towards the storm because completely fighting against its pull was too tiring. Passing through the several layers of wind-whipped clouds took a couple of hours and then they burst through the cloudtops. This perspective was even more unnerving than seeing the twirling solid wall of the funnel below.

Above them, the pale golden atmosphere quickly disappeared into the ebony of space. As they were south of the equator, Quroak could see the underside of Jupiter's rings glowing startling grayish white against the blackness, like a ghostly curved blade slicing open the cosmos.

Tortured Io, with its surface covered with yellow, orange and green bruises with rings of red showing its volcanic tears from being trapped in the middle of the gravitational tug-of-war between Jupiter and Ganymede, hung close by as a reminder that space was an unforgiving place.

Mighty gray Ganymede, larger than four of the Solar System's planets, was also visible with its surface white pockmarked from asteroid collisions, yet seemingly serene in its supremacy of all the moons, indifferent to the cruelty inflected upon its brother, Io.

Europa, looking like a bluish-white opaque globe that had been smeared in mud and thrown against a huge rock causing cracks to snake across its surface, was about to disappear below the horizon.

He could see about a dozen other moons, all tiny compared to the other three, scattered across the heavens like dirty pearls from a broken necklace and in the background were the ever present uncaring but curious stars bearing witness to all that occurred.

He redirected his attention to his immediate surroundings. He and Zwane were a few kilometers above the storm clouds at the edge of the Red Storm, though from their perspective there was no clear edge like there was when viewing from space. Here, all they could see was a wall of bronze clouds below them that almost stretched towards the horizon with a barely visible sea of lighter brown clouds beyond the bronze wall.

Trying to put their location in perspective, he brought forth in his mind an image of the Red Storm as he had once seen it from hundreds of kilometers away in space. The Red Storm was the size of the whole planet Earth and was made up of swirling masses of burnt-orange, ochre, salmon, peach, coral, and sandy-brown clouds racing around the faded brick-red Pluto-sized center of the storm with the whole encircled by a bronze oval band with that in turn embraced within churning cloud eddies in every shade of tan imaginable, all of which plowed through the banded cloudic ocean of browns, whites and blues that was Jupiter. He knew right now they were hovering above the bronze oval band.

Though the comparison was in no way apt, he couldn't help but imagine that he was at the edge of an unseen, cosmic-sized drain that was about to suck him down to a place outside of the universe, a place *under* the universe from which he could never escape.

After spending a few hours flying over the bronze swirling wall, they reached the dark tan sea of clouds and without a word between them, just a 'here we go' glance, Quroak and Zwane dove downward at a slant towards the center which was still about 20,000 kilometers away, too far to be seen, but was felt with its powerful cyclonic suction.

CHAPTER 26

As they sunk into the swiftly moving, reddish sand-colored cloud current, Quroak could feel Zwane's nervousness like waves of heat emanating from his body. This current was racing along the bronze wall at about 500 kph which was much faster than any Jovian had ever attempted to travel through. Zwane was unprepared for the wind velocity as he was sucked into the current uncontrollably and then slammed sideways as if hit by a comet. As Zwane battled the cyclone over control of his own body, his mind was whipped into a whirlwind of panicked thoughts that were as loud as a tornado to a telepath, assaulting Quroak's mind.

Quroak could hear the Jovian's thoughts as clearly as if Zwane had been verbally shouting: *This is crazy. What are you doing? No one can do this! Are you completely out of your mind? ARE YOU CRAZY?*

But underneath the panic, Quroak felt the Jovian's

determination to not let anything stop him from finding Zola, who he believed was in the center of this hellish storm. When Zola was stolen from him, Zwane felt as if his heart had been physically ripped from his body and a cold emptiness rushed in to fill the void. Her absence was a vacuum in his soul, empty of all light and life. He had been hoping that Quroak would be able to help him by reducing his mass in this dimension. Since that was not an option, Zwane felt alone and knew he was going to have to rely on his own strength and determination.

All of this hit Quroak like a tidal wave before he could put up his mental defenses to block out his companion's thoughts. He sent thoughts of strength and encouragement to Zwane and thought-said, "I'm here. Be calm."

Quroak was able to handle the crazy wind speed better than the Jovian, though not by much, and he flew up to Zwane, wrapped four of his arms around Zwane's body and steered them both to ride with the rushing cloud-river instead of fighting against it.

"Relax your body and let the wind carry you." He could feel the tenseness in Zwane's body and felt the Jovian shiver uncontrollably in his arms. He didn't know how much of that was caused by fear. However, for the first time he noticed how cold it was this high up in Jupiter's atmosphere. His mind had been too focused before, but he now realized it must be around 160 Celsius degrees below zero.

Zwane recovered quickly, managed to calm himself and said, "Thanks, I'm okay now."

Quroak unwrapped his arms from around Zwane and glided within arms' length beside him in case he needed Quroak's assistance. "Sunghost, but its cold here."

"Yes, but it will get warmer the further down we go."

Knowing the Jovian's desire for privacy from telepaths, Quroak felt he should apologize to his companion. "Zwane, when we entered this current and you lost control, your thoughts became like thunder to me, very loud, before I had a chance to block them out . . ."

Not wanting to face Quroak, Zwane kept his eyes forward but whispered, "I understand, it's not your fault."

"And I want you to know, that you are not alone. We are in this together and I feel the same way about Xelrine as you do for Zola. Xelrine means everything to me. She's been my dream, in more ways than you can imagine, and now that I'm finally this close to her, nothing is going to stop me from finding her. As far as I'm concerned, failure is not an option here. Okay?"

Moved by Quroak's words, Zwane glanced at the Cloudotian with watery eyes and simply shrugged his smaller wings in thanks and acknowledgement.

"Okay then, now what we have to do is . . . what . . . sunghost, what's happening?" Quroak fell quiet, turning a yellowish purple, utterly surprised by what had just happened. Or rather, what *had* not happened.

To escape the full affect of the frigid atmosphere, Quroak had naturally tried to shift some of his mass as Cloudotians instinctively do when in the vacuum of space or when in hostile environments. Also, as they were being carried by the sandy brown current, buffeted about by smaller eddies, a small, burnt-orange whirlpool suddenly appeared before them and Quroak's idea was to de-solidify enough to escape its powerful suction, but not too much that he couldn't help Zwane.

But he found he couldn't shift his mass, not at all! This was like a bird that couldn't fly or a fish that couldn't swim, it was unnatural for him. He felt perfectly fine, but he couldn't transfer any of his mass to the other dimension. He felt oddly trapped within his own body!

Before he had a chance to react any further, the orange whirlpool grabbed them, started to whip them around in a circle. Caught by surprise, Quroak tumbled over and over and became entangled with Zwane as the Jovian slammed into him headfirst.

Quroak instinctively reached out, grabbed Zwane with four of his arms, and performed a flip where he actually seemed to have turned himself inside out so that now he was hurtling headfirst around the curve of the whirlpool. Before completing the circle where they would have just spiraled downward into the funnel, he put on a burst of speed while towing Zwane so that he were able to slingshot around and out of the whirlpool's grasp, like a spacecraft doing a gravitational slingshot around a planet.

Back in the sandy-brown cloud-stream again with the orange storm leaving them behind as they slowed down to the slower speed of the current, both Quroak and

Zwane glided quietly for a while, shaking a little from the adrenaline rush and giving their hearts a chance to slow down from their thundering pace.

Finally, Quroak said, "We are going to have to avoid those things from now on."

"What happened?" Zwane asked.

"I was caught by surprise by that small twister."

"Yeah, I know, but why were you surprised?"

"Because I can't shift," Quroak said slowly, disbelievingly.

"What do you mean, 'shift'?" Zwane asked.

"I can't transfer my mass to the other dimension. I'm totally stuck here, to feel the full affects of this place. Shifting is as natural to us as breathing is for you. We just take it for granted. This has never happened before in the history of my people." Quroak tried to shift again but nothing happened.

He was really worried because he now had no advantage; he was going to have to tackle the Red Storm full-bodied, as it were. Whenever Cloudotians storm-surfed, they always shifted their mass to some degree when dealing with the fiercest winds and there was no fiercer windstorm than this newly created, out-of-control artstorm.

Plus, he wasn't exactly at his best now because he hadn't been given the chance to recover from the four-month strain of guiding the Jovians home from Uranus. He was extremely tired and somewhat weakened. But he knew he had no choice and knew his determination to find Xelrine would give him whatever strength he needed.

The thought of Xelrine brought forth an image of her with her eyes smiling and he reached out again with his mind. "My love, I'm coming for you."

To his shock, he heard a sweet flavored thought-reply, "Quroak, where are you?"

"Xelrine!" he thought-shouted. "Are you all right? Are you hurt? Where are you? What happened? I've been so worried!" His thoughts tumbled out like waves crashing against a rocky cliff. He turned a dark turquoise tinged with sea green from excitement and happiness from hearing her mind's sweet, melodious voice.

Meanwhile, not knowing about the non-verbal communication going on, Zwane asked, "So will you be able to make it through to Red Storm's center?" He was obviously worried that he might have to go this alone after all.

Quroak sent a quick thought to Zwane, "Wait a minute Zwane, I've contacted Xelrine!"

"What? Great winds! Is she with Zola? Are they unharmed?" Zwane waved his tentacles in anxious excitement as he stared at Quroak with concerned eyes shining like lighthouses on a dark stormy night.

But by the time Zwane had verbalized his questions, as immediate as they were, Quroak and Xelrine had already completed the following rapid-fire exchange at thought-speed:

Xelrine: *I'm not hurt.*

Quroak: *I'm so glad to feel your thoughts!*

Xelrine: *Me too.*

Quroak: *If I lost you . . .* Waves of love from Quroak washed throughout Xelrine's being, saying everything that words and thoughts could never adequately express.

Xelrine: *You're not going to get rid of me that easily. Besides, I kept you company during your little excursion to the edges of the universe so the least you can do is talk to me now. You owe me.*

Quroak could feel the giddiness of relief in her thoughts and he responded in kind. *If you insist but I can't promise how long I can suffer through such a torturous task.* Then his thoughts hardened with determination. *I'll do you one better. I'm coming for you. Where are you?*

Xelrine: *I don't know where I am exactly, but I think I'm inside a ship.*

Quroak: *Is Zola with you?*

Xelrine: *Yes and she's okay. There are also about twenty other Jovians trapped here with us.*

Quroak: *Trapped?*

Xelrine: *Yes, we are all locked in a large room with opaque yellowish doors.*

Quroak: *Are you sure you're okay?*

Xelrine: *Other than being a prisoner, yes. But all the others, including Zola seem to be weak, lethargic, like they have little energy or strength to do anything.*

Quroak: *They're slowing dying. They only have a few days to live.*

Xelrine: *What? Why?*

Quroak: *I can't tell you now. I'm afraid the Venusians might find out somehow. Just try to take care of them.*

Xelrine: *Okay.*

Quroak: *I've missed you and been so scared, worrying about you. Zwane and I think you are being held inside the Red Storm. We are coming to get you.*

Xelrine: *Be careful, Quroak. We are being held by Venusians.*

Quroak: *Yes, we had guessed that.*

Xelrine: *I don't know why they took us.*

Quroak: *Have they done anything to you?*

Xelrine: *Until now, they've been keeping me unconscious. I just completely woke up for the first time now. Before, every time I was coming out of it, they gave me a shot to put me out again.*

Quroak: *Oh, so that's why I wasn't able to reach you.*

Xelrine: *Yes. There's something else. There's something wrong with me. I can't shift. I know that's hard to belie–*

Quroak: *I believe you. Unfortunately, I believe you all too well. I can't shift either.*

Xelrine: *How is this possible?*

Quroak: *I don't know but since ELEFANT is involved, it's got to be them causing this.*

Xelrine: *I love you. Do be careful!*

Quroak: *I love you and I'm getting you out of there.*

Then Quroak heard Zwane's questions. "Yes, Zola is unharmed. She and Xelrine and all the others seem to be held captive on a ship, though Xelrine doesn't know where. But she did confirm that it is the Venusians."

Relief at knowing Zola was alive shined from Zwane's eyes like the morning light after a long, cold night.

Though they were being carried in an unstoppable wind-current at a mind-whirling speed of 500 kph, a sudden gust hit them from the left side, sending them tumbling a couple of kilometers across the rusty, swirling nightmare of a sky. Before they could regain some semblance of control, they were slammed by another howling gale which pounded them downward.

After straightening themselves out and flowing with the main stream again, feeling somewhat bruised and battered, Zwane requested, "Please let Zola know that I'm near and will soon touch her."

After marveling again at the Jovian's ability to make himself clearly heard through the deafening roar of the cyclone, Quroak thought-sent to Xelrine Zwane's message.

The thought of the wind's noise prompted him to ask her, "Xelrine, can you hear anything?"

"No, why?"

"Ask the others if they hear anything." Ever since Cloudotians became civilized and developed telepathy their sense of hearing had been weakening and he knew Jovian's hearing was much more acute.

"Zola says she never doubted Zwane would rescue her and that she loves him. She and the others agree that they can hear the wind. They say it's not close but far in the distance."

After relaying Zola's message to his Jovian companion,

Zwane stated excited, "Then they must be in the calm center of the Red Storm! We must hurry."

Quroak tended to agree. If the prisoners can hear the storm in the distance, then they were probably in the storm's eye. Of course, that was still assuming they were *in* the Red Storm. However, the fact that something was preventing both he and Xelrine from shifting, something that didn't seem possible before, told him that they must be in close proximity of each other.

And they did have to hurry. He figured the Jovians had only about seven days before they totally succumbed to the softra. That was seven days to find them, rescue them from the Venusians and then get them back to their lifemates to be healed with live-saving caresses of love. So, about forty lives hung in the balance, depending on him and Zwane: the twenty one held captive and each of their lifemates. *No pressure at all.*

So Zwane and Quroak started to cut across the five thousand kilometer wide sandy brown cloud-stream, which on any other world would have been considered an ocean, but on this leviathan planet was only a narrow river within the cyclone that was an Earth across. They tackled the current at an angle, heading both inward and downward but still letting it carry them forward in order to conserve as much energy as possible.

"Xelrine, what happened?"

"Zola and I were on a tour of the bottomside storm, Orange Wonder, which is absolutely amazing, by the way.

We stopped to admire a rare emerald green eddy of clouds that was being pulled into this golden-orange cloud-devil on the edge of the storm's eye while the rest of the group went on ahead of us. We suddenly felt sleepy and the next thing we knew we woke up in this room. We must have been gassed. Until now, our captors have kept me unconscious the whole time. But the others tell me that they have each been taken out of our cell by the Venusians and led to some kind of laboratory where they are immediately knocked out. So they don't know what's happening to them while there." Quroak could feel the uneasy disgust in Xelrine's thoughts.

"So you think the Venusians are doing experiments on the Jovians?" he asked.

"We can't think of any other explanation."

"How do they feel when they awaken? Are they in pain?" he asked.

"They are hurting and growing weaker but they insist it has nothing to do with their visits to the laboratory. But they won't tell me what's going on." Frustrated concern colored her thoughts.

"Xelrine, listen to me. It's important that you don't push them on this. I think the Venusians are studying the process that is slowly killing the Jovians. I'm not sure to what end but it can't be good."

"But why was I taken? Wrong place, wrong time?"

"They seemed to have found a way to stop us from shifting. Maybe they are testing whatever device is causing this on you," he conjectured.

"Sunghosts! I wish the Uranians had wiped out ELEFANT after their world was attacked!"

"Yeah, too bad they're pacifists," he agreed.

As he and Zwane continued to the fight the river of sandy brown cloud mass, Quroak continued conversing with Xelrine but as most of his attention was focused on avoiding the sudden eddies, whirlpools and twisters that appeared with no warning, he couldn't remember most of the conversation.

Zwane was mostly quiet the whole time, concentrating his flagging strength on his struggle with the insane velocity, trying to maintain the correct body position to go with the wind flow as much as possible with his wings continuously changing color to blend into the surrounding clouds.

It took about a day for them to fly across the taupe river of clouds. Quroak felt *fly* was too generous a word to use since it implied *controlled flight* whereas it felt like they were anything but in control of their tumbling, erratic progress towards the Red Storm's center. He was just wondering if they were ever going to reach the inner-side of this endless sea when he heard Zwane yell out in pain at the same moment his own body screamed in agony as he slammed into a burnt orange solid wall that appeared out of nowhere, knocking him unconscious.

CHAPTER 27

Quroak must have been knocked out for only a second or two because his next impression was that the rust colored wall reached out and plucked both him and Zwane out of the ruddy sand swirling river and threw them in front of a racing tsunami wave that painfully slammed into them and was now carrying them as if they were strands of seaweed stuck to the prow of a seafaring ship that was being demonically pulled into a whirlpool strong enough to pull planets from their orbits.

With his own mind a swirling storm of confusion made up of half-formed thoughts, vague images and shifting colors of oranges, browns and reds, he dimly realized they must have reached the inward side of the river current and were now in the outer fringes of the reddish maelstrom that swirled in the middle of the Red Storm. Even as he was tumbling out of control, he guessed the wind must be traveling at an inconceivable velocity of around 600 kph.

He instinctively tried to shift, immediately remembered he couldn't. *Sunghosts!* He then did his best to make himself as thin and long as possible by stretching his head and arms in opposite directions and aimed himself with the wind's flow so that he was like an arrow in a gigantic maelstrom; a whirlpool so immense that it would takes days just to travel the circle once.

He carefully looked around, trying to not disturb his delicate aerodynamic balance with the windstorm, in search of Zwane as he also called out with his mind, "Zwane, are you all right?"

Through the numbing, roaring noise of the cyclone that made him think of worlds colliding, he barely made out the Jovian's soft trilling voice, "I'm okay, though my body hurts so much I feel like some god just threw Callisto at me!"

Quroak concurred, he also felt like he had been slammed by a moon. "Where are you?"

"I'm three meters below you, to your right."

Quroak cautiously rotated so he could see the Jovian. Zwane had his larger set of wings folded tightly against his body with his tentacles streaming behind him and his smaller wings making minute movements trying to keep himself relatively stabilized in the furious wind.

Xelrine's thoughts sweetly caressed his turbulent mind, "Quroak, are you okay?"

"We're okay. We just weren't prepared for – whoa!"

All of a sudden, he and Zwane were caught by some kind of wandering pocket of still air and they both lost their equilibrium, unprepared for the calmness that was like a slight breeze compared to the hyper-hurricane they were riding. It was like a small bubble in the storm where the dull scarlet clouds swirled all around them in a sky gone crazy while they were somehow outside of reality, safe in their bubble of stillness, untouched by the chaos outside.

"Quroak, what's going on?" Xelrine queried anxiously.

Zwane and Quroak both collapsed upon themselves, totally exhausted, just letting themselves be carried by the heaven-sent pocket of peace. Every muscle in Quroak's body felt mushy, as if he had been trampled by a stampede of Earth elephants scared silly by a mouse. *I really have to stop watching their cartoons.* Every movement was a herculean effort like he was trying to move a mountain.

Any energy he had was now coming straight from his willpower and the effort of trying to fly in this vermilion storm from hell was draining that strength at a prodigious rate.

Blackness was hovering at the fringes of his awareness, threatening to rob him of consciousness. It reminded him of when he was caught in the snare of the Neptunian vampires.

However, though his emotional strength was flagging as well, he knew he would never give in or give up. Xelrine was real, no longer a dream and no longer a question regarding his own sanity. She was real and he was going to find her and finally be with her. She was not a fantasy but she *was* the fantasy of his heart and nothing was going to stop him from living his dream of happiness and true sharing of his life with another, with her.

But being in this pocket of stillness, where he wasn't fighting the turbulent wind eddies and currents that seemed to have been hell-spawned, made him realized just how tired and weak he really was. *And we've only been in this crimson tornado-within-a-cyclone for a few minutes!*

Plus, he could feel waves of exhaustion flowing from Zwane who was curled up in a ball. *Being emphatic as well as telepathic certainly had its downsides.* It just made it harder for him to fight his own exhaustion while feeling the Jovian's as well, weighing upon him like Olympus Mons. *I have to take Xelrine to Mars; I think she'd enjoy seeing the largest volcano in the Solar System.*

His mind floated in free association for a while, trying to escape the agony of his body and the encroaching darkness threatening his consciousness even as his love for Xelrine fueled his determination and strengthened his willpower.

"Quroak, talk to me! What happened?" Xelrine's caress in his mind was a lifeline, towing his mind back to the present.

"Xelrine. We're okay, just exhausted. We were swooped up by some kind of huge air pocket of stillness.

Sometimes you don't realize how hard something is until it stops. Just need to rest for a few moments."

"Where are you?" she asked.

He pictured the Red Storm in his mind and tried to estimate their position within but he had lost track of their progress. His best guess was that they were about twelve thousand kilometers from the storm's center. He sent her a 'you are here' mental picture of his best guess.

"Xelrine, I'm worried about Zwane. I can hear his mind screaming with exhaustion, begging his body to stop fighting, to just give up. I need to fortify him."

"What about you? Who's going to fortify you?"

"Are you kidding? As long as I have your sweet mental caress and warmth soothing my soul, I'm invincible! I would take on a thousand Red Storms just to be by your side. You are going to have to try a lot harder to keep me away, lady." He tried to project as much levity and confidence into these sentiments as possible, though his own body was currently plea bargaining, begging and threatening all-out rebellion if it didn't get rest: *NOW!*

"I see I'll have to try to come up with something more challenging for you next time," she joked, matching the mood he was trying to set. "The Red Storm, a rogue black hole, soul-sucking vampires, nothing can beat my handsome knight."

"Not when it comes to being with you, my love, my light." The lightness of their conversation was pushing back the darkness surrounding his consciousness with strength and determination flowing through his aching body.

"I love you, Xelrine."

"I know. I have always known, long before our minds touched. I've been waiting for you. I've been waiting all my life for you. I love you, too."

"I've always dreamed of you, Xelrine, also before our minds touched. But I didn't dare hope that you were real. But now, after I found you, nothing will ever keep us apart again. No runaway storms from hell, no black holes, no freeze-shifting force . . . black holes . . . hmmm, I wonder."

"What?" queried Xelrine after a moment of mind-silence.

"Hmmm, I was just wondering about –", a shrill moan from Zwane called Quroak's attention.

"Zwane, how are you doing?" Quroak asked quietly.

"Did anybody see the runaway moon gone berserk?" Zwane complained lightly.

"I know what you mean. I can't move a muscle without starbursts going off in my head." Quroak tried to send subliminal messages of strength and encouragement to the Jovian. He didn't want to hurt Zwane's pride by suggesting the Jovian needed help so he sent warm, soothing thoughts that his companion wouldn't pick up consciously.

"I really hate to say this," said Zwane, "but we have leave this little paradise."

"I know," Quroak sighed. "This pocket isn't really going our way. We need to cut towards the storm's center."

"I'm all topsy-turvy. Do you know which way the eye is?" Zwane spread his tentacles showing confusion.

"I don't know exactly where we are inside the storm, but I can still sense the general direction of the center." Quroak pointed one arm towards their bottom right.

They were silent for a few minutes, enjoying the calm while the world roared in fury all around them; as if angry they had temporarily escaped and was reminding them their fate when they were once again in the storm's clutches. The crimson clouds swirled furiously, forming monstrous shapes that instantly dissolved into chaotic nightmarish mists.

Quroak was still trying to psyche himself up for the upcoming abuse when Zwane said firmly, "Let's do this."

Gathering himself together, forcing his mind to ignore the pain, Quroak flew out of the pocket of stillness into the howling hell with Zwane right behind him. Their brief stay in the calmness must have dulled his body's memory, for the hyper-velocity wind felt worse than he remembered, spinning him out of control. He heard the Jovian scream out in pain, for coming out of the bubble and into the full fury of the storm was like being struck by that moon gone berserk.

Just as he was able to straighten himself out and ascertain that Zwane was still with him, they were slammed by a dull orange mini-hurricane which painfully hurled them sidewise to slide across the wall-like force of the scarlet main headwinds.

The next two days were a blur for Quroak. His mind was entirely concentrated on surviving and on getting him and Zwane to the runaway artstorm's center, with all his attention intensely focused on their immediate surroundings with everything beyond non-existent to his consciousness. Details were washed out by exhaustion, one moment sharp when they mattered, the next, faded by the next crisis overwhelming his immediate attention.

His mind swirled with chaotic images of them seemingly bouncing from one mini-hurricane to another, dodging energy-sapping eddies which appeared out of nowhere, gusts of wind pummeling them with unheard of insane speeds of up to 740 kph and nightmarish crimson cloud formations conjured up by an exhausted mind.

The constant struggle towards the storm's eye drained them physically and mentally with the ever-present planet-shattering howl of the wind grating on their nerves, causing Quroak's head to throb intensely.

Quroak and Zwane communicated solely with vague gestures, too tired to talk, which conveyed all the meaning necessary as they were now reacting automatically to each obstacle with their instincts now honed by constant perils over the past couple of days. Plus at this point, they were highly attuned to each other's thoughts and reactions by now so that they were acting as one, synchronized, as if they had been practicing for years.

They had not been able to rest at all and Quroak was now beyond exhaustion, running fully on automatic with his mind frozen in an orange haze, over-stimulated by the wind's raging howl and the screaming of his own body begging his mind to stop fighting the inevitable and his mind pleading with his willpower to give in, to let unconsciousness take over and give him peace, or at the very least, sweet unawareness of whatever would happen to him if he simply gave up. But his heart overruled both his body and mind, fueling his willpower with a soft mantra of *Xelrine, Xelrine, Xelrine.*

He was vaguely aware that Zwane's mind was mostly quiet, having stopped screaming at his own willpower hours ago, too numb with agony to protest anymore. However, without conscious thought, out of concern for his companion and against his policy of never intruding, he listened to the Jovian's mind and discovered that Zwane had his own mantra going on: *I need your touch, your sweet light caressing my heart.* Between the *softra* slowly killing him, the battering of the storms and the emotional distress caused by Zola's absence, Quroak knew Zwane might not last much longer.

Off to their left appeared a dark red tear in the clouds. Without thinking or communicating, they both dove into the hole to find a small horizontal vortex slicing through the clouds which sucked their exhausted bodies through its twirling walls of super-speed-hardened, crimson clouds which they painfully scraped along as they spiraled uncontrollably. Even as his body yelled in agony, his mind screamed *I can't take anymore!*

Quroak snapped out of his encroaching hysteria when Zwane's limp body slammed into him. Quroak wrapped the unconscious Jovian in his numb arms (which barely responded to his mind's commands anymore) as he himself felt his own mind succumbing to an enclosing circle of hazy darkness. His heart cried out *No, you can't give in!*

Even though he had never actually met her, during the time he had been communicating with her during his odyssey home from the Solar System's boondocks, he had gotten to know her very well for they really bared their souls to each other.

(Note to readers: while Quroak downloaded memories regarding himself and his emotions to my library, he was not willing to share most of whatever personal things Xelrine shared with him, out of courtesy and respect for her privacy.)

He never knew before how strongly he could feel for another. Now, she was the only thing that truly mattered to him and he longed to be with her. He couldn't imagine how it would be when they first touched, but he yearned for it as a physical need and he craved to melt into the enticing sweet scent of her skin. He also wanted to drown in her lovely bronze eyes where he imagined he'd be able to see all of his desires and his future. But more than that, his heart and soul were overflowing with the desire and need to share his life with her.

So, he had to save her no matter what. If he died before saving her, before being able to share love and life with her, his spirit, his essence, would never rest and his next reincarnation would be haunted by it.

But though he fought valiantly against the encroaching darkness, with Xelrine's face the only light in his desperate mind, Quroak unwillingly succumbed to the pure exhaustion and numbing pain of his body that tumbled uncontrollably through the crimson vortex, finally surrendering to the sweet and warm sea of unawareness where nothing mattered.

CHAPTER 28

Quroak awoke to find himself sliding through the deep red whirlpool with Zwane still miraculously embraced in his arms, unconscious. He wasn't sure, but he figured he hadn't been out for more than an hour or so. Luckily, they were no longer bouncing off the vortex's curved walls but were sliding straight down the middle in the crimson colored light and they seemed to be traveling quite fast, with something pulling them forcefully.

Unbidden, his mind instinctively reached out for Xelrine, "Xelrine, are you there?"

She immediately responded, "Yes, Quroak, I'm here. I've been trying to reach you."

"Oh, I was bored and so took a nap." He sent her a mental image of him and Zwane sliding through the mysterious tunnel through the clouds.

"And here I was waiting around for you to rescue me. I guess I'll just have to tell my Jovian friends here to cancel the rescue celebration because you lost interest. It looks like you decided to go cyclone surfing."

"Oh, well, if they have *already* planned a party in my honor, then I wouldn't want to disappoint anyone, so I'll be there as soon as I can."

"Why, how kind of you not wanting to hurt anyone's feelings like that. I knew I liked you for a reason," she thought-said with a sarcastic flavoring.

"Well, you know, I'm a nice guy. Really, just ask anyone." The light banter was helping him to focus his mind's attention and to summon his emotional energy which was coalescing into renewed determination, revitalized by her mind's loving caress.

Watching the swirling deep red walls racing past him, he said, "I'm kind of embarrassed to ask you this, but I don't want to be late for the celebration; can you give me the directions again? I think we may be lost."

"Let me guess, you didn't want to stop and ask anyone for help, did you? Honestly, you men!" she retorted.

"Well, *I* wanted to, but Zwane insisted we figure it out for—"

Then suddenly, they shot out through the end of the vortex and out into . . . . a place of utter calm and emptiness. The shock of not being forcefully sucked through the vortex and not fighting against a horrendous wall of wind was such that they fell for several kilometers before Quroak's mind snapped out of it and gained control of their flight, for what seemed like to him, the first time in days.

"Quroak?" Xelrine asked anxiously.

"Yea, I'm here. We're okay. We just exited the vortex unexpectedly," he replied.

"Where are you now?" she asked.

He paused, looking at his surroundings. Behind him and stretching in all directions as far as the eye could see, was a rushing, tumbling mass of orange and red clouds that looked as solid as a brick wall with the mouth of the crimson vortex, which had carried him and Zwane here, a churning opening a few kilometers above them. But where they were now and ahead of them stretching into infinity in every direction was a clear, cloudless sky suffused with a soft burgundy light with only a slight breeze flowing over his body.

A chill ran through his whole body and at first he thought the breeze was cold but then he realized the air and wind were warm and that his body was thawing out for the first time since leaving the ocean on Oberon. He was too tired to remember how long ago that was but it was long enough that he had forgotten what it felt like to be warm again.

"We made it! We're in the storm's eye!" he excitedly told Xelrine.

"Great!" she responded. "Do you see anything? The ship?"

"No, but I'm sure the eye is probably as big as Mars, so I'm not surprised," he answered, being careful not to disappoint her.

Meanwhile, he gently shook Zwane, trying to wake him up. After a few moments, the Jovian started to mumble incoherently as he began to come around. He finally opened his eyes with a snap and asked, "Where are we?"

Quroak first asked, "Are you all right? Can you fly?"

"I'm fine!" Zwane said rather irritably, realizing that the Cloudotian was carrying him.

Quroak let him go as he said, "I believe we are in the eye. It should be smooth going here on out."

"Oh yeah, all we have to do is find the spaceship, knock on the airlock and politely ask the Venusians to let their prisoners go and while they're at it, give us a ride out of this crazy storm!"

Taken aback by the Jovian's unbidden hostility, Quroak asked again, "Are you all right?"

"Yes, of course I'm all . . . ." Zwane stopped, took a deep breath and let it out slowly before continuing. "I apologize. I guess the softra has taken a bigger toll on me than I thought. Plus being battered around like a feather in this cyclone from hell didn't help any. I know I wouldn't have gotten this far without your help. I'm sorry."

"It's okay. We helped each other get this far. I don't know about the rest of it, but as for finding the spaceship, I can feel the ship's mass. It's in that direction," as he pointed ahead and down.

"Good winds! Let's go." Zwane started to fly forward.

After a few hours of flying towards the eye's center,

Zwane asked doubtfully, "Are you sure we're going in the right direction?"

"Yes, I can sense it quite strongly now, it's not too much further ahead." Quroak replied confidently.

"We've been flying for what seems like forever without seeing anything! Even the inner walls of the Red Storm are far away now!" the Jovian stated irritably.

Quroak was slow to respond to the implied criticism of his abilities. He slowly counted to ten in his mind to calm down. The Jovian had been making small complaints and hints of discontent the whole time since entering the eye and was really getting on the Cloudotian's nerves.

He tried to remind himself that Zwane was being affected by the softra and was only a few days away from dying. And he realized there were probably a couple of other considerations making the Jovian nervous. The first was being out in the open like this in a perfectly clear sky. Jovians spent most of their lives in the clouds and didn't venture too often below Jupiter's multiple cloud layers where it was clear before eventually turning into a sea of metallic hydrogen as you drop towards the planet's core. And when they do visit underside, they go in a large group as protection against the many large predators living there. When he and Zwane had flown below the cloud deck to reach the Red Storm as quickly as possible by bypassing some of the planet's curvature, the Jovian had insisted they fly close to the cloud ceiling since both the Jovian and Cloudotian could blend in with the oranges, bronzes and reds of the cloudy background with their ability to change their body coloring.

The second thing making them both anxious was that after spending so much time fighting the horrendous winds of the Red Storm, now that they were traveling through the tranquility of the cyclone's eye, it didn't really *feel* like they were actually doing anything to affect a rescue of their loved ones. He knew it was an illusion, a letdown after the days spent with their adrenaline flowing like a waterfall from dealing with the hardships.

But that was all about to change as Zwane pointed ahead, "I think I see something in the distance."

Even though Quroak could see more in the spectrum range, his acuity did not match the Jovian's for he still couldn't see anything. However, he could feel the mass of the large object up ahead.

With his hearts racing now in anticipation, Quroak suggested, "We should probably approach the craft from underneath to try to avoid detection."

Zwane agreed with a flap of his smaller wings, "Sounds good to me."

So they dove downward about six kilometers, hoping they were now below the ship, before they continued flying towards it. It turned out that the ship had been about thirty kilometers away when Zwane had first spotted it. *Still can't get used to the scale of Jupiter!*

A few minutes later, they flew up to within two hundred meters underneath the ship. *More a monstrosity than a ship!* Quroak always thought the Losians had the strangest sense of beauty of all the known species. To him, the spacecraft looked like the designer was trying to create a personification (or whatever you would call it for a ship) of chaos itself. He supposed the basic structure was a cross between a flat oval and an oblong rectangle about a hundred meters or so long and forty meters wide, but it was buried under dozens of different sized triangles sticking out at weird angles from the ship's body with the whole painted a sickly yellow mottled with ugly shades of greenish browns and grayish tans.

If there ever had been any doubt before about who was behind the kidnappings and the runaway Jovian artstorm, it was blown away with the sight of this ship for no one but the Losians could design such an ugly and ungainly craft. While he knew the shape of a spacecraft didn't matter in the vacuum of space, he couldn't figure out how this nightmare that looked like it had escaped from an Earth cubist painting could possibly fly in the wind-whipped atmosphere of Jupiter.

"This is a ship?" wondered Zwane. "It looks like something dragged from a junkyard!"

"You've obviously never seen Losian ships before. This one actually looks quite beautiful to others I've seen," Quroak joked with a straight face.

At the same time, he thought-sent to Xelrine, "Baby, I feel real sorry for you for being swallowed up in the belly of this hideous monster. I don't know if I can come get you. Next time, can you please arrange it so I can rescue you from a beautiful castle high up in the snow covered mountains?"

"I'll see what I can do," she replied sarcastically. "But if you don't mind and have nothing better to do at the moment, can you please get me out of here!"

"Your wish is my command, my queen."

"And don't you forget it!" He could feel the smile in her thoughts. *Guiding Star, I love her!* as his heart swelled with emotion.

"Now what?" murmured Zwane.

"I guess we have to find a way in – wait, look over there!"

They were currently underneath one end of the ship and near the other end they could see four Losians in spacesuits with small claw-held weapons, which Quroak recognized as stun-guns, pushing two Jovians through a portal on the side of the ship.

"This is our chance! Let's go!" Zwane urgently whispered even as he shot down the length of the craft's belly towards the portal, almost caressing the ship in his attempt to avoid detection by the Losians.

They were still about ten meters away when the last Losian disappeared into the ship.

"Hurry!" urged Quroak as the door started to slide downwards.

They both dove forward and barely squeezed through the closing portal a mere second before the heavy door slammed shut, creating a dull metallic boom, both masking any noise they may have made and sounding like fate was sealing their doom.

"We made it!" Zwane whispered, throwing his tentacles up in relief.

"Yes, let's hope our luck holds out." Quroak replied, looking around at their surroundings.

They were in an empty square room where there was another closed door on the opposite wall. Through the small triangular window in the door, Quroak saw a Losian removing its space gear.

"Down!" thought-shouted Quroak as he dove to the floor before he could see anything more.

Zwane dropped like a puppet whose strings had been cut. "What did you see?"

"They're in the next room. They are removing their spacesuits."

A few moments later, they heard a door open and then slam shut with a metallic bang.

Quroak cautiously inched up the door to peek through the window. He saw another square room holding a row of low lockers, but it was empty of any living beings. He could see through the window of the door exiting the room and it showed a short corridor where he saw the Losians just turning a corner before disappearing. He assumed the prisoners were in front and had already turned the corner because he hadn't seen them.

He slowed grasped the odd looking handle and opened

the door and they quickly floated into the second room and closed the door.

Two things happened at once. A blast of hot, stuffy air slammed into them like the heat from a metal-melting furnace with such force and so unexpectedly that they both recoiled backwards. However, they were also pulled upwards suddenly like a pin exposed to a giant magnet, crashing them against the ceiling.

"Sunghosts!" thought-muttered Quroak, as Zwane exclaimed something unintelligibly in pain.

"We weren't beaten up enough by the storms, now this ship wants a piece of us!" complained Zwane.

"Yea, I've had enough of these tests by the universe." Quroak twisted and rubbed his arms together, trying to remove the sting from the collision with the ceiling from his already tortured muscles.

"So am I! Why is it insufferably hot and why are we plastered to the ceiling like paint?" Zwane gingerly peeled himself from the ceiling but found that he had to keep pushing with his tentacles to fight against its magical pull.

Quroak's body felt so light, as if it weighed almost nothing at all. After pondering for a moment, he exclaimed, "Oh, of course. They have it so it's comfortable for them. To make it feel like home, Venus. Everyone knows that planet is infernally hot, about 450 Celsius. And if I remember my astronomy correctly, Jupiter's gravity is something like two and a half times that of Venus. And we may be able to use that fact."

"Oh, how so?"

"Well, if we feel extraordinarily light in their gravity, the Losians would feel two and a half times heavier than normal in Jupiter's gravity and they wouldn't be able to move around so freely. Not only are their environmental suits protecting them from your atmosphere, it also allows them to move around outside, though they would need that anyway since Venusians can't fly."

Quroak paused for a second as he thought-asked Xelrine, "Do the Losians usually wear their space gear when you see them?"

She replied instantly, "No. Why?"

"Oh, just an idea I have," he answered her.

With barely a noticeable pause to Zwane, he continued, "If we can destroy their gravity making machine –"

"We could slow them down!" cried out Zwane enthusiastically. "I guess that explains that awful smell, too! This must smell like their planet."

"Yes, Venus has a lot of sulfur dioxide in their atmosphere. Now, let's go find our sweethearts."

"There's just one problem, though." The Jovian grimaced in pain.

"Oh? Just one? Then things are looking up!" Quroak answered lightly, though he was feeling somewhat queasy.

"I don't think we can stand this heat. I feel like I'm on the surface of the sun!"

Quroak knew the Jovian was exaggerating, of course.

But not by much! The heat was like being inside a furnace and he knew he couldn't take it for long and neither could the Jovian. They both were accustomed to temperatures ranging from zero to thirty degrees Celsius, though Quroak, of course could handle the cold vacuum of space. *But four hundred degrees! Sunghosts! How are we going to survive this? Guiding Star, but I miss shifting!*

Already, the superheated air was taking its toll on them; their movements were sluggish and their skin was wrinkling up, drying out and it felt like he had a ton of sand in his eyes, they hurt so much.

In desperation, he reached out to Xelrine. "Is it hot in your cell?"

"No. Our prison is at normal Jupiter atmospheric conditions. Why?"

"Because we are in the changing room outside the airlock, and it feels like we are on Venus! Remind me to never take a holiday there!"

"Whenever the Jovians are taken away to the labs, they are made to put on specially designed suits. I guess that's to protect them from the ship's environment."

"Great, thanks, Xelrine." As he sent her warm feelings to indicate a tender embrace, Quroak pulled himself down the wall and started opening the lockers quickly. He found an environmental outfit suitable for Jovians and passed it up to Zwane. "Here, get into this. It will help you." The weight of the suit brought the Jovian down from the ceiling.

After another moment he found one designed for Cloudotians and he donned it as quickly as possible. The moment he sealed it up, it automatically provided an atmosphere comparable to his homeworld's; Sea of Clouds. *Much better*, he sighed.

"How are you doing, Zwane?"

"I feel like I'm in heaven after just visiting hell!" the Jovian answered contently.

"Yea, I know what you mean. But they will hamper us, as well. At least we can still fly, though," as he floated experimentally. Quroak flexed his arms but the suit was stiff so that he couldn't be as flexible as usual, but he would just have to deal with it, he grumbled to himself. But they were light enough to allow flight, at least, in this gravity setting.

Zwane's suit was a little more flexible, at least, the part that held the wings. Nature didn't design Jovians to be able to move about on land, since there was none on Jupiter except at the very core of the planet. So the Losians had to design the suit so that the Jovian's could move about using their wings.

"Okay," Quroak said, "we're ready to go."

"Great," Zwane replied wearily, "but unless you know where to go, we're just going to have to start searching."

"Wait a second. Maybe we can get help with that." Quroak then communicated with Xelrine, "I don't suppose you have any idea where you are?"

"I don't since I've never been conscious outside our

cell. Let me ask the others." In a few seconds she came back with, "They say we are in the rear of the ship on the bottom deck."

"Sunghosts! We're near the front. Do you have any idea how many Losians are on board?"

"No, but we think we've seen twenty five different individuals."

"Okay, Zwane, they're in the stern." Quroak looked through the window into the corridor and seeing no one, he slowly opened the door.

CHAPTER 29

So with an actual strategy in mind for the first time other than 'rescue them', Quroak and Zwane left the airlock room carefully and entered the corridor. They moved slowly, trying to get used to the stiff environmental suits.

They found themselves at a T where they were at the intersection. The Losians had gone straight ahead so they didn't want to go that way.

"Which way?" wondered Zwane.

"Well, I think we entered near the port bow of the ship, and I'm guessing the engine room would be in the stern, so we should go right. Assuming, that is, the artificial gravity controls are in the engine room. Although," he mused, "the Losians did go straight. Does that mean –".

"Xelrine, when they bring their prisoners onboard, do they go straight to the holding cell?"

"No, Zola says they are first taken to a laboratory for some tests."

"Okay, Zwane, Zola says to get to the lab, you go straight. So, I still say we go right."

"Well, we've got to start somewhere." The Jovian led the way down the corridor, hugging the ceiling.

Quroak actually felt thankful for the reduced gravity because he felt so weak and tired he didn't think he could have gone on much further without this unexpected assistance, especially in these spacesuits.

The atmosphere was very hazy, thick with the gaseous elements that made it seem like home to the Venusians, but it wasn't much of an issue for him since his visual range of the spectrum allowed him to penetrate it. Since Zwane wasn't so lucky, Quroak took the lead.

Skimming along the ceiling, they quickly discovered that the ship was a confusing maze of corridors that didn't seem to make any sense. The corridors twisted and seemed to cut back on themselves with dozens of intersections. It was quite difficult to maintain a stern-ward direction.

While exploring the maze of corridors, they were able to escape detection by the few Losians that scurried below them by ducking into other corridors. Having the better hearing of the two species, Zwane was able to hear the Losians well in advance as the insectoids could not move on the metal deck without creating a clicking sound from their chitinous exoskeleton.

The Losians always reminded Quroak of stick bugs from Earth, though being able to walk on their four hind legs while holding the rest of the body upright to work with the forelegs. *It would be really funny if Earth was inhabited not only by forms of life from Sea of Clouds but also from Venus as well. Of course, the Losians did create the platypus.*

The layout of the ship was not noticeably organized in any conventional way and the pattern of the grayish yellow corridors seemed to be only decipherable by an insectoid mentality, for Quroak and Zwane were hopelessly lost.

Looking at the walls more carefully, Quroak noticed for the first time that when viewed in the ultraviolet wavelengths, they glowed in an iridescent sort of way. And each corridor was slightly different in color. *Maybe they're color coded.*

"Hey Sweetheart, what color is the corridor outside your prison?"

"A sick, yellowish gray. Does that help you in some way?" she responded.

"No, look at it more carefully. Notice the color in ultraviolet. What do you see now?" he instructed hopefully.

"Oh! I've been too distracted to notice, but it is a glittering bluish-green."

The corridor in which he and Zwane were currently in ran a more greenish-orange.

"Thanks, I think the corridors are color coded which should help, though this ship is a wandering maze of hallways that has no pattern. At least, not to a non-Losian."

"I thought you were supposed to be my knight rescuing your damsel in distress. What are you waiting for? I'm all dressed up and ready to go!" she jokingly scolded him.

"Oh, I'm sorry, I didn't know you meant right away. I was just enjoying the scenic route." Quroak made his thoughts drip with sarcasm.

"Zwane, the womenfolk are getting restless. I guess we should do something about it."

"Well, if they insist!" The Jovian rolled his eyes expressively.

After searching for what seemed like forever, they finally found the engineering section at the rear of the ship. Unfortunately, it was crawling with about a dozen Losians doing maintenance and monitoring the heart of the ship.

Quroak and Zwane slowly inched along the ceiling into the large engine room and slid along the wall by the door, all the while keeping a wary eye on the Losians, until they were safely hidden behind some big conduit piping in the corner which extended up through the ceiling to the deck above.

After studying, from discretely peeping around the piping, the hundreds of bulky equipment crowding the engine room, Quroak focused on a low, flat box studded with thin conduits that flowed into the floor. He reasoned this was the device controlling the gravity within the spacecraft, though he had to admit, he only came to that conclusion by a process of elimination. He also noticed a control panel on the far wall with a display screen showing the current environmental conditions.

Quroak sent-thought to Zwane, "We can't risk being heard. Do I have your permission to use strictly telepathy to communicate with you until we are through this? I promise not to invade your privacy. Just think loudly what you want me to hear and I will only focus on that."

After a moment of hesitation, Zwane thought-responded loudly, "Okay."

So Quroak pointed out the gravity control machine and the environmental control screen on the opposite side of the room.

"That gives me an idea," mused the Jovian.

"Well, what is it?" when Zwane didn't clarify.

"Oh, you'll see. I'm not sure destroying the gravity machine will be enough to *freeze* the Losians in their tracks," Zwane replied, silently laughing at his own joke.

"Okay, so what's the plan then?" queried Quroak. His head throbbed a little from reading the Jovian's thoughts which had a strange shrill, yet fuzzy, quality to them. *Something about the brain biology, I guess.*

"You go for the gravity machine and I'll take the environmental controls."

"Okay, but we have to coordinate this," Quroak cautioned. All three of his hearts were racing and if it weren't for the spacesuit, his skin would have advertised his feelings like a billboard sign, with the dark turquoise and light blues and sapphire blues with green rings flashing across his body like racing neon lights showing his mixture of excitement, fear and anger all boiling within.

When the immediate vicinity of the gravity machine was clear of Losians and there was only one near the environmental controls, Quroak and Zwane exchanged a quick glance then quickly but quietly flew from their place of concealment towards their respective targets, going for the element of surprise since they were far outnumbered.

Quroak dove towards a discarded metal tool, grabbed it and flashed over to the gravity device where he quickly smashed what he figured was a crystalline energy junction providing power to the machine. With crystal shards flying everywhere, a small explosion erupted as the power flow was disrupted, throwing him a few meters until he was slammed into the corner of another machine.

Sunghosts! It was like the spacesuit not only didn't provide any protection but seemed to have magnified the impact somehow. With his body already badly bruised and beaten up from his struggles to get here, the impact made Quroak shake uncontrollably in agony as he slumped to the floor. Despite his stunned condition, he vaguely realized that the gravity was now at Jupiter norm, more than twice what the Losians were accustomed to.

Through his pain-hazed vision, he saw the insectoids move slowly under the increased weight of gravity to what was for them, nearly crushing. Their previous scurry was reduced to a slow crawl as they carefully moved their thin limbs forward. The heavier gravity was not life-threatening but it definitely slowed them down. Even so, they were slowly closing in on him.

He tried to float up to the ceiling, but he was too weak with the increased weight of the spacesuit holding him down.

With his whole tortured body enflamed with agony and his mind threatening to shut down from exhaustion and the overload of pain signals flooding his brain, Quroak tried to struggle up off the floor, knowing he had to assist Zwane any way he could so the Jovian could implement the rest of the plan immediately or all of this would be for naught, he would die and will have failed Xelrine and the others.

But his body was refusing to obey his desperate commands to move. His mind raged and whirled in a frenzy, but his body refused, insisting on rest and then four Losians reached him and started to pummel him with metallic tools. Fortunately, the insectoids couldn't lift anything too heavy in the, to them, crushing gravity, so they were using light tools. However, even through the spacesuit, each strike still sent agony through his arms as he flailed them about, trying to both ward off the blows and protect his head.

He was able to wrench the tool used by one Losian and bash him over the head with it while simultaneously wrapping two of his arms around another, effectively immobilizing that attacker, leaving him with two arms to protect his head and the last three warding off the other two insectoids.

Just when he thought there was hope of him overcoming them all, three more insectoids joined their brethren and pinned down his arms. One of them unlocked and opened up his protective spacewear, exposing him to the Venusian fiery heat. His remaining strength immediately vanished like a teardrop on the face of the sun. He collapsed, limp, and as he felt consciousness start to slip away, images of an old Earth movie flashed through his mind as he wearily thought, *Kung Fu doesn't work very well when you have no bones!*

Then he felt a sweet warmness flow through his mind, like a tender kiss from a midnight sun, that swept away the encroaching darkness with its soft light caressing his being with the simple message of *I love you.*

Xelrine! I won't fail you! He tried to override his body's overwhelming weakness with his willpower. With a surge of burning determination and adrenaline, he grabbed two Losians and smashed their heads together, knocking them out.

All of a sudden, there were multiple explosions reverberating throughout the ship, most of which were faint, but one was close by that was loud and metallic sharp and then there was a loud *whoosh!* with a sudden gust of wind and the temperature dropped three hundred degrees Celsius, almost instantaneously. All the Losians froze in place instantly.

Zwane! Quroak had almost forgotten about the Jovian and his task. *He must have done it!*

"Zwane, are you okay?" Quroak reached out with his mind.

"I'm still alive, anyway," the Jovian answered, his soft voice a welcome sound.

Quroak laid there for a few moments trying to regain some strength, enjoying the soothing coolness of the Jovian atmosphere.

"Xelrine?"

"Quroak, what happened? Our guards are like statues!"

"I think Zwane got mad at them. Hold on, love, we're coming to get you."

Eventually, Quroak pushed the unmoving Losians off his body, removed the spacesuit and floated over towards the environmental station in search for Zwane. He found a pile of Losians frozen in various positions near a wall. Sticking out at the bottom of the pile a wingtip was visible. "Zwane?"

"If you don't mind, I could use some help here. I can't move!"

With his body flushed a light orange spotted with red rings indicating his distaste of touching the insectoids, he slowly removed the Losians from the pile until Zwane was able to push himself off the floor. The Jovian promptly tore off the spacesuit and slammed it against the wall.

After making sure Zwane was not injured beyond

the green and blue bruises blooming on his face, Quroak gazed around the engine room to notice that there was a large opening in the wall beyond which was the vast sky of Jupiter. He looked at Zwane with a questioning look.

The Jovian grinned widely. "After I turned off the environmental controls I found the emergency controls that blew open all the external hatches on the ship."

Quroak laughed appreciatively. "Well, my friend, that's what finally stopped the Losians."

Looking over the controls, he saw a display screen showing an internal diagram of the ship, which was color coded. He located the area that was colored a bluish-green and figured that was the holding cell area. "Come on, this way," he motioned to Zwane as he dived into a corridor.

Though he was exhausted all around, his main heart was racing like a cyclone, excited that he was finally going to lay eyes on the person he had dreamed of all his life: Xelrine. Having memorized the route from the diagram, he tore through the twisting maze until he saw the bluish-green corridor, which he flashed down.

When Quroak turned the last corner he saw the Jovians locked behind solid opaque doors guarded by six insectoids, though now frozen. He opened the doors and the Jovians poured out, their eyes beaming with gratitude. The Jovians that had been captured first were too weak from the *softra* to leave the holding cells, just laying there while attended by newly made friends. Then he saw her, the only Cloudotian in the cell, staying near one of the Jovians lying on the floor.

He froze for a moment, too stunned to move. He could see an aura of light around her and she was simply more beautiful than he had ever imagined. Then she turned her head and gazed at him with her luminous bronze eyes and his heart cracked open, flooding him with love and tenderness. Then his body moved on its own volition, flashing over to her and gently enfolding her in his arms.

Though to the watching Jovians, it appeared to be a simple embrace, Quroak felt the universe crack open and his reality change in an instant. The moment they touched, a warmth flooded his body as the years of cold loneliness was swept away by her loving embrace and the magic of love.

Though no true thoughts were exchanged, they telepathically merged; their minds becoming one as they hungrily explored and cherished each other. His heart wept from relief as his mind and essence merged with hers with a hunger that would not be denied until all of her was ravenously savored by his need.

All of his love radiated into her essence, making Xelrine mentally gasp from its intensity before allowing herself to dissolve gratefully into its tender warm, ocean. He sank into the sweet scent of her and lost himself in the sensations created by the feel of her softness as rapture replaced the despair that had taken him over since her capture.

The darkness in his heart receded before the onslaught

of the light created by her touch where instead of drowning in sorrow, his heart soared freely, light as a cloud.

All the tension melted from his body and the whirlwind of his mind slowed to a calm breeze allowing peace to settle in. With his love freely flowing, Quroak gained a sense of harmony with Xelrine in his arms, his heart became whole and a new zest for life brightened his soul.

After melting into each other's presence for a long while, both Xelrine and Quroak let out a sigh of relief, contentment and happiness, flushed turquoise with waves of sea green showing their love and happiness.

Xelrine thought-whispered quietly, "I knew you would find me."

He replied with a smile, "Of course I had to find you. I got tired of eating alone."

Punching him playfully, Xelrine cried, "You uncaring monster!" causing Quroak to yelp in pain for his whole body ached terribly.

Quroak then somehow found the will to pull his gaze from the depths of her bronze eyes, realizing for the first time that he had been drowning in them since first embracing her, and turned to look at Zwane and Zola holding each other with love and deep affection shining in their eyes.

Zwane looked up and said, "Quroak, I would like you to meet my lifemate, Zola."

"Pleased to meet you, Quroak" she said with a soft yet lyrical voice.

"The pleasure is all mine, Zola. What do you say we get out of here?"

"I thought nobody would ever ask," she replied as everyone laughed.

CHAPTER 30

The next few days were a blur of activity with all the details washed away in both exhaustion and happiness; the happiness, of course, was from finally being with Xelrine. A couple of the captured Jovians were engineers and were able to fly the Losian ship up through the Red Storm safely to reunite all the Jovians with their lifemates in time so that no one died.

The Jovian authorities decided to keep the ship to study it and they stranded the insectoids on the moon Io to live out their lives under what the Jovians considered hellish conditions with the many sulfuric volcanoes covering its surface. However, most suspected the Losians might have found it paradisiacal and thus let off too easy.

The true intention of the Losians regarding their kidnappings was never discovered for it is almost impossible to gain information from an uncooperative Losian. However, it was clear that they were doing experiments regarding the Jovian's physiology, especially concerning the softra. To what end, no one knew, but everyone agreed it was for no good. All the data concerning their experimentation was destroyed with the hope that the Losians hadn't shared their findings with their homeworld.

The engineers found a strange device onboard that was responsible for Xelrine and Quroak's inability to shift. Apparently that was the reason why Xelrine had been kidnapped; to test and refine the machine. Out of respect for Quroak's assistance in rescuing the Jovians, the engineers thoroughly destroyed the device without trying to figure out how it froze the Cloudotian's dimension-shifting abilities. Quroak hoped he wouldn't come to regret that decision, but at the time he felt the knowledge was too dangerous for his people.

Another device was found that was responsible for the Jovian's new artwork, the Red Storm, to be sent out of control. Though studying the device allowed the Jovians to figure out a way to prevent this from happening again, they still couldn't do anything about the Red Storm itself. However, the super-massive cyclone had finally stabilized in that it was no longer growing in size or velocity and Jupiter was certainly gigantic enough to be able to accommodate the storm without too much trouble.

The most surprising find, however, was of extreme interest as everyone began to realize just how industrious this fanatic sect of Losian society, ELEFANT, really was.

The science was way beyond Quroak's understanding, but the Losians were experimenting with *micro black holes*; more specifically, on how to *create* an artificial black hole.

Based on documentation found in the ship's computer, ELEFANT had created the micro black hole aiming it at one of the moons around Sea of Clouds to see what would happen. One could only imagine what the affect would have been if the black hole had actually collided with the small moon. Fortunately, the black hole had been unstable and had exploded. Unfortunately for Quroak, he happened to be at the wrong place at the wrong time, sending him on his unplanned journey.

With all this nefarious activity by ELEFANT, Quroak and Zwane met with the Jovian authorities to open up a dialog with the Cloudotian government to decide what would be done for these offenses. With the experimentation on the Jovian softra, the Cloudotian's shifting abilities and the creation of black holes, obviously the Losian sect presented a very grave and immediate danger that needed to be addressed firmly.

After being debriefed thoroughly by both governments, Quroak and Zwane left the authorities, with their boisterous politicking that had ensued, hoping that something would actually be done about ELEFANT.

Zwane was considered a hero by many for his bravery, determination and strength for doing what had always been considered impossible before: diving into the heart of the Red Storm. Whenever asked how he was able to do it, Zwane simply answered, "By my love for Zola."

Quroak and Xelrine spent most of their time with Zwane and Zola, recuperating, relaxing, and just hanging out, getting to know each other better. After feeling well enough to travel, the Cloudotians said goodbye to their Jovian friends, promising to keep in touch and to get together soon, Xelrine and Quroak left Jupiter to travel home.

As they flew past the Guiding Star's pale gossamer rings, Quroak felt a mixture of emotions roiling inside. Though he felt some sadness for leaving such good newfound friends, he was extremely happy to be with Xelrine, his dream come true. And though he had been gone from home for a long time, seven and a half years, and missed his homeworld, he realized he had just really found his home by meeting Xelrine.

It felt so right to be with her. He finally found what had been missing from his life all along. He belonged by her side. He was glad his odyssey from the edge of the Solar System was over and he looked forward to what he thought would be his greatest adventure of all; sharing life with the beautiful person flying beside him.

This was the first time they had a chance to have some quiet time alone and he was enjoying it immensely as they flew past colorful Io. For a second, his thoughts turned to the stranded insectoids. *Good riddance!*

With the glow of Xelrine's presence beside him and the comforting warmth of her thoughts and essence entwined with his, he looked around and saw a beautiful universe, filled with wonders to be explored. *Wonders? Dream comes true?* These words resonated within him for a moment, echoing in his consciousness before they finally triggered a memory.

Turning towards her, trying not to lose himself in the brilliant depths of the pools of bronze light in her eyes, he said, "Xelrine, I still don't understand something."

"Oh, only one thing?" she teased.

Determined not to be knocked off track, he continued, "After I escaped the Neptunian vampires, I thanked you for saving my life, that I'm forever in your debt and that I could never repay you. You said, 'I know you will'."

"Then, while I was following the dragon-cats in the underground ocean of Oberon, you said, 'I also know that just as you say I helped you at Neptune, you will help me in the future'."

When she didn't respond, he continued, "And how do you explain the heartlink? We had never even met before, yet somehow we had the heartlink established. That's impossible. Yet, it happened. And ever since I can remember, I have always dreamed of you in some way. While I was growing up, you were just a vague dream, like a wisp of clouds with no definition. You were more like a feeling of comfort, warmth, love, of a *home*."

He paused, thinking with wonder of what he had just said, knowing it was true. "Then you became more than mist, more than a cloud, for you became my dream, my fantasy and my reality all rolled up into one. I dreamt I met you after that accident where my friend Tsin almost died. It felt so real. And ever since that dream, you were always a big part of me, always there with me. I thought I was going insane because it really felt you were with me, sharing my experiences, talking with me, but you weren't really there."

"And I knew that you were the one I had been dreaming of, that you were my comfort, my warmth, my love, my home. And when I was blown out to the edge of the Solar System and couldn't feel you anymore, couldn't communicate with you, I was so lost. I felt more lost from losing you than I did from being six billion kilometers away from Sea of Clouds. And I didn't really understand why, since at the time I just thought you were a figment of my lonely heart. I thought the explosion had done brain damage so that the dream-fantasy-reality had been blown apart, leaving me with only reality. A reality of true loneliness which I hated and despised, which always haunted me with its darkness of depression and sadness of what wasn't, but should be."

He looked down, trying to derail the emotions that were steamrolling out like a freight train and compose himself, not wanting to go down that track anymore, wanting to forget all that pain and darkness. Looking up again, he gazed into her eyes with pure affection. "But you are real. You are here and I'm here and I'm so happy and I love you so much. I never want it to end. I guess I shouldn't question my good fortune." He quickly embraced her as if she might dissipate right before his eyes into that mist of cloud that had formed his earliest dreams.

After a moment, Xelrine pulled away slightly so she could look him in the eyes. "Quroak, my love, you weren't going crazy. I was there with you. I was always with you. At least, in your mind with my thoughts and in your heart with my love. You see, I discovered at a very early age that I'm different than most Cloudotians in a few ways. One way is that I have premonitions of a type. I can't see the future or anything like that. But I do get these feelings, very real and strong feelings of what will come, at least for me."

She paused to let this sink in and to see his reaction but he simply gazed at her with fascination and affection. Thus encouraged, she continued, "When I was around five, I knew I was going to get sick somehow and come close to dying. My parents didn't believe me when I told them. That is, until a year later when I contracted lightsickness and almost died. Then they believed, but more importantly, I believed."

Xelrine paused again to see if Quroak was with her. "Then when I was around nine, I dreamed of you. But it wasn't really a dream as you think of a dream. There are ancient legends of our people where there were some whose essence, or soul, would reach out while sleeping in search of their soul mates, as it were. I had never heard of this until it happened to me and I did some research. On the first night this happened to me, I found the warmest and kindest soul I could ever imagine. A soul I knew was destined to love me, to cherish me. That soul was you. After that night, every time I went to sleep, my essence would go to be with that soul, to feel comforted and loved. So you see, Quroak, those earliest dreams you had weren't really dreams at all, but me visiting you in your sleep."

Quroak just gazed at her in wonder, letting her words sink in. Before he could think of what to say, Xelrine smiled deeply with her light bronze eyes, making his heart skip a few beats and then she continued. "That happened every time I went to sleep and I always woke up feeling warm, safe and loved. Then a few years later, I knew something else terrible was going to happen to me, though I didn't know what, but I was convinced that if something wasn't done to stop it from going too far, I would surely die. However, though I was worried, I wasn't too scared because I was also convinced that you were going to save me. I knew you were strong willed and that you wouldn't let anything stop you from coming to my rescue. And you did rescue me."

Feeling a little overwhelmed and flustered, he said, "But you weren't about to die. Were you?"

"You remembered I disappeared two days ago, telling you I had to visit a friend visiting Jupiter? Well, it was actually a Cloudotian doctor that was there for a conference. She examined me and found that the Losians had been injecting me with some kind of drug that was slowly causing my organs to fail. I didn't want to worry you even more by telling you just how bad I felt or how much pain I was in during my captivity. Apparently ELEPANT was trying to discover how we shift in the hopes of being able to create a corresponding DNA gene sequence in their own physiology. The doctor was able to cure me but she said if the Losians had continued their experiment for another day or two, there would have been no hope of recovery and all my major organs would have failed in a matter of a week or so. So you see, again my premonition came true."

She stopped for a second, while warmth and love filled her beautiful eyes, gazing at a dumbfounded Quroak. "Actually, that's the third time my premonitions came true, at least in a major way. Another way I'm different than most Cloudotians is that I'm a very powerful and unique telepath in that I don't just read thoughts but can truly see into one's soul. Because you were under extreme exhaustion and stress from your experience with Tsin, I was able to reach out to you in a stronger telepathic link than usual so that you truly felt I was there with you. From that time on, I was able to visit you during waking hours, not just when we both were asleep and make it seem so real to you that you actually believed I was with you. And during all that time, I saw into your soul and knew without a doubt that you truly do love me and will always cherish me. So that was the second time a major premonition came true. For I knew I really had found my soul mate."

Laughing gaily, she finished with, "I never knew just how strong a telepath I was until I was able to communicate with you when you reached Pluto. But I was so relieved and happy when I found you again after losing contact after the black hole explosion. I had never felt so lonely in all my life. Of course, up till then, I had always visited you at night and then later during the day, too. I love you very much. And I guess because of my telepathic strength coupled with my love and my visitations, I unconsciously created the heartlink between us, which I didn't even know was possible since we hadn't actually physically met."

Quroak was so overwhelmed with joy and relief from understanding the mysteries of his dreams that had always seemed so real, dreams that had driven him and carried him through a life of intense loneliness, overwhelmed with happiness of finally being with her, *truly* being with her, and flooded with love that he simply had no words, no thoughts to speak so he simply embraced her as they floated in the velvety night studded with thousands of colored diamonds with the majestic panoramic of *Guiding Star* with its white ghostly rings and loyal companions in the background, letting her simply feel the love and happiness flow through his mind and soul into hers.

CHAPTER 31

"Me." I said firmly, withdrawing from the memory bank.

I've relived thousands of memories during the course of my career, ranging from the bland everyday routine to heart-pounding terror caused by either real danger or extreme paranoia. I've experienced other people's happiness, sadness, ecstasy, depression, joy, loneliness, and anger, all from the mild to the extreme. I've studied the whole range of the emotional scale, from quiet unemotional beings to raging uncontrolled emotions, from the emotional numb to those whose emotions were apparent but totally unknown by the *feeler*. I have studied individuals who lost the capability to feel emotions due to brain damage.

And lastly, I relived the memories of individuals from the one species I know, other than the Neptunian vampires, who never evolved with emotions, just to understand what it was like to truly be emotionless. I admit this last was largely just out of personal curiosity. This species is totally alien in every way and it would be extremely hard to give a description that would be understood by corporeal beings. However, besides the experience scaring the hell out of me, it did give me some more insight into the huge and critical role emotions play in everyday decisions, both minor and major.

Out of all the memories I've relived, Quroak's is one of my favorites. His story says so much about facing adversity with determination and growing in the process, about not giving up hope and never letting go of your dreams.

Quroak shows that you can still learn a lot of positive things even while in a negative situation. Look at everything Quroak learned on his return journey after a terrible accident left him stranded so far from his home, putting him in a desperate situation. He learned about patience and creating an inner calm from the Quaoarians. To accept *what is* and to just deal with it and that you can't let things you *can not control, control you*.

Though, he would be the first to admit, he is still working on the patience thing because he also learned that the longest Monopoly game he can comfortably handle is only two months, not the nine months the Quaoarians enjoy!

He learned about having a sense of purpose, a feeling of destiny from the *Guardians of One*. About the unstoppable drive towards fulfilling that destiny against all odds until it is reached.

He discovered how much inner strength he possessed from his ghastly ordeal with the Neptunian vampires. Before, he never knew about the deep reservoirs of strength he could call upon to carry him through a crisis.

He also gained knowledge of what hope can do from the dragon-cats of Uranus. That when all else is lost, hope can push back the dark curtains of despair letting in the light necessary to guide you onward and forward to a better place, a better tomorrow.

And though he may have wanted to at times on some level, he never gave up when everything looked bleak. Quroak was stranded impossibly far from home after the universe seemed to have conspired against him. He could easily have given in to despair and not even tried to get home. Or let depression permanently strand him in the frozen darkness of the Kuiper Belt. Who would have blamed him? He was so far from Sea of Clouds that not only was the sun just a glimmer in the deep night but so were his chances of returning. But he never gave up even when all seemed lost, even his life, while ensnared by the vampires. He kept fighting onward and kept looking for and finding ways to not only survive but to get closer and closer to home.

I believe with the right attitude, you can make your own luck. Or if you will, attract the right events or coincidences to help you achieve your goals. There were times when Quroak despaired, but he kept his hope and determination alive, and he attracted each stepping stone to himself until he succeeded.

And of course, Quroak never gave up his dream, even when he thought he was going insane. Though he had his doubts about Xelrine being real, he still held onto his hope that she was real and not just a lonely mind's desperate fantasy. And when they finally met and spent time together, they formed a bond that grew into a cozy blanket of intimacy where love's warmth protected them from the coldness of life. It was like they created their own private oasis within the chaotic universe where the sun always shined with love and a warm breeze caressed their hearts with tenderness and within each other's eyes they always found safety and acceptance. It was within this protective oasis that Quroak was finally free to be himself, free to open his heart completely without fear of his trust betrayed, and free to love fully for this is what his heart needed above all else. It was within her arms that he found paradise, within her eyes all of his tomorrows, within her heart his home and within her soul his destiny.

In essence, he found his home, his true home, within the true intimacy created and shared with Xelrine, true love.

This is why I love my profession of emocology. I gain a lot of insight into the motivations of individuals and of societies as a whole. It makes me reflect upon what motivates me, what drives me and what dreams I hold safely cradled deep in my heart. Experiencing other's journeys makes me ponder on whatever lessons I've learned during my own journey. About what is truly important to me. About what I've done or would do to pursue a dream.

Stories like Quroak's also give me hope for myself. Hope that I will eventually find my *home* within true intimacy and real love where the sun shines brightly every day, not from without but from within my heart. Hope that I could truly be myself with my heart completely open with someone really accepting me for whom I am without fear of rejection or deep pain. Hope that my heart's dream will materialize where I can truly share myself, completely express the deep love my heart is capable of, and share life's experiences with someone. Hope that my heart will no longer be a haunted empty abode but a magnificent mansion filled with warmth, light, happiness, love and *life*. I have as many character flaws as any other being, but doesn't everyone deserve to be loved and to love?

There are no right answers, for what is right for one is not right for all. It all depends on your dreams, your agonies, your heart, your emotions and the strength and depth of any or all the above. If you're very passionate you'll probably risk more and have a stronger drive to make your dreams a reality. A less passionate person is more likely to be content with just *wishing* for the dream to come true while not putting much effort into making it happen.

And of course, while there's greater reward for trying and winning, there's greater pain with trying and losing, whereas not trying at all is the safest way to go with the least amount of pain, but also with less chance of fulfillment.

So each must choose to follow their own heart. Or not. Of course, you must be open enough to listen to your heart in the first place; otherwise you may live your life like a leaf on a breeze, letting circumstances decide your fate on the careless whims of an arbitrary universe.

As for Quroak and Xelrine, they finally made it home to Sea of Clouds. For Quroak it had been a journey over seven and a half years. He was vastly relieved to find that someone had remembered to feed Qat, his pet. Otherwise, who knows what the resulting chaos would have been, like Sea of Clouds thrown into another dimension, lost to Quroak forever.

Our young Cloudotian became a legend among his people for everything he had gone through and all the discoveries he had made while in the outskirts of the Solar System.

The Cloudotians now have a legend that once a year on the same day, as God's eye watches over Sea of Clouds with its golden pupil, the *Blue Guardian* will blink from a bright royal blue to a deep shining violet then instantly back to blue in celebration of the day Quroak and Xelrine met. Violet represents true love to the Cloudotians and folklore says that if you're lucky enough to catch that flash of violet then you will rejoice in true love. So on that night every year, thousands of hopeful couples fly to the highest clouds and carefully watch to see if God will wink his violet blessing upon their togetherness.

I hope I haven't unbalanced your sense of your pride

too much regarding your place in the universe. Now you know you are not alone, that the Solar System is teeming with life. By the way, as you send your probes to other planets, make sure you sterilize your robotic explorers more thoroughly. The following probes that you sent to Mars either crashed or were lost due to damage done during our sterilization process when we discovered microbes hitching a ride: the Soviet Union's probes Mars 1, 2, 4, 6, and 7, Phobos 1 and the American probes Mars Observer, Climate Orbiter and the Polar Lander.

We are highly protective of the red planet. And when you finally decide to set foot on Mars instead of sending your delicate toys, be kind to the sandtigers. They were just playing little tricks on your rovers, Spirit, Opportunity and Beagle 2, like when they made Spirit spew gibberish and beeps instead of sending scientific data for a few days. On the other hand, they did help Spirit find a safe haven during the winter. The sandtigers are completely harmless, just playful and are under the full protection of the Cloudotians and, for some unknown reason, the Losians.

Also, don't try to interrogate your cats. Just be kind to them and leave them be and they will leave you alone and continue to perpetuate your belief that you're in control. But if I were you, I wouldn't look too long or too deep into their eyes. You might lose yourself or even lose your soul. Hey, just trying to give you fair warning.

On the journey of life, we all reach the same destination at some point, unless you believe in multiple levels of existence like the glow-bats or are immortal like the *Guardians of One*. It's up to you to decide what you will learn and how you will grow from this journey based on the openness and receptiveness of your mind and heart, especially during hardship. I for one intend to be able to say truthfully at the end of my journey that I followed my heart's dreams with passion, honesty, kindness to all and with everything that I am, trying to live up to my potential and fulfill my purpose in life, though it may be a mystery.

Enjoy your journey.

NOTES

Perspective on Distance:

Consider: light travels at 299,338 kilometers/second (186,000 miles/second)

The Earth's Circumference at the Equator is 40,075 km (24,902 miles)

This means in ONE second, light can circle the Earth 7 ½ times!

The approximate time it takes sunlight to reach and distance:

Mercury	:	3 ¼ minutes	.38 AU
Venus	:	6 minutes	.72 AU
Earth	:	8 1/3 minutes	1.00 AU (149,600,000 km)
Mars	:	12 2/3 minutes	1.52 AU
Sea of Clouds	:	25 ½ minutes	3.00 AU
Jupiter	:	43 1/3 minutes	5.20 AU
Saturn	:	79 ½ minutes	9.54 AU
Uranus	:	2 2/3 hours	19.22 AU
Neptune	:	4 ¼ hours	30.06 AU
Pluto	:	5 ½ hours	39.50 AU (average)
Quaoar	:	6 hours	43.61 AU (average)

GUIDE TO LIFE IN THE SOLAR SYSTEM

1) Unknown origin : *Sunghost*

2) Mercury : *Bloodeagle* – used to create measurement of the *zulat*

3) Venus : *Losians* – insectoid, aggressively competitive, stay at home

: *ELEFANT* – fanatic sect living on invisible moon, goal is to hinder other species' advancement

: *Toadfly* – has extremely acidic, yet sweet tasting, saliva

4) Earth (non- indigenous) : *Octopus* – exiled Cloudotian criminal that's been de-evolved

: *Jellyfish* – separated individuals from 1 united creature w/ hive mind that formed living spaceship carrying exiled Cloudotians

: *Platypus* – created by ELEFANT to create oil fields to slow human's progress

: *Cats* – classified: penalty of death

5) Mars : *Sandtiger* – playful, yet harmless, protected by the Cloudotians & Losians

6) Sea of Clouds (€☾⊖℘⚭♅℩☾☞♐) : Home planet of the Cloudotians but appears to be the asteroid belt between Mars & Jupiter

: *Cloudotian* – telepathic, change colors when emotional, transfer their mass to another dimension, love windstorm surfing

: *Dimenhopper* – pet that can jump between dimensions but tied to each, when hungry creates chaos

: *Glow-bats* – live on the moon Curon (♌℩♈&⚭), believe in Ascendancy to next level of existence

318

7) Jupiter (*Guiding Star*)   : *Jovians*   – create world-size artworks, afraid of windows

                    : *Glowmouse*   _ Considered as good omen when spotted

8) Saturn   : *Blue-winged Sunsurfer*   –

9) Uranus   : *Uranians*   – created subspace tunnel between Uranus & Neptune, current whereabouts: unknown

                    : *Dragon-cats*   – feed off planetary rings, trying to save population on Oberon in underground ocean

10) Neptune   : *Shadowcasters* – Jellyfish like creatures living in Neptune's ocean

                    : *Wraiths*   – Emotionless replicas of the shadowcasters

                    : *Emovamps*   – Invisible vampires, feed on emotional energy

11) Pluto   : *Kulan (Ice-worms)*   – live on the moon Nix

                    : *Guardians of One*   – the moon Charon was their temporary base before leaving to save another galaxy

12) Quaoar (planetoid in Kuiper Belt)   : *Quaoarians*   – live in underground crystal city, mine Kuiper Belt, love the game Monopoly